continued . . .

An Unforgettable Rogue

"Never has a hero submitted to such sweet seduction while making it clear that he is still very much a man in charge . . . Spicy sensuality is the hallmark of this unforgettable story."
—*Romance Readers Connection*

"After *An Undeniable Rogue*, I never expected to read such a wonderful story again. *An Unforgettable Rogue* proved me wrong."
—*Huntress Reviews*

"A beautiful blend of humor, pathos, and passion, with the added bonus of outstanding supporting characters."
—*Reader to Reader*

"'Knight In Shining Silver' Award for KISSable heroes. Bryceson 'Hawk' Wakefield is most definitely an Unforgettable Rogue."
—*Romantic Times*

"Ms. Blair is such an awesome storyteller . . . *An Unforgettable Rogue* is a mesmerizing tale that sweeps the reader into the Regency era."
—*Scribes World*

"Annette Blair creates another memorable and refreshing love story . . . a charming read."
—Jan Springer

"I recommend *An Unforgettable Rogue* as an entertaining book in its own right, even more as part of the must-read The Rogues Club series."
—*Romance Reviews Today*

An Undeniable Rogue

"A love story that is pure joy, enchanting characters who steal your heart, a fast pace, and great storytelling."
—*Romantic Times*

"An utterly charming and heartwarming marriage-of-convenience story. I highly recommend it to all lovers of romance."
—*Romance Reviews Today*

"Awesome! To call this story incredible would be an understatement . . . Do not miss this title."
—*Huntress Reviews*

"Annette Blair writes a very good story and has created some unforgettable characters in this excellent tale."
—*Romance Review*

"Annette Blair skillfully pens an exhilarating, humorous, and easy-to-read historical romance. You don't want to miss *An Undeniable Rogue*."
—Jan Springer

"Ms. Blair has a delicate touch with love scenes . . . none of her characters are insignificant."
—*Romance Readers Connection*

"A feel-good read that shines with warmth, wit, and passion."
—C. L. Jeffries, *Heartstrings*

My Favorite Witch

Annette Blair

B

BERKLEY SENSATION, NEW YORK

THE BERKLEY PUBLISHING GROUP
Published by the Penguin Group
Penguin Group (USA) Inc.
375 Hudson Street, New York, New York 10014, USA
Penguin Group (Canada), 90 Eglinton Avenue East, Suite 700, Toronto, Ontario M4P 2Y3, Canada
(a division of Pearson Penguin Canada Inc.)
Penguin Books Ltd., 80 Strand, London WC2R 0RL, England
Penguin Group Ireland, 25 St. Stephen's Green, Dublin 2, Ireland (a division of Penguin Books Ltd.)
Penguin Group (Australia), 250 Camberwell Road, Camberwell, Victoria 3124, Australia
(a division of Pearson Australia Group Pty. Ltd.)
Penguin Books India Pvt. Ltd., 11 Community Centre, Panchsheel Park, New Delhi—110 017, India
Penguin Group (NZ), Cnr. Airborne and Rosedale Roads, Albany, Auckland 1310, New Zealand
(a division of Pearson New Zealand Ltd.)
Penguin Books (South Africa) (Pty.) Ltd., 24 Sturdee Avenue, Rosebank, Johannesburg 2196, South
Africa

Penguin Books Ltd., Registered Offices: 80 Strand, London WC2R 0RL, England

This is a work of fiction. Names, characters, places, and incidents either are the product of the author's imagination or are used fictitiously, and any resemblance to actual persons, living or dead, business establishments, events, or locales is entirely coincidental. The publisher does not have any control over and does not assume any responsibility for author or third-party websites or their content.

MY FAVORITE WITCH

A Berkley Sensation Book / published by arrangement with the author

PRINTING HISTORY
Berkley Sensation edition / January 2006

Copyright © 2006 by Annette Blair.
Excerpt from *The Scot, the Witch & the Wardrobe* copyright © 2006 by Annette Blair.
Cover art by Masaki Ryo.
Cover design by Rita Frangie.
Interior text design by Kristin del Rosario.

ISBN: 0-425-20723-4

BERKLEY® SENSATION
Berkley Sensation Books are published by The Berkley Publishing Group,
a division of Penguin Group (USA) Inc.,
375 Hudson Street, New York, New York 10014.
BERKLEY SENSATION and the "B" design are trademarks belonging to Penguin Group (USA) Inc.

PRINTED IN THE UNITED STATES OF AMERICA

10 9 8 7 6 5 4 3 2 1

With love to Chris Cabral—
awesome friend, calming force, revitalizing spirit,
who enhances my life and every life she touches
without ever using a wand.

One

NHL Wizard Jason Pickering Goddard left the battered podium to a round of applause and sat beside his grandmother on the gym stage of St. Anthony's Home for Boys. "Dreams die," Jason whispered. "Life sucks. *That's* what they should learn. I didn't do them any favors with that 'dreams do come true' crap."

His grandmother bristled without ruffling a manicured feather. "Reality, they've got," she said. "*Hope* is what they need."

Jason winced. She might as well have said, "They're a hell of a lot worse off than you are, so stop feeling sorry for yourself," and she was right. But he sure as hell wished the boys heading for the gym exits would stop looking back at him with all that misplaced hero worship.

Damn it. He'd screwed up. It didn't make sense, him talking about dreams, not after he'd drunk himself senseless and lost his.

Wait a minute. . . .

Jason raised his chin and gave the woman who raised

him a sidelong glance. What he saw should not have surprised him: a manipulating matriarch running a power play. Well, well, well. He relaxed in his chair, stretched his legs to ease the ache in his knee, and folded his arms across his chest. "Gram, why did you really drag me here today?"

"What? Well . . . you never get to see the good that the Pickering Foundation does."

"Good? This place is falling apart."

Every inch the society matron, his grandmother barely winced before she tilted her head in belated approval. "My point exactly."

She was angling for something, Jason knew, but what? "You want a bigger donation, just say so."

The benevolent old fraud cleared her throat, fidgeted with her Dior handbag, and looked everywhere but at him before she patted his hand. "Thank you, dear."

"I'd rather write a check any day than—"

"Raise a finger to help?" Sheer annoyance filled Gram's snapping hazel eyes. "You and every other member of the idle rich!" She rose, braced on her ancient umbrella, chin high, head at a regal angle, indignation in the set of her shoulders and the straight of her spine.

"Give me a break," Jason said. "I wouldn't be idle if—"

"Enough with the self-pity." She tapped his cane with her umbrella. "*This* is only a setback," she said, echoing his tired litany.

Jason squared his shoulders. "I *will* play hockey again. I'll be back on the ice in no time. You'll see."

"Not according to the majority of your doctors."

"The majority of them are wrong!"

"Of course they are, dear."

"Don't take that patronizing tone with me, young lady."

Bessie Pickering Hazard, seventy-seven-year-old chairman of the board of the Pickering Foundation, laughed like a schoolgirl.

Jason grinned. Glad the old twinkle was back in her

eyes, he still wished to hell he knew what she was up to. He'd seen this act before, and it didn't bode well for the poor sucker she'd picked as her latest mark . . . him.

Gram had accomplished some great deeds in her day, and to pull them off, she'd played some steep angles. Just thinking of the ways she might try to play him made Jason's tie so tight, you'd think somebody pushed a choke switch.

Best rebound now, he thought, self-preservation riding him. "How the hell does a gimp jock fit into whatever scheme you're trying to hatch this time?" he asked.

"Jason, dear, whatever are you— Ah, here comes the director. You remember Sister Margaret?"

They were force-fed sugar cookies and watered-down cherry punch in the old art deco reception room, a showplace of mission furniture and teeming glass-faced trophy cabinets. Untouched by time, the room remained the sanctum where hopeful childless parents met with more-hopeful potential adoptees.

Gram had purchased the turn-of-the-century, brick-and-granite school building in the fifties specifically to house St. Anthony's, likely to keep herself busy while his grandfather pursued other "interests."

That she'd named it *Saint* Anthony's after her faithless husband, Anthony Bannister Hazard, was one of Gram's private jokes with God. Or perhaps she'd thought to redeem the philandering old buzzard. No one knew but Gramps himself whether she succeeded, because he had resided in the hereafter for more than twenty years now.

What Jason liked best, and feared most, about his grandmother was that in her entire life, she'd let nothing and no one stop her. She was the strongest person he knew, man or woman, and he loved her in the rare way she loved him, faults and all.

As Jason opened the outside door, the scent of pine-pitch wafted up from the sun-soft, cracked-tar schoolyard, reminding him of the afternoons he'd spent waiting for Gram to pick him up and sneak him off to hockey practice. She'd said these boys needed hope, and hope, by damn, he'd had aplenty back then.

Now, as then, Chilton, her octogenarian driver, saw them and came around to open the door of her pristine, sixty-three white Rolls, and stood waiting at attention.

The moment they exited the building, the boys at play hushed and stood like statues, making Jason's awkward cane-clicking trek across the yard seem endless.

"I wish you had let me drive my Hummer," he told his grandmother, as if that might have given him control over anything but the next brick wall that got in his way.

After the last brick wall, his glory days of voluptuous female groupies and instant male bonding had come to an abrupt, if temporary, halt.

Like the fans who'd once rushed and crushed him, but now avoided meeting his eyes, the boys from St. Anthony's emanated a kind of disappointment and pity, and remained a safe distance away.

As if to disprove that theory, a three-foot carrottop began a lone, tenacious approach his way, from across the schoolyard, capturing Jason's full and curious attention.

Though they had already made eye contact, the eager boy found it necessary to tug on Jason's cuff when he arrived.

Jason grinned despite himself while something pulled at his chest like an invisible thread that connected his shirtsleeve to his heart.

Ignoring the pain in his knee, Jason stooped to the boy's level, bit off a groan, and received a wide, deep-dimpled grin for his efforts. "I'm gonna play hockey, too," the outgoing boy said.

"Good for you," Jason said. "What's your name?"

"Travis. Travis Robinson."

"Well, Travis, if you want to play hockey, you do know that you have to practice every day?"

The tip of his grandmother's umbrella made hard contact with Jason's right shoulder blade.

"Ouch! What?" he asked, turning.

"No rink to practice," Travis said, reclaiming Jason's attention. "No money for ice time, Sister Margaret says."

An incoherent apology died on Jason's lips when the boy threw his small but steely arms around Jason's neck. "Take me home," Travis said, his voice choked and desperate. "I want 'dopting *bad*. You don't even have to teach me hockey."

Poleaxed, Jason inadvertently embraced the tiny, reed-thin body in a bid for balance, and when he felt those fragile bones against the muscles in his arms, a wave of protectiveness assaulted him. His cane hit the blacktop with a clatter, but it didn't matter, because the boy's stranglehold kept him from falling on his ass—figuratively as well as literally.

An old nun rushed forward ringing a handbell. "I'm sorry, I'm sorry," she said as the schoolyard cleared of boys and she grabbed Travis by the shoulders and wrenched him from Jason's arms. "Don't mind him," she said. "He asks everybody to take him."

Chilton handed Jason his cane.

His name is Travis! Jason wanted to shout at the nun as he rose and watched the boy get dragged away, his green eyes huge and pleading as he looked back.

Hope now had a face—dirt-smudged, freckled, and about six years old.

A minute later Jason slipped into the backseat of the limo beside his grandmother and released a long slow breath. "Son of a—"

"Watch your language!"

"I hang out in locker rooms, Gram," Jason said, stretching his leg and rubbing his knee. "Believe me, I *am* watching my language. Did you pay him to do that?"

"Don't be an idiot, and don't let him rattle you. You

heard Sister Estelle, Travis asks everybody to adopt him . . . as if he wants parents as much as you wanted to play hockey."

"What's that supposed to mean?"

Gram shook her head. "What boys like Travis Robinson have to give can't be bought; it's called love. Scares you doesn't it?"

Jason did a double take. "What scares me? Love? Hell no."

"Possibly not. Possibly you haven't learned to recognize it. Who could blame you with parents like yours? Plus you've been kissing too many starlets and models, on and off that absurd celebrity reality show. *The Best Kisser in America,* indeed."

"Yeah, well, I didn't realize my contract said I had to make an ass of myself. You know damned well that as soon as they called the show 'promo,' I was tied to it. Hell, Gram, give me a break, I gave the prize money to the foundation."

"Yes, and we're grateful, but it wasn't enough."

"Ah, here it comes," Jason said with relief. "Play your angle and get it over with. You're killing me here."

"Angle? I don't know what you're talking about." His grandmother opened an engraved oval compact—a twenty-four-karat guilt gift from the rogue—and pretended to check her hair in the mirror.

Jason silently applauded the innocent act. "Gram, nobody plays more angles than you."

"Except maybe you."

"Hey, I learned from the best."

"Your grandfather?"

"Yeah, right." Jason knew he'd inherited his "unfortunate roguish ways" from his grandfather, but his skill for playing angles was pure Gram. "Give it to me straight, damn it. I'm tired and my knee is killing me."

"Straight? You don't hear straight."

Jason clenched his jaw, trying not to snap. "Try me."

"The doctors give it to you straight and you don't listen."

"'Cause they're wrong! All I need is six more months off the ice and I'll be leading the Wizards to the Cup."

"Fine then, give *me* those six months."

Another double take. "Instant replay, please."

"The Pickering Foundation is in trouble," his grandmother said, "therefore, St. Anthony's, which we were founded to support, is also in trouble."

"*Money* trouble."

"Of course, money trouble. Is there any other kind? Think of it this way, if the foundation's floundering, then Travis and all his friends—"

"I get it, and now I *know* you paid him." She might walk around disguised as a four-foot-ten, ninety-seven-pound granny, Jason thought, but when she dug in her heels, Bessie Pickering Hazard was one immovable object.

"You owe me," she said.

Her words struck like a puck in the face. And damned if she wasn't right, Jason thought, when he got past the sting, but damned if he'd let her know he agreed. "What is it you think I owe you?"

"I will *not* let the boys at St. Anthony's down." She firmed her small steel shoulders. "If we lose the foundation, we lose four of Newport's finest, if not its biggest, mansions, which amounts to a pretty amazing chunk of history, hundreds of jobs, employee homes, and most important, we'd lose our support structure for St. Anthony's.

"If that happens, those boys will be given over to the state's already-overworked and understaffed foster-care system."

"I won't kid you, Gram, you have my attention, but how do the foundation's problems fit in with my supposed debt to you?"

"*Supposed* debt? Are you, or are you not, the Jason

Goddard I sneaked off to Mite Hockey when you were too young to blow your own nose?"

She had him there. He'd played for years before his parents stayed around long enough to catch on, and then it was too late.

A top draft pick of the NHL, he'd risen to glory, to the very top of his game. He'd played his heart out, until the blonde driving his rented Peugeot along a mountain road in France—him passed-out in the passenger seat—took a wrong turn through a brick wall and walked away without a scratch. Unlike him.

Jason grimaced. Gram believed the doctors, plural, who said he'd never play again. He believed the *one* who said he would. He had a right to suspect Gram's motives. "How can a few months of my life make a difference? I don't know anything about raising money. Why me?"

"We need to get more people on more tours, or have more fund-raisers. I figure a celebrity like you would lure some high-stakes donors to some big-ticket special events."

Jason mocked himself with a laugh. "I'm old news."

"Nonsense, even if 'The Ice Wolf' was, and he's not, 'The Best Kisser in America' still carries some pretty amazing clout." She pulled out a copy of *In the Know* magazine and flashed it. The cover read "Newport, Rhode Island's Brightest Star" with a picture of him in his Wizards uniform, sitting on the ice, playing kissy-face with the Hollywood goddess straddling him.

Son of a bitch. Jason raised a brow. "Wait a minute; the reality show's not absurd when there's money involved?"

"Not when it means money for our kids, it's not. Hey, we might as well make it work *for* us. All I want from you is six months of special events, the type of functions you did all the time for team promo."

Jason sighed. "Which functions?"

"You get to choose." His grandmother's eyes twinkled brighter than they had in years, more enticing than any argument she might make, but he couldn't shake the fear that she was doling out the penalties in small doses when she really wanted to bench him . . . for life.

"Why not just put another few million into the foundation?" he asked.

"Good long-range planning calls for keeping the principal—ours, and the foundation's—intact, and utilizing only the interest from both to keep the foundation running," she said. "Otherwise, in a few years, the money's gone, and St. Anthony's and the mansions become condos or parking lots."

Jason knew she was right. He'd seen it happen.

"To preserve the mansions and support St. Anthony's in perpetuity, I intend to increase the foundation's principal," Gram said, "and protect it, on several fronts. We need more donors to solicit. Therefore, we need some headline-making special events to bring the foundation's causes to the hearts, eyes, and bank accounts, of some high-stakes donors, events that will bring philanthropists to us."

"Sounds ambitious," Jason said.

"I have no choice," Gram said. "Neither I, nor my money, will last forever." She regarded him measuringly. "You know what the doctors say about my heart."

Jason winced. "You know, Gram, I do know what the doctors say about your heart, and I also know that there's a word for your current exploitation of the diagnosis, and it isn't pretty. It's called blackmail."

The wily old vixen tried to contain her grin. "You're gonna be the best director of special events the Pickering Foundation has ever seen."

"The director? No way. Absolutely not!"

"Hey, I'm making you the brains of the outfit, the head coach, the idea man. You won't have to lift a stick. I hired you an incredible new coordinator who can work magic."

"Not for me, you didn't, because I'm not gonna be the director."

"Jay," she said, using the nickname his parents hated,

the one she'd whispered only with a good-night kiss. "Think of this as my final wish."

"Another one? I think this makes about eleven. I swear, Gram, one more final wish and I'm gonna *make* it your last."

She laughed, because she had him and they both knew it.

Two

THE day after she was supposed to have been married, Kira Fitzgerald sat with her back to her desk at the Pickering Foundation, systematically and symbolically ridding herself of the dick-wad she'd caught screwing her sister.

She emptied her desk and purse of anything that reminded her of the jock. Then she tossed the debris into her metal trashcan with gratifying force, and broke a tiny but expensive vial of his favorite perfume with great satisfaction. She took each of her addressed, ecru parchment wedding invitations that she'd been saving in self-torture for months and finally tossed them in as well.

Taking this job had been a first step in rising from the ashes of her life. Performing this spell was the second. She'd turn everything that reminded her of the snake into ashes.

She added a pinch of healing herbs from her pouch, lit a long tapered match, and touched it to the edges of her shattered dreams. "I hate jocks!"

As a number of pearl-embossed calla lilies, and ridiculous, romantic words began to singe and curl, Kira raised her amethyst-tipped wand, tempted to give the jerk what he really deserved. "I wanna wither your Charlie, Penis!" But like any witch worthy of the title, she would harm none.

Kira wielded her wand with a flourish.

> *"Charlie Tillinghast,*
> *Reap what you sow.*
> *Recall your faithless past.*
> *Travel the row you hoe,*
> *And grow a heart to last.*
> *Though I wish you no ill,*
> *Begone from screwing me.*
> *This is my will.*
> *So mote it be."*

Whoosh! The fire flared to bright and vigorous life, releasing a sickly sweet scent into the air. "Shit!" She'd forgotten perfume was flammable.

As the flames and the flowery smoke rose, Kira grabbed her consolation bouquet from beside her computer, rescued the yellow roses, poured the water on the fire, and doused the small inferno.

That was when she saw the crisp blue vellum invitation atop her stack of mail, sitting there, free of its envelope, mocking her.

"Cripes, not another wedding." She leaned forward to read it.

> *You Are Cordially Invited*
> *to Jason Pickering Goddard's*
> *Ghost & Graveyard Tour of Rainbow's Edge*
> *Narragansett and Ochre Point Avenues*
> *Newport, Rhode Island*
> *Sunday Evening, October 30, 2005, 7 P.M.*
> *Donation: $1,000 per person*

"What idiot thought this up? There are no ghosts at Rainbow's Edge."

"Damn!" came a deep, sexy voice. "I should've thought of that."

Kira yelped and whipped about to gape at the hunk of manhood who'd materialized behind her, her heart beating double time.

How long had he been standing there?

He made her think of a wolf, hungry yet calm, every nuance of his aquiline features sharp, like the gleam in his silver-gray eyes, and the disapproving dimple cut deep in the center of his chin.

Like a lazy predator, he leaned against the connecting doorjamb between her office and the next, arms crossed, sculpted lips firm, an antique walking stick at his side.

Kira's heart shifted into overdrive. For half a beat she thought he was gorgeous, flawless, but no. He needed a haircut, a bump spoiled the precision of his nose, and his square chin bore a decidedly stubborn set, not to mention that five-o'clock shadow at eleven in the morning.

The small scar that crossed his left brow intrigued her, but his lips—too perfect for a man—seemed carved in granite, and the orgasmic promise in his eyes should have come with a warning label. Nevertheless, all the odd parts formed such an attractive whole, Kira had to catch her breath and rub her arms against a sudden chill. "How long have you been standing there?"

"Long enough to be glad my name's not Charlie."

"Shit!"

"Nice talk. Little hormone problem going on there?"

Kira bristled. "Little attitude problem going on *there*?"

"Sorry, geez, but that penis talk was seriously scary."

"Who are you?"

The intruder extended his hand with a wolfish grin that made her wonder why his teeth weren't sharp. "I'm the new director of special events," he said. "And you?"

Just call me screwed. "Kira Fitzgerald," she said, unable

to extend a hand because she held an empty vase in one, and dripping roses in the other.

She placed the flowers in the vase, glanced behind her at her smoking trashcan, and opened the window above it. Then she wiped her hands on the skirt of her smocked tube dress, glad it was black, and eyed her matching blazer with yearning. "I'm the coordinator of special events," she said.

"Son of a . . . I mean, glad to meet you." The wolf warmed her with his sweeping glance, and when she took his offered hand across her desk, the heat his gaze had ignited escalated.

He let her hand go so fast, she thought he might have felt the burn as well.

"I guess . . . you're my new boss." Kira took her blazer from the back of her chair and slipped into it.

"You guessed right," he said.

"I've been alone in this office for two weeks," she said. "I didn't expect—"

"Not last week, you weren't. I started last week."

"Well, no, I was on . . . vacation last week. Personal stuff . . . to settle." Like getting her things from the Penis's apartment, finally.

Her hot new boss waited, for more of an explanation, Kira supposed, but she preferred not to elaborate. "I wouldn't have cast—I mean, I thought I was alone or . . ." She pointed over her shoulder and down toward the trashcan.

"Ah . . ." He winced. "Is the Penis begoned forever?"

"Nah. I'm sure he's screwing somebody."

"Okaaayyy."

Kira bit her lip and shifted her stance. "Anything in particular you'd like me to . . . coordinate this morning?"

"Now that you ask." Her boss gave her another deadly wolf grin, but fortunately for her, she'd mastered the art of hunk-resistance.

"I don't suppose you could scare up a few ghosts for

Rainbow's Edge," he said. "You know, say something that rhymes, and twirl that . . . thing in the air, the way you . . . toasted . . . Charlie."

"Do you honestly believe in magic?" Kira asked.

"I'm reserving judgment, but threaten one penis and a guy will usually believe about anything you tell him."

Kira bit her lip, refusing to be charmed. "Did *you* have this invitation printed?"

"Seemed like a good idea at the time," the hunk said. "How do you know Rainbow's Edge doesn't have any ghosts?"

"I've read histories on all our mansions."

He tilted his head. "Maybe you need to get a life?"

Kira slapped her palm with the invitation. *Bite me,* she thought. "Good thing these haven't been mailed yet."

"Oh, but they have."

She glanced at her desk calendar. "You ordered them *before* you started the job? What are you, some kind of overachiever?"

"I wanted to get a head start, but I didn't mean to put you on the spot. Nevertheless, I was assured that you could work, ahem, magic, and coordinate any event I thought would bring money into the foundation."

Kira thought about ways to put *him* on the spot to raise money for the foundation, like . . . selling him to the highest bidder. Hmm. Revenge for fun and profit.

She smiled, and reread the invite. "The phantom ghost *is* a problem, pun intended, though the event is perfect for All Hallows' Eve. But if anybody's willing to pay a grand to attend, which I seriously doubt, they're gonna expect to meet this drive-by playboy, and I don't think we can depend on him to show, even if he is Bessie's—"

"I see you two have met." Bessie Pickering Hazard, chairman of the board, swept into Kira's office, making for an awkward moment, as Kira had been about to trash her neglectful grandson.

"I came down to perform the introductions," Bessie said, "but no need, I see."

Kira and Bessie embraced like the friends they'd become in the past month, because it was Kira's first day back after a week of canceled-wedding damage control. "I missed you, Bessie. How *are* you?"

"Glad to see you back. When you didn't come home last night, I was worried. Everything okay? You okay?"

"I drove down from Boston this morning," Kira said. "Everything is . . . as expected."

"What do you mean, she didn't come *home* last night?" the wolf asked with snapping eyes. "Gram?"

Gram? Kira felt herself go cold. She wished a vanishing spell existed that she could perform lickety-split. But she remained visible, if the focused glint in Mr. Tall, Dark, and Incredible's eyes was anything to go by.

No wonder she'd thought of him as a wolf; they called him an Ice Wolf in the news, for pity's sakes. Now that she knew who he was, she saw that his stance, his demeanor, belonged to every arrogant jock she'd ever encountered.

Come to think of it, hadn't her ex looked up to this guy as some kind of role model—less for his skill on the ice than for his money, women, and cars, it was true, but what could you expect from a penis?

Talk about your worst nightmare.

"Didn't I tell you?" Bessie said, with such innocence, Kira became as suspicious as her grandson. "I couldn't pay Kira as much as I wanted," she said, "so I gave her an apartment at Cloud Kiss, rent free, as a job benefit. She's been with me for a month, now."

"No, you didn't tell me, but I think you might have mentioned it before I sublet my condo and moved home."

"Oh, no," Kira said.

"Oh, yes," Goddard said. "It appears, Miss Fitzgerald—"

"*Ms.* Fitzgerald."

"*Mizz* Fitzgerald. It appears we're neighbors, here and at home."

Bessie gave them an "Isn't this cozy?" smile, and Kira began to understand the wolf's simmering anger.

"As a matter of fact," Bessie said, "you'll be sharing a kitchen."

"Wait a minute," the kitchen-sharers said as one, surprising Kira and making her stop and regard the jock, as he regarded her, with even greater mistrust, if that were possible.

Bessie waved away their concern. "Don't worry. It's not like you'll be tripping over each other. Neither of you bothers to cook." She patted Kira's hand. "The kitchen separates the suite. You'll hardly know he's there."

Oh, she'd know. They'd both know. After all, she'd insulted the hell out of him. Worse than that, ever since he'd opened his mouth, she'd had this hormone thing going on, like popcorn on high heat, which really pissed her off, because that made him right. She did have a hormone problem.

The fact was, if he caught her raiding the fridge at midnight—which she did in her sleep—she just might . . . pop.

Kira gave herself a mental shake. According to the Penis, her new boss was the best Wizards goalie in thirty years, a wolf on and off the ice. Just what she needed, another jock in her life. A player. A man who collected women like loose change.

And hadn't Bessie said that this one had been named the best kisser in America or some such nonsense?

Air. She needed air. She should have realized that the slash across his brow and the bump in his otherwise perfect nose meant that he'd been kissed by sticks and pucks as well as starlets.

"Listen," Kira said, raising her chin as she regarded him. "I didn't know you were Bessie's grandson."

"The fact that I'm Bessie's grandson has no bearing on my ability to do my job!"

Kira stepped back. "Okay."

"And what's with you? How could you not know? You don't read the papers, watch TV?"

"Not for sports or reality shows, I don't. I like the movie channel."

"So you hate jocks *and* reality shows?"

Damn, he had been there for a while.

"Let's get something straight," he snapped, a miffed ice jockey in wolf mode, shooting hard sparks of silver her way. "Whoever I'm related to, whatever I used to be, or will be again, by God, I'm on board right now to get the Pickering Foundation back on its feet, and while I'm here, I plan to work myself, and everyone else, *to the bone*. Are we clear on that?"

"Sure. Of course. No problem."

"Glad to hear it." The jock turned on his heel for a last-word exit, but he gasped, faltered, and grabbed his cane. So much for a spectacular retreat, Kira thought, wishing to hell she hadn't witnessed it.

"Gram!" he shouted. "My office. Now!"

Bessie winked at Kira. "Yes, dear."

"Jason!" he snapped from his office. "You will call me Jason! No, maybe you should call me Mr. Goddard when I'm on the job, and I'll call you Mrs. Hazard."

"Yes, dear."

"Six months," he said, with no less bite. "You have me for six months and not a day more."

"Yes, dear," Bessie said with a last grin for Kira before shutting herself into his office.

If Kira hadn't been so shaken, she might've laughed— so sweet and innocent had Bessie looked before facing the snarling wolf in his den. Snarling and angry with the world.

But the closing click of that door had Kira covering her heart. Six months with eyes like his gazing down at her— as if in heated expectation . . . of . . . *not* what every other woman was willing to put out.

Would she be able to interact in a businesslike manner, in a sane manner, at least in the office, for six months on a daily basis with a man who looked like every girl's fantasy? A man with the eyes of a predator, an irresponsible jock who'd been chased by, and slept with, every acclaimed beauty in the Free World?

Kira wasn't certain, but no way could she bear the heat Goddard seemed to generate day *and* night. She didn't know what his problem was: a personality clash, plain old dislike, the nepotism chip on his shoulder, or maybe it was her magic spell. Whatever. It didn't matter, because they were stuck working together, and they'd both best get over it.

At least the electricity between them wasn't sexual. She'd already failed that test. She didn't have enough sex appeal to interest her own bridegroom, never mind a brazenly rich, sexy playboy jock.

She knew by Goddard's reputation, and by her ex's praise, that the hockey wolf was the kind of cocky jerk who needed no more than to snap his fingers, or flash his smile, to get a woman into his bed. "Well not me, buddy."

The man was spoiled—that was a headline-making fact—spoiled and rich, and so well put together that women followed him as if they were pups and he had a bone in his pocket.

Kira clamped a hand over her mouth when she caught her pun. A pretty meaty bone, too, as far as she could tell. Made Charlie look like he kept a cocktail frank in his pants, which pretty much defined the sex.

Now Goddard, on the other hand, had a reputation as a world-class lover, a winning kisser, and . . . selling him to the highest bidder was beginning to sound brilliant.

Kira grinned, but she groaned inwardly. The thought of working with Bessie's world-class hunk of a grandson spelled danger—a spell greater than any she could conjure—the kind with a heart-thrumming excitement attached, heaven help her, which meant she needed to remain *in control* at all times.

She'd surround herself with a white light so no emotion could touch her, because the last time she let down her guard and relaxed around a jock, she got caught in a three-way face-off without a stick.

She might be a solitary white witch, who'd vowed to harm none, but she wasn't stupid. She would not allow, or accept, or open *herself* to harm.

Now that she knew how faithless jocks could be, she wouldn't trust any of the breed again.

Nevertheless, the anger in her, the need for a bit of revenge, made Kira want to call her two-timing ex and brag about working with his idol.

She might do it, too, if she could erase the picture of Charlie and her sister in bed together long enough to make the call. Regan, her slut of a sister, had tried to say that "it" had never happened before, though as Kira watched them writhe in naked harmony—like a deer in headlights, unable to take her gaze from the sight—she thought they looked like they'd rehearsed, and plenty. Charlie's enthusiasm had been like nothing Kira had ever known . . . until he saw her and had the balls to be pissed by her interruption.

An eye-opener . . . in so many ways.

True, her sister had tried for months to talk her out of marrying Charlie, and ultimately Regan had not only saved Kira from a close call with a ball-fumbling jerk-off, her sister had kept her from having to explain what a loser she was to everyone they knew, because, *lucky for her,* she'd caught them *before* she mailed her wedding invitations.

Maybe someday she *would* thank her sister, as Regan had brazenly predicted. She might even be able to forgive her. Maybe. But Kira knew that she would never be able to trust her own judgment again, not where cocky jocks were concerned, and especially not in regards to a certain infamous silver-eyed jock of the wolf variety.

"*Mizz* Fitzgerald!" Goddard's growl crackled through the ancient intercom, as if to confirm his predatory nature. "Staff meeting in five minutes," he snapped. "The boardroom."

Kira rose and saluted . . . and Goddard opened the door.

Three

JASON stopped dead at the sight of the copper-haired witch mocking him. "At ease," he said, tongue in cheek, more charmed than annoyed by her salute, though, truth to tell, he had been a bit of both since he'd caught her casting a man-withering spell on foundation time.

A witch. His grandmother had hired "an honest-to-goddess witch," to quote Gram. Kira Fitzgerald, it seemed, had raised a great deal of money at the Museum of Witchcraft, and Gram expected her to do the same here, under *his* directorship—if he, and all his man-parts, survived, that was.

She stood there in an edgy black dress that raced his blood and turned it south, sliding notebooks, files, a day planner, pens, and highlighters into her briefcase, like any normal businesswoman . . . radiating pure sex.

Jason shifted his stance to ease the weight on his bad knee, not sure if he was grateful, or sorry, that he'd sworn off women, especially since this one made fiery magic, only one of the reasons he found her fascinating . . . and dangerous.

Damn it, he always did like to play with fire.

He'd come in for a pre-meeting briefing, but his focus had changed in the face of the paradox, or to put it more bluntly, in the face of his need to keep the paradox from noting his interest.

She slipped her wand into her briefcase and brought him crashing to earth. "Wait! You're not taking that mandrooper into *my* meeting."

"What?"

He crooked his fingers. "Give me the wand."

"This?" She dangled the smooth sensually carved staff by its lavender-faceted tip, as if it were a prize. Her sable lashes lowered over her gleaming emerald eyes, daring him to come closer.

Damned if she wasn't taking a fiendish delight in making him work for it, or in finding a reason to "stick it to him." She wasn't even waving the wand, and she was working a brand of sorcery.

Worse, he was exhilarated by her challenge. "Yes, that," Jason said on a scowl—or he hoped he'd scowled, because the sparkle in her eyes made it difficult to be stern.

"Why shouldn't I bring it to the meeting?" she asked with deceptive innocence. "I like to keep my wand handy."

"So you can take a shot at my . . . hockey stick? That would be a *no*. I wouldn't be able to think straight."

"Hah! I knew it! Men *do* think with their . . . sticks."

Jason frowned and remembered how much she annoyed him despite the attraction, so he presented his open palm with firm finality, to remind her who was boss. "Give it here, Mizz Fitzgerald."

He stepped toward her and she stepped back.

"No!" She brought the wand to her heart as he reached for it, and he came away with nothing but the heat of one fine firm breast scorching his hand.

Jason reared back, stung . . . and ready, and closed his fingers into his fist to retain her heat. Lush breasts, tiny waist, a bottom to fill his hands, and sink into. An hourglass figure that the women who'd once run this house would envy. Or . . . as the guys in the locker room would say: excellent butt, great rack.

They both chose to ignore the unexpected body check, though it was all Jason could do not to reach for more.

He didn't need to wonder whether she'd felt the shock of it. He could tell by the slow-rising soft russet stain washing the freckles from her pale Irish complexion.

Mesmerized, Jason watched each speckle blend with the blush and wondered how many freckles dotted the landscape where the blush began. He'd like to explore that uncharted territory at his leisure.

The way her tube dress was slipping, and her full alabaster breasts were emerging, it looked like fate was setting up his shot.

Their eyes met and held. Could she read him? Did he want her to?

She whisked her wand behind her back. "Hey," she said, as if challenged by that hot bit of eye contact. "It's my wand and it's important to me." She brought the slender wooden rod forward, stroked and regarded it with the kind of affection usually reserved for a lover.

Was she coming on to him?

"You wouldn't let just anybody touch *your*—" Her head snapped up.

"Hockey stick?" Okay, so she hadn't intended a come-on. Given the size of her eyes, she'd only just caught her own meaning. Her chin rose and her freckles disappeared again.

Jason thought it best to deny his fascination over the process and went around her desk to open the top drawer. "Let's leave the wand here while we go to the meeting, shall we?" He opened his hand again, but to no avail.

The witch went to the opposite side of her desk and faced him over the expanse. "No. I mean it. You can't touch it. A magic wand is personal. It symbolizes the life-force within the witch to whom it belongs. You could ruin it with negative energy, bad vibes, bad karma, dark moods, whatever. The damage would be unseen, but devastating. Your very touch could spoil my magic."

She took a long, slim purple velvet drawstring bag from her blazer pocket, slipped her handy-dandy man-drooper inside, pulled the string tight, and placed the package lovingly in her briefcase. "There, it's safe, and so are you . . . for now."

Jason faltered in his walk back her way.

She backed up, and bumped her hip on her desk. "You wouldn't want a rookie playing with your stick, now, would you?"

He cocked a brow, but she'd turned to her desk. "Someday, after I know you better," she said, searching her desk, "I might let you touch my wand, but don't count on it."

"Ditto," he said, raising the smoke-scented tension.

She froze, bit her lip, and searched harder.

"I apologize," he said, and she nodded.

With nothing more to be said—nothing safe to be said—she returned to her cubby, where the window met her computer table, which met her desk. There she sat, showing him her back, and giving her keyboard her full and fast-fingered attention.

Jason entered his office and closed the door between them.

"Ditto?" he repeated incredulously. "Ditto?"

Shaking his head over his idiocy, over his big mouth, both feet inside, he wondered what else Gram had been angling for, and it had better not be a rebound.

He really had given up on women, though he could never prove it by his reaction to this one. Berries, he thought; she smelled of ripe summer berries, and carried a lethal weapon.

Jason didn't know Gram's office staff well, but he was reasonably certain that Little Miss "Wither Your Penis" was not his grandmother's standard choice.

Plus, Gram had never before opened their home to a

foundation employee. Then again, as she had just finished reminding him, the foundation had never been in such dire straits before.

Fine. So Kira Fitzgerald might be able to get them out of this mess. Fine, so he was her boss—the *director* of special events—and she was his subordinate, his *coordinator*. Which meant that they should *not* be playing word games.

He should, without doubt, not have the feel of her breast programmed into his sensual memory banks, and they most categorically should not be about to share an apartment. More to the point, anticipation should not be riding him.

Oh, the apartment was big enough. His own suite on one side, and his parents', opposite, where the witch now lived, were separated by a good-sized kitchen. Like the red line in the center of the ice, their kitchen could serve as the neutral zone, but there, as here, nothing but doors would stand between them.

Suppose one of them sleepwalked. Yeah, he wished.

Okay, so he had already imagined sifting his fingers through that lush tumble of cinnamon corkscrew curls, of tugging that single tight coil on her brow to see if it would spring back.

He'd already admired the splash of freckles across her tip-tilted nose, so pale, he could only see them up close, in bold contrast to the eloquence in her snapping verdant eyes, visible and deadly at any range.

Jason paced his time-worn oriental rug to work out the kink in his bad knee, and avoid thinking about the atypical sorceress his grandmother had hired. He had a lot of work to accomplish in six short months.

Too bad the witch thought he got this job because Gram was Pickering's chairman of the board.

"Well, Mizz Fitzgerald, you're in for a surprise, because I intend to earn my title by working us both until we drop from exhaustion." She'd hate him by the time his stint at the foundation was up, which would be best for both of them.

It really irked him that he'd been comfortably celibate since his accident, and now in struts Little Miss Freckled Shoulders, who jump-starts his libido with a flick of her wand, never mind that she's shrinking somebody's dick at the time.

What a contradiction—small in stature, big on impact. Chic, sassy, bold, hard-hearted, tough as nails, and very much a woman of today. In contrast, she exuded a rather Victorian air, an innocence that had caught his attention.

At first glance she'd appeared wounded and vulnerable, then she'd turned witchy and bone-shriveling. Hot in barely there black, her strappy high-heel sandals topped with crystal butterflies, her ears rife with hoops and studs, she looked at a man in a way that could shrink him or harden him without a wand.

Jason took another awkward turn about his office, wishing he could toss his damned cane out a real window. Fortunately, neither of his windows opened, not the small clear oval in the corner, nor the rare, multipaned Tiffany behind his desk. Damned cane.

Could Kira cast a spell to make him heal? She'd sure cast one to make him ache.

Did she honestly have any true magical power? And could she be as innocent as she seemed?

If he weren't her boss, he'd try shock tactics to find out, like lowering the top of her strapless dress.

"Don't go there, Ice Boy." Jason rubbed the back of his neck and turned to his desk. "Help save the foundation."

He sat down and went through his papers, and found Kira's job application.

Impressive.

Maybe *innocent* wasn't the right word; nor *Victorian.* Kira Fitzgerald was more of a Gilded Age throwback— soft, he remembered well, feminine, sexy, wholesomely endowed, in a cutting-a-man-to-his-knees sort of way, but stiff-spined, determined, and willing to fight for what she believed in, chin high, eye to eye.

He looked up at the portrait above the claret marble mantelpiece. Like the siren in the Gay Nineties ballgown overseeing his office from on high, Kira Fitzgerald could hold a man in thrall and not let him go, until she was ready, and most men would allow it, wallow in it, and beg for more.

Let her try, Jason thought, denying his instinct to add, *please.*

He cursed. This mansion was getting to him; there was no other explanation. He wished they hadn't been forced to house the foundation offices here. It felt too personal, like . . . playing house. Not good in the circumstances.

Their offices had obviously been someone's private suite—his, the sitting room, while his coordinator's connecting office would have been the bedroom, which explained her private bath, complete with claw-foot tub.

Jason envisioned her using it, cinnamon curls damp and coiled on her head, bubbles to the crown of her round lush breasts.

Like his Gilded-Age mantel Madonna, Kira Fitzgerald, sexiest witch in the East, gave the impression she was waiting to be set free . . . or awakened.

"Shit. That's the last place you wanna go."

The clocks in the mansion chimed in sync, a swift but hearty echo, over, above, and around him, and Jason scrambled to put his notes in order. "Great start, Ice Boy; late for your own meeting first day on the job. Way to make a good impression on the witch."

He heard her hall door shut and her heels clicking away. He gathered his things, opened the door between their offices, and went to her trashcan.

Holding his breath at the stench, he retrieved a barely singed scrap of what she'd been burning . . . an invitation to her wedding . . . yesterday. Son of a . . . Envelope fragments were addressed. Wedding invitations never mailed, ergo, wedding canceled.

Jason wondered why, precisely, but he did know that Charlie's penis must somehow be the culprit.

No wonder the hard edge, the fight one minute and vulnerability the next.

"Poor wretched little witch . . . just keep your vengeful wand away from me."

"HE'S thirty-one, single, and dynamite," Michaela Dennison said as Kira entered the boardroom.

The development director was, no doubt, talking about America's best kisser, and, *no doubt,* calculating the ways she could use him as her . . . personal . . . assistant.

"Yes," Kira said, looking through her folder to be certain she'd brought the Ghost Tour invitation. "But watch out, his people skills su—"

He stepped into the room and skewered her with a look. Talk about eye contact. "His people skills *sure* can't be beat," Kira said.

Electric eye contact. He zapped her with a scowl and a cocked brow. Okay, so he wasn't buying her save.

She really would need to think about moving out of Cloud Kiss, because she wasn't even gonna catch a break when she went home tonight. Except she needed a break in rent more than she needed to get away from the wolf.

The Penis had bailed on his half of the nonrefundable wedding expenses, big surprise, and she couldn't lay the cost at her parents' faded door; *they* were still putting their sixth through private school.

When the staff was seated at the jade marble boardroom table—Goddard the only male present—Bessie cleared her throat and stood, upstaging him, or so his surprise seemed to indicate. "You all know my grandson," she said, "but what you don't know is that besides being the director of special events, he's the vice-chairman of the board."

Goddard raised a brow Bessie's way, his promise of retribution clear, though the old dear simply grinned, and indicated that he should take over.

Kira wished again that Bessie had *said* it was her grandson she was bringing onboard, and when he would arrive, but that was dirty water under a broken bridge.

Goddard took the floor, but he didn't act like the savior who would rescue the foundation. He failed to mention his star status and connections, and what his famous presence could accomplish.

Score one for the jock.

When he shared his vision for the foundation, Kira saw why Bessie thought he might be the man who could pull Pickering out of its slump.

Jason Goddard spoke with knowledge and determination. He oozed charisma, vowed to work hard, asked for their help, and at least eight of the ten women around the table were drooling, which pretty much left her and his grandmother with the only semblance of sanity in the room.

Except that Kira wasn't taking any bets on herself.

Four

KIRA stopped salivating and tried not to give in to her hormone surge.

She reminded herself that Prince Charming was a jock, however jump-my-bones captivating he may appear at this moment. He was a natural seducer, always irresistible, mostly unreliable, a wart-making, lily-pad-sitting, smarmy-type jock.

"Every *mansion* is now more of a liability than an asset," Goddard said, reclaiming her attitude-adjusted attention. "And we have to turn the equation around. The profit we used to give away, mostly to St. Anthony's, is being devoured by rising overhead."

Kira found it difficult to picture him as a toad when he looked so hot and sounded so informed.

"We also need to turn the foundation's image around," he said, "because people like to give to a winning organization. I have a few ideas about how and where to begin."

Ah, here it comes, Kira thought, all the reasons that

would make her want to pin the croaker to a slab of wax and start cutting.

She'd be the one forced to coordinate their way out of his schemes, and if his new ideas were anything like his Rainbow's Edge ghost fixation, she was gonna need her dissecting kit real soon.

"Basically, work at the Pickering Foundation is going to turn into one big party," Goddard said, "and what more could we ask of life?"

"Par-tee," Kira said below her breath.

"What was that?" he asked.

She looked up, surprised. "I . . . get to plan the party."

"Yes, you do." He proposed events twice a month at first, weekly down the road. "I was thinking of a Christmas Ball; sleigh rides; a dress-as-your-favorite-lovers Valentine Ball; garden parties; candlelight water tours."

Yeah, right. "Excuse me," Kira said, "but how can you see a mansion from a boat by candlelight?"

"Good point," Goddard said, clearly ticked. "I should have said *moonlight* water tours *to* the mansions." He took a breath. "We could have scavenger hunts, vintage-car races; hot-air-balloon tours . . ."

"And sweep our donors out to sea; that'll bring in the bucks."

Goddard skewered her with a look.

Kira felt the sting. "We're on the coast," she said. "I mean, personally, I've always wanted to take a ride in a hot-air balloon, but . . ." She shrugged. "Over land would be good."

Goddard bent to confide in her. "If you got swept out to sea," he whispered, "you could ride your broom back."

Kira bit off a giggle, which earned her an eye roll from the development director, who was trolling for donors. Part of rich boy's job would be to find Michaela more wealthy women to solicit.

Hmm. Rich *female* donors needed. Rich, powerful *male* on board . . . equals celebrity bachelor auction . . . equals spectacular event. Kira added the auction idea to her notes.

The rest of Goddard's ideas ranged from off-the-wall horrible, to impossible, to doable, to brilliant.

Lucky her, Kira thought, she'd get to weed out the nightmares.

Mizz Fitzgerald," Goddard said. "You have something to add?"

"Yes, I've put together a list of events myself."

"Such as—"

"I think we should do more for St. Anthony's, like bringing the boys together with couples looking to adopt."

"That'll bring in the bucks," Michaela said.

"Money isn't all we're about," Goddard said. "The boys are my primary concern, and I think the idea is an excellent one. Please, continue Mizz Fitzgerald."

Kira now saw him as a respectable frog-toad kind of jock. "In addition to events for the boys," she said, "which we can discuss, later, how about a horse-drawn fund-raising sleigh tour of the mansions decorated for Christmas, an interactive murder-mystery tour, a celebrity bachelor auction? I'll bet some woman would pay big to win the Best Kisser in America for a night . . . I mean a date." Kira flushed.

Goddard growled, but she didn't know if he was angry about the auction idea itself, or her slip implying he'd sleep with his date, or both.

Whatever it was, Kira had to look for something in her briefcase on the floor, while her face cooled.

When she rose, Goddard was waiting to pounce. "Some of your ideas are excellent," he said. "Some are impossible, impractical, out of the ques—"

"As are yours."

The silence around them pulsed.

To give the toad his due, he acknowledged her point with a nod, which caused a slight relaxation of shoulders and an easing of the collective tension around the table.

He scowled. "A people auction is—"

"Perfect," Kira said. "I mean, how many famous kisser guys are there? You can get your famous jock friends to join you. The cheerleaders you date hang with some pretty illustrious names. Invite them to be auctioned off. Your models and starlets would be a draw, plus they'd bid high."

Jaw set, chin dimple deep, Goddard gave a lengthy negative head shake, while Kira nodded for the same length of time, simply to tick him off.

"You're on board to get the Pickering Foundation on its feet," Kira quoted. "You'll work yourself and everyone else to the bone."

Okay, so the toad was morphing back into a wolf.

Kira tried an encouraging smile, not easy in the face of his blood thirst. Any minute, she thought, he'd go for her throat with his pointy teeth dripping saliva.

"Come on," Kira said, taking her life in her hands. "It could be fun, the kind of upbeat high-profile party you're used to, and it would mean big bucks for the foundation. I'll bet we could clear a hundred grand in a night."

"Two hundred," Michaela said, and Kira knew what it cost the development director to side with her. Kira could hear the fund-raiser's brain ringing like the vintage cash register at the mansion tour desk.

Goddard shook his head again. "While I'm sure a bachelor auction is not without merit—"

"*Celebrity* bachelor auction," Kira clarified.

"I like it," his grandmother said, catching him off guard. "An auction is a great idea. November would probably be best." Bessie patted her grandson's hand. "Call your friends, dear." She turned to Kira. "You two can work out the details later."

Goddard bit off an argument, his mottled complexion a dead giveaway, and appeared to swallow his pride and his objections.

Squaring his shoulders, he returned to his notes as if the debate had not taken place, as if it had not gone against him, which meant it was not over, not by a slap shot.

Great, Kira thought. She could hardly wait for the grudge match.

He checked his notes. "Mizz Fitzgerald, let's talk about those events for St. Anthony's."

Bessie cleared her throat. "Spending more money on St. Anthony's is the only suggestion I *can't* agree with," she said. "I regret that our donations and expenses for St. Anthony's must be lower than usual this year. We don't have the ready funds, and I won't dip into the principal."

"There must be ways to save money, Gram, er, I mean, Mrs. Hazard," Goddard said, "than by cutting St. Anthony's."

His grandmother opened a folder. "I send only rare and valuable items to conservators. As workers retire, I try not to replace them. We have two gardeners, instead of four; they travel from property to property. At Kingston, after the housekeeper retired, I left a small cleaning staff and a caretaker."

Bessie checked another list. "The Deerings at Rainbow's Edge took the gatehouse as a life residence, in lieu of raises. That saves them rent, and the gatehouse is maintained at no cost to us, though that did take the gatehouse off the tour."

Goddard placed a hand on his grandmother's. "Of course you tried. I apologize." He shook his head. "We're walking a fine line, and I know we have no choice, but if we're not careful, cost-cutting could lead to higher maintenance later."

"My worst fear," his grandmother said.

"So . . . now I know why I'm here," Goddard said. "Ideas for St. Anthony's, Mizz Fitzerald."

"I have two," Kira said. "A theatrical that the sisters would prep the children to perform, followed by a dessert buffet and games, where people interested in adopting could meet and interact with the boys."

Kira opened her publicity folder. "I can advertise on the cheap, in community bulletin boards, TV, the papers. Maybe get a feature story." She made a note. "We'll post a phone number so people can call to make reservations, no charge, so we know how many we're seating and feeding."

Goddard's expression turned to respect. "I like the idea. Thank you, Mizz Fitzgerald." He made a note. "Your second idea?"

"A gift of time and service, something that would save St. Anthony's money to make up for what we're not donating."

"I'm for it," Goddard said. "What do you have in mind?"

"You could give the boys hockey lessons at the Cloud Kiss rink, and cut the cost of after-school supervision."

Jason felt as if he'd been board-checked by a bulldozer. He shook his head to clear it. "No," he said, dazed. "No."

"Well," the witch said, "you gave *that* a lot of thought."

Jason had noticed that everyone at the table spent a great deal of time looking from him, to his coordinator, and back. Gram's smile was broad, while everyone else looked as if they wanted out.

"I'm a player," Jason said, knowing if he could make his grandmother understand, everyone else would, but though he saw empathy in her look, he knew that she thought he should forget hockey. She probably thought coaching would be good for him. Son of a . . . witch!

He turned to the thorn in his side. "I'm not a coach, Mizz Fitzgerald. When I'm on the ice, I skate," he said. "I play hockey; I *have* to, which is impossible right now."

She didn't understand any more than his grandmother.

"You wouldn't have to skate," the witch said. "Give the boys directions from the sidelines. Whatever they learn would be second to working with you, to the exercise, the *fun,* the opportunity to leave a building, in which they live *and* attend school, to do something different with their mundane lives."

She was right, damn her, but it would kill him to spend time in that rink and not be able to skate. It would eat him from the inside out. Jason shook his head. He wasn't ready. Not to coach, and not to face those boys again. He certainly couldn't bear to see the need in Travis Robinson's eyes again. "Gram, I don't think—" Jason felt like he was begging, so he shut up.

"I think," his grandmother said. "I know," she corrected, seeking his understanding, "that this is the solution. We can't give them money, but we can save them money." She covered his hand. "You can do it, Jay," she said softly.

Great, he thought, another minute and she was gonna pull out choo-choo doggie and his blankie. But she squared her shoulders and became all business again, and he was grateful.

Jason hoped no one else had seen the vulnerability his grandmother had addressed. He couldn't even look the witch's way to see what she thought of the exchange.

Gram caught his eye. "Since you have physical therapy on Mondays, Tuesdays, and Thursdays, you'll coach the boys after school on Wednesdays and Fridays," she said, "starting next week. That will give me time to talk to Sister Margaret, and it'll give you a week to prepare. Kira, I'm adding assistant coach to your job title and duties."

The witch bit off a protest, as ready as he to argue, but God herself had spoken, and there wasn't anything either of them could do, because Bessie Hazard's head was as hard as the brick wall that got him here.

Better men than he had tried, and failed, to sway her.

For the next six months, he was gonna have a sexy-as-hell witch by his side day and night and in between, Jason realized. Talk about a bad time to be celibate. He might spontaneously combust.

Jason gave the witch a hard stare, because he wanted her to squirm, but she raised her chin and gave as good as she got, her eyes hot with something that shot straight to his—

Damn, but she would be a handful, if he ever got his hands on her, minus the wand, of course, which would be stupid in the extreme, and dangerous, and impossible, Jason reminded himself.

He opened the floor for questions. The development director licked her lips when their gazes met, and he almost laughed. He'd had more subtle come-ons from a pole dancer.

"Your celebrity status could make you quite an asset to the Development Office," Michaela said, lashes at half-mast. "Any chance I can take you on the occasional weekend? You know, do some 'one-on-ones' together?"

Could she be any plainer? Did his grandmother understand?

Since Gram was examining a plastic pen with great attention to the casino ad on the side, he figured: Yeah, she knew.

Okay, so Michaela was assertive, but who better to ask for big bucks, right? He simply needed to find her some top-notch donors. He nodded. "If I can help secure a major donation, I don't see that doing a face-to-face would be a problem. On occasion. Mizz Fitzgerald? Did you have a question?"

The approving smile the witch turned his way made Jason feel as if he could do anything.

"Yes, I do," she said, "about the Ghost and Graveyard Tour of Rainbow's Edge."

"Shoot," her boss said, flashing his first easy smile, and making her damned-near forget to breathe. No wonder women followed him like puppies.

"Mizz Fitzgerald?"

"Oh, yes. Sorry." Kira tossed the end of her scarf around her neck to hide her blush. "One: A thousand dollars per person seems a bit pricey for a ghost tour. And two: More of a fact, but important—Rainbow's Edge doesn't have any ghosts."

Goddard chuckled with everyone else; she had to give him that. "In my . . . enthusiasm," he said, "I did fail to confirm the existence of ghosts, but with a little research, I'm sure *we* can come up with enough titillating ghostly activity to keep our attendees happy."

Kira took the bait. "*We*, meaning?"

"*You*, of course," Goddard said with a smile that could only be termed vengeful. "You'll pull off every event I plan with class and flair."

And that, Kira thought, was an order.

Five

"YOU think we can give our guests a thousand dollars' worth of ghostly titillation in a mansion with no ghosts?" Kira said, making everyone else in the room shift uncomfortably in their chairs.

"The fact is," Goddard said, "the ghosts won't be the draw, if you'll excuse my—" He blushed; the Best Kisser in America actually blushed.

Kira was charmed, despite herself, and to remain objective, was forced to recall her previous image of him.

The toad sat straighter. "Let me say this another way. The upper stratum, or shall I be blunt and say the moneyed hoards, will attend the Ghost and Graveyard Tour because it'll be my first public appearance." Pain etched his features, giving him a wounded look and making Kira want to take his healing process into her own hands.

"My accident made the national news," he said, almost in apology. "According to the press and Mrs. Hazard, everybody who is anybody with a buck is clamoring to attend my . . . coming-out, shall we say?"

That was true, Kira thought. Maybe the ghost thing wouldn't be such a big deal.

"I don't understand the draw, myself," Goddard said, "but there you are. We may as well take advantage. Soon enough people will see an invitation from the Pickering Foundation and say, 'Oh no, not him again.'"

Disarmed, Kira looked around and saw she was not alone.

"While I plan to have several pricey events over the next few months," Goddard continued, "a thousand will not be the cost for all attendees or for every event."

His gaze lit on each woman in turn, raising the estrogen level to catfight proportions. "In addition to the Sunday-night tour, we'll give the tour after school on Halloween the following day to about two hundred children. Some will be from St. Anthony's and others will be selected by social services. No charge, of course, with games and Halloween treats. Do you have another question, Mizz Fitzgerald?"

Kira felt small and she wasn't certain why. Her questions had been valid, but his answers had been better—professional and self-effacing. How did a living legend pull off "humble" with such apparent ease?

Kira sighed. "No more questions."

"Good," Goddard said. "I'm looking forward to working with all of you. I hope the foundation will profit from my six months here while I have the chance to heal and rejuvenate, and figure out what I want to be after my hockey career ends, which won't be for some years yet."

"Most people our age know what they want to be when they grow up," Kira said, her quip hitting him like an unexpected dart. Without meaning to, she'd opened a wound and made him bleed.

"Hockey was practically my first word," he said, tossing his own quip, which fell as flat as hers. "I knew what I really wanted to be when I was three, but it's the nature of the game for hockey players to go on to a second, less strenuous career, eventually. Any other questions? Anybody?"

She'd really liked living at Cloud Kiss, Kira thought with a sigh. Who wouldn't want to live in one of Newport's finest Gilded Age mansions? But it was definitely time to go apartment hunting.

Damn. She hated the thought of moving, but fighting her inclinations, as in allowing herself to become tinder to this man's spark 24/7, would suck.

If she stayed, she'd hate herself in the end . . . and so would he.

Cloud Kiss was incredible, and Bessie was sweet, but the old dear couldn't use living alone as an excuse to keep her any longer, job perk or . . . rent. Crap, she'd be forced to pay rent anywhere else.

She couldn't afford to move, damn it. How could she forget that little detail, even for a minute?

Kira closed the folder on her notes. She had to face facts; she had no choice but to stick it out at Cloud Kiss. She'd simply take steps to avoid the Big Bad Wolf after hours.

He checked his notes. "I guess that's it for today. A light lunch is being served in the dining room, compliments of Mrs. Hazard, to celebrate my first day. You're all invited."

He checked his watch. "Since it'll be late when we finish eating, why don't we make this a real celebration, call it a day, and start fresh tomorrow morning."

Kira saw that Bessie approved his move. With his decision and his announcement, Goddard made it clear who was in charge.

Everyone left, except Michaela, who eyed their new leader with determination, and more on her agenda than Pickering's development program. Kira could have sworn Goddard caught her approach, but he turned away.

"Mizz Fitzgerald," he said. "Can I speak with you for a minute before you go?"

Michaela turned on a proverbial dime, broke her heel, faltered, and kept going.

Kira stifled a grin.

Goddard gave her an assessing look, causing another hormone surge. I am woman; hear me sizzle. How weird was this? Kira could have sworn she'd iced over months ago.

Yeesh, Goddard shows up and her hormones rush out to greet him with hot popcorn dances and full-bodied sociability.

Hell, she guessed she'd been handling her jilt pretty well . . . until today.

"You didn't do that?" Goddard asked. "Did you?"

"Do what?"

Again, that appraising look. "The broken heel," he said.

"Ask me again when her hair falls out."

"You couldn't?"

Kira laughed. "You look so serious."

"And you look so dangerous."

"Dangerous, huh?" Kira liked that, however wrong the call.

Okay, so she'd admit it. She was a sex-starved jilted bride, who'd sworn off men, dealing with a slightly broken, vulnerable ex-jock, who just happened to be drop-dead gorgeous, with eyes sad and intense enough to turn her to Jell-O. Cherry Jell-O, with whipped cream, and . . . popcorn on top. Yum. She would share. They could wallow in it. Make love in it. Kira covered her lips with her fingers to keep from betraying a vocal and hysterical reaction to the thought.

Goddard regarded her quizzically.

"Hiccup," she said, feeling as if the words *loose cannon* should be stamped on her forehead.

"Mizz Fitzgerald—"

Kira groaned. "I hate it when you call me that."

"You *told* me to."

"But you say *Ms.* as if it has *three* z's. Mizzzzzz."

Her nemesis rose, winced, and sat again. "Of all the—" He shook his head, rubbed his knee, and gave her a near grin. "Perhaps we should . . ."

Oh, yeah, she thought, *we should.* "What?" she asked.

"Bury our pasts and work together?"

How could she argue, when burying her past was exactly what she'd come to Newport to do? "Listen, Mr. Goddard, I didn't intend to—"

"Call me Jason, will you? My father is Mr. Goddard, damn it, and neither of us appreciates the comparison."

The dysfunctional disclosure resonated in the silence of the empty boardroom. He stopped rubbing his knee and looked up, as if he'd just heard himself. "I can't believe I said that."

Kira felt normal in the face of his admission. "Wow."

"You never know, though," he said, "I might be in favor again, now that hockey's temporarily out of the picture."

Kira relaxed for the first time since meeting him. "That's okay," she said. "I like you better flawed."

He removed his hand from his bad knee, his expression hard.

"I don't mean physically flawed," Kira rectified. "Yeesh. Sorry, again. I mean the kind of flawed that negates the silver-spoon, rich-pampered-brat image."

Jason barked a laugh. "You wouldn't think me pampered if you saw me on the ice."

"No, I'd imagine that rather than a silver spoon, you'd need a silver stake to stop you on the ice. That's what they use on wolves right? Or is that vampires? Which are you? I can't keep my wolves and vampires straight."

She was glad he'd found the grin she was going for.

"Seriously," she said. "You might want to talk to somebody about that father issue."

"Why would I want to dredge up all that crap?"

"You're right," she said. "Let's leave our pasts at the door and be ourselves, shall we? No walking on eggshells. You're the Ice God and I'm the Ice Maiden. Deal?"

"Already, I disagree with you."

"I'm well aware of that."

"I mean, if I'm a god," he said, "then you're a goddess."

"Yeah, right."

"Fine then; I *play* hockey, and you *play* ice maiden."

Kira shrugged. "If you say so."

He damned near smiled. "Why do I think you won't always be this agreeable?"

"Search me."

He gave her his cockiest grin, but Kira refused to blush. "So," she said, "I guess we *are* free to be ourselves."

"I'm almost afraid to agree."

"Too late. That was definitely a yes, in which case, hello, Jason, I think a ghost tour in a house with no ghosts is a blatant misrepresentation, and smacks of questionable ethics. Oh, and please call me Kira." She didn't extend her hand this time, which would be about as smart as sticking it in a fire.

Goddard—no, Jason shook his head. "Hello, Kira. I expect we'll find *something* spooky at Rainbow's Edge, because we're going to look *very hard,* and if we don't, it doesn't matter, because I'm the boss for the next six months, right?"

"Right," she said, as ordered.

"Three hundred invitations have already gone out, so you'll coordinate this event, and any others I hand you, with that special magic my grandmother assures me you possess, misgivings or not, until I go back to the NHL." He waited for her to accept his authority.

She gave it with a nod.

"After my grandmother and my hockey career, the foundation is my top priority."

"And you said *I* needed to get a life."

He gave up the point with a gracious nod. "It appears we're in the same situation."

"Not quite," she said, "but I won't argue."

"Already I find that suspicious."

Kira shrugged, grabbed her briefcase, and rose. "I'm picking my battles."

"Good game plan. I'm sorry about your wedding."

He knew. Damn. She sat down again. "I made my own bed, as they say, except that somebody else . . . Well, *c'est la vie.*" She popped back up. "Lunch?"

AFTER lunch, Kira returned to her office and found she had company. Castleton Court's jet-setter in residence, heir to the Castleton fortune, Mr. William Castleton—bronze, blond, and beautiful—sat slouched in her cordovan leather armchair, ankles raised and crossed on her desk, a martini in his hand.

Another charming toad of the lily-pad set.

Billy's family had donated Castleton Court to the Pickering Foundation some thirty years before, with the stipulation that their descendants, in perpetuity, occupy the family apartment on the top floor. Billy was the last of the line, thus far.

Definitely a silver-spoon kind of guy, Billy also owned a silver Ferrari, a Lamborghini, an Aston Martin, a Porsche, and a Jag. Bewitching Billy collected the world's most expensive cars the way her grandmother collected silver snuffboxes.

Frankly, Billy's I-can-have-anything-I-want attitude got old fast. His style made Goddard seem like an everyday-Joe, a regular nine-to-fiver. Even the tennis outfit Billy was sporting right now probably cost more than her weekly paycheck.

Not that Goddard dressed off-the-rack. His dapper double-breasted suit of dark eggplant, with pale blue pin stripes, felt like silk to the touch. She'd discovered that by accident when he leaned over to suggest she use a broom for transportation, but keeping herself from touching it, or him, again had turned into a study in control.

The difference between the two men stood out, however: Billy didn't play tennis, hence his tennis clothes were no more than a pricey male-peacock type display, while Goddard had just put on a great show of working for a living.

"Anybody home?" Billy asked, waving a hand in front of her eyes, to reclaim the attention he craved. "Got something on that pretty little mind of yours?" he teased.

"Yeah, like my job. Hello."

But Billy only heard what he wanted. "How about we go"—he sipped his martini, as if she had time to waste—"for a spin?"

Kira sat at her computer to look up Sister Margaret's phone number on her database. "Which car?" she asked, typing Sister's name into the "find" field. Billy's cars were beautiful.

"Who said anything about a car?"

Kira turned a look his way.

Billy winked. "Four-poster, upstairs, my suite. Whadya say?"

Kira shook her head at his nonsense. "Did you hear? I have a new boss."

"Yeah, Bessie's puck-stoppin' grandson, Mr. Kissy Face Goddard, himself, is hanging here these days, working, no less, or pretending to. Imagine that."

"Billy," Jason said, his greeting frosty.

Again, Kira didn't know how long Jason had been standing in the doorway behind her. This time he stood like a stone statue, jacket gone, ice blue shirtsleeves rolled up, muscular arms crossed, perfect lips firm, the scar on his brow white against his tan. His cane, she noticed from her vantage point, he'd left against *his* side of the connecting door.

By the matching expressions of distrust on the faces of the hard, dark jock, and the soft, fair jet-setter, Kira thought a new-millennium pissin' contest, rich-boy style, might be brewing.

She leaned back in her chair, tapped her pencil against her smile, and crossed her ankles to wait for the show.

"Kira," Goddard said, using her first name for the first

time since their postmeeting chat, making her name sound like honey on his tongue, probably for Billy's benefit. "I thought I gave you the afternoon off. What are you still doing here?"

"I wanted to call Sister Margaret and give her a heads up on the play. She'll need to get started, and we should set a date for the sake of publicity. Then I want to call a friend on the *Journal,* see if we can get some buzz going. I think I can get a story in the Boston papers, too."

"Go *team,*" Jason said. "Want to iron out a few details before you call?"

"Sure. I'll be ready in a minute," she said, going for her notes, pleased by her promotion to the team.

"Well." Billy pouted as he rose, ignoring Goddard. "I guess that's our spin canceled for the day."

"Right," Kira said, waving him off without looking up.

JASON smiled in approval at Kira's response to Billy. He and Billy had been rivals through high school, whether it was drinking, sports, cars, or girls, but they'd grown up now . . . for the most part.

It wasn't his fault, Jason thought, that the people who worked here at Castleton Court called Billy the Court Jester while they called him the Boss. Sweet.

Kira stepped into his office, notes in hand. "What are you smiling about?" she asked.

"Progress," Jason said. "By the way, I'd like to do a ghost hunt at Rainbow's Edge tomorrow. How does first thing in the morning sound?"

"What are we gonna do," she asked, "sit and wait for something to spook us?"

"Of course not," he said on a frown. "I thought we'd check out the library, see what we can find on the history of the place."

"I read only one history on each house, so who knows?" she said, choosing a sofa. "Maybe we'll get lucky and find a tunnel . . . with a skeleton . . . and hidden treasure, so we can improvise."

Jason didn't seem to appreciate her sarcasm. "We'll find something."

"I still can't believe you invited people to a ghost tour without making sure the house had ghosts."

Jason opened his notebook with a hard flick of his wrist. "Had this talk," he said. "Didn't appreciate it then. *Don't* appreciate it now. Moving on."

Six

JASON took the sofa opposite Kira while she reviewed her notes. An art deco coffee table stood between them, but he suspected that a referee would be a smarter bet.

Over the next hour they discussed the Rainbow's Edge Ghost tour, disagreeing often.

The last time he felt this exhilarated, Jason thought, he was gearing up for a championship game.

The ghost tour quarrel led them to his giving the boys at St. Anthony's hockey lessons, over which they outright battled, Jason playing offense loudly, Kira playing defense brilliantly.

"Bottom line," she said. "They're boys in need, and you're an adult who can help them. So, you've been benched for a while. Tough cookies. Suck it up."

With those words, she'd kept him from scoring. The game ended at one-to-nothing in her favor. Jason was beginning to see his coordinator in a whole new light, while trying not to imagine her in a lot less clothes.

His luck. He had himself a sexy "witch" with a brain, a heart, and a smart mouth.

She argued for the sake of the boys, for foundation ethics and good planning, which could only spell success in the end. He'd never admit she was right, but he respected the hell out of her feisty spirit.

By the time they finished, Jason felt justly pleased with his first day's work. He'd survived an invigorating battle of wits, and made strides to benefit both the foundation and the boys at St. Anthony's, but not without the witch's annoyingly excellent input.

She was right, damn it. Hockey lessons would be good for the boys.

Every clock chimed six as he stood in the dim upper hall of Castleton Court locking his office door, satisfied and impressed with his adversarial coordinator, while she locked her own door, twenty feet away.

Gram had chosen well. Kira Fitzgerald knew special events, and Jason could already tell that she gave her work 110 percent, even if it meant being a pain in the ass.

They discussed their projects as they walked through the mansion, parting at the base of Castleton Court's sweeping staircase. Jason headed for his Hummer, in a reserved spot out front, Kira, for her car in the employee lot out back.

He arrived at Cloud Kiss and headed for the family garage while she drove around the house to park out back. They met at the elevator and rode up together.

The dim, Gilded Age old box had always reminded him of a canary cage, still bearing the fussy traces of its era, though its guts were now state of the art. The scents of nutmeg, cinnamon, and apples permeated the air inside. "This goes down to the kitchen," Jason said. "I'm guessing Rose baked apple strudel today."

Kira chuckled. "No wonder I'm always starving when I walk into my apartment."

"Good day," Jason said.

"Is that a good-bye," she asked, "or an observation?"

Jason shook his head at her nonsense. "An observation, and you may as well take it as a compliment."

The witch clapped a hand to her heart. "Such exalted praise. I'm all aflutter." Her emerald eyes danced.

He could drown in those eyes, Jason thought, eyes as green as a stormy sea, a good way to describe Kira's sudden presence in his life. A storm. A wreaker of havoc . . . and magic.

The elevator doors opened and they stepped onto the fourth floor, its black-and-white diamond-shaped tiles gleaming.

Their respective "front" doors, at opposite ends of the family apartment, opened to foyers and living rooms. The "back" door sat between the two and led to the neutral zone, their dreaded community kitchen.

That door, they avoided like the penalty box. He'd starve before he'd breach the sanctum that separated them, and he thought she might, too.

When she turned her key in her lock, their gazes caught and slipped away. Jason bit off an invitation to supper as she disappeared inside. A narrow escape, but at least *he* could go down and beg from Gram.

An hour later he regarded the witch across the linen-covered expanse of Gram's long, polished mahogany dining table, with its gargoyle-carved chairs that had scared him until he was seven.

"Isn't this cozy?" Gram said. Like a queen, she presided, while Jason faced his nemesis in black. On Kira, tights and an oversize hoodie looked sexy, because her zipper stopped at her ample cleavage, and she wasn't wearing a blouse . . . maybe not even a bra.

Jason fumbled and dropped his fork.

Her red curls fought their confinement, as unruly as the witch herself, while her haphazard ponytail made her look young and innocent. Hah!

Not having expected her presence, Jason felt gauche and embarrassed in faded gray sweats with a hole in one knee. "I would have dressed," he said sharply, "if I'd known we were having company."

Gram squeezed Kira's hand, taking the bite out of his words.

"Our Kira's not company."

He hadn't meant to be rude and she wasn't theirs. She lived in a world of magic wands and— "Wait!" He skewered the witch with a look. "Where's your wand?"

She whipped the man-drooper from her pocket and held it up.

Jason raised a staying hand. "Stop!"

The wand-bearer froze, mocking him.

"Now put it on the table where I can see it," he said. "Nice and slow, no false moves or sudden swishes."

Eyes twinkling dangerously, Kira did as she was told.

"What was that all about?" Gram asked.

Jason cut his steak. "I don't want her waving it under the table when I'm not looking."

Laughter burst from Kira, the first Jason had heard, and she couldn't seem to stop any more than he could look away.

Napkin to her lips, the witch's eyes were as bright as the amusement she failed to suppress.

Gram looked pleased by her display.

And him? Well, he was straight-out bewitched, or enchanted . . . or both, damn it. He'd move out tomorrow, he was so spooked, except that Gram would be hurt if he did.

He now had proof of two things. Kira hadn't waved her wand beneath the table, because everything down there worked fine, thank you very much. And this was indeed going to be a long, hard six months.

THE following morning Kira noted the difference between Goddard's ebony Hummer and Billy's exotic toy cars, which gave her a bit of insight into her new boss. For one thing, she suspected that a scratch would not put Jason into cardiac arrest, which is what she'd always suspected would happen if one of Billy's cars got maliciously keyed.

"Is this the only vehicle you own?" she asked as they drove toward Rainbow's Edge.

"You like the Court Jester's stable of cars, do you?"

"Yeah," she admitted. "I do."

"Well, sorry, but this is what I drive, and it's the only vehicle in my garage, besides the Zamboni, of course."

"Of course." She gave him a sidelong glance. "I wouldn't mind taking a spin on the big Z someday, though. Can you drive it?"

He gave her a double take. "Who else? Gram?"

She was comfortable in his company today, Kira thought, relaxed.

"I'm sorry about dinner last night," he said, surprising her. "For acting as if you were unwelcome. I was embarrassed for dressing like a slob."

"I liked you as a slob. I like a guy in torn sweats better than a super-jock stud." She could curl into Jason the slob, and sleep . . . or not.

He perked up. "Stud?"

"Did I say stud? I meant dud."

He chuckled. "So," he said, hanging a right turn. "Do you own a pair of skates or do we have to buy you a pair?"

"Skates?"

"You're helping me give hockey lessons, right?"

"Who? Me? I haven't seen a hockey game since my twenty-six-year-old brother quit playing in high school. I thought I'd sit on the sidelines, kiss the boys' boo-boos, and hand out hot chocolate and . . . tissues."

"Some of those boys are no more than babies, so you'll have to wipe their noses *for* them, and anything else that needs wiping, and that's strictly written under *your* job description. I'm not happy about giving hockey lessons, but I am resigned. Gram gets what Gram wants. And I get an assistant who's gonna pay for her bright idea with grunt work up the Zamboni, got that?"

"I'm shivering in my sandals."

"You think you're sassing me, don't you? But you're shivering because it's fifty degrees outside. Aren't your feet cold?"

"I like sandals. My feet can breathe in them. I like being barefoot better; makes me feel rooted to the earth. I can't even stand to have my feet covered when I sleep," she added. "The Penis said I was hot-blood—"

Jason did a double take, and Kira realized her statement could be taken two ways. She shrugged. Let him think what he wanted. She'd already admitted to being an Ice Maiden.

Jason regarded her so long, she was afraid he'd drive off the road. "Hot blood is good," he finally said. "You won't mind the ice time. We'll buy you a pair of skates."

"Fine." Kira bit her lip, wondering whether to confess her shortcomings or let him find out for himself. "If I could skate."

"What? Did you have a deprived childhood or something?" Jason sighed. "I guess I'll have to teach you, but you should watch a couple of hockey games with me, too, so I can give you pointers. Here we are."

"Crap!"

"What?" he said again. "You don't want to hunt ghosts today?" He put the Hummer in Park.

They were already at Rainbow's Edge? That was fast, she thought.

"What's the problem?" he asked.

She huffed. "I never thought watching *sports* would be part of my job description. Yuck."

"Just hockey, no baseball."

She faced him in the seat. "How did you know? Bessie

can't remember the dick-wad's name, never mind what he did for a living. How did you know he was a ballplayer?"

"I went through your stinking trashcan yesterday, all right? I was nosy. I think it was the penis thing. I'd like to keep mine in good working order, if you don't mind."

Kira snorted. "Going through my personal possessions was *not* a good way to begin."

"It was trash," Jason said. "I might be wrong, but I don't think trash is considered private property."

"Crap," Kira said, laying her head back and closing her eyes. "You know everything. I'm such a loser."

"Why? Because Tillinghast couldn't keep it in his pants? Please. He was compensating for his other short-comings. He's never gonna move up from the minors. Everybody in sports knows that. He'll be off the farm team and out of Pawtucket in less than a year."

That cheered Kira big time. "Really?" She couldn't keep from grinning.

"What's with Dick-wad, by the way? I thought you called him the Penis."

"Hey, give me a break, thinking up crud names for the scum-sucker is the only pleasure I have left."

"Remind me not to get on your bad side," Jason said, putting his weight on his good leg as he got out of the Hummer. He grabbed his cane, then came around to open her door.

"A gentleman wolf," she said. "Retro."

"Remember that the next time you're tempted to point your wand."

"You really aren't spooked, or turned off, by the fact that I'm a witch, are you?"

"Only insofar as the well-being of my penis is concerned. I don't judge nor do I appreciate being judged. Besides, *fascinated* would be a better assessment, about your witch status, I mean, but don't let it go to your head. Gram told me you've sworn off men, and I'm here to tell you that

I've sworn off women, which in my estimation makes our working relationship perfect."

"Commitment-phobia? No kidding," she said. "Now, there's a cause I can get behind."

"I get the distinct feeling you're pleased to hear it, unlike every other woman in my memory."

Kira extended her hand. "Welcome to the club."

"But you were engaged and about to be married."

"Yeah, engaged and screwed over. That's why I joined the club. It was a close call, and I am *not* going there again."

"Got it," Jason said. "Great."

Kira looked up at Rainbow's Edge. "Thirty rooms," she said. "Hard to believe it's the foundation's smallest mansion. I love it, though."

"Pure Gothic Revival," Jason said. "Our only mansion made of wood. Nate Winthrop, who built it, was a true visionary. This was open farmland, but Nate saw its potential and bought the land to the sea. He used to watch his ships sailing to and from the Orient."

"Then why is that house standing between the Edge and the ocean?"

"You said you read the history."

"Of this place, not that one."

"One of Winthrop's heirs sold the land to maintain his opulent lifestyle."

"How long have we owned the Edge?"

"Bessie started the foundation to acquire this house in the early sixties to keep it from being torn down. She fixed it, gave tours herself, and discovered she could preserve history and support St. Anthony's at the same time. Thus her crusade to acquire more houses was born. Since this is your first visit," Jason said, "I'll give you the grand tour."

The minute they entered, Jason began to reveal a side of himself that surprised and delighted Kira. He loved history as much as she did.

Give the toad a princely crown.

In the stairway leading to the third floor, a draft of cold air rushed up Kira's skirt, teased her, like icy fingers against her skin, and made her shiver. As she did, a weird noise grew, and swelled, into a cacophony of excited squawking. "What *is* that?"

"We keep birds, but I've never heard them go ballistic like this."

"How many birds?"

Jason allowed her to precede him into a sunny pink-striped sitting room, sparse of furniture to one side, with a wall of glass on the other, a window through which Kira saw a huge bustling birdcage.

"That," he said, "is our working aviary."

"Big birds, and . . . noisy. Is that a crow?"

"They're all crows," Jason said, "two blacks, two black-and-whites, two grays, and a pair of browns. Mated pairs."

"A *murder* of crows," Kira said.

"No, we keep them healthy. They live for years."

"No, a group of crows is often *called* a 'murder,' because in folklore, crows are believed to punish rogue members of their flocks by— Never mind. It's gross."

"Look at the way they're screeching, and jumping, and flapping their wings," Jason said, "almost as if they're . . . happy to see you."

"Yeah, right," Kira said. "Sorry—though they are thought to carry messages from the spirit world—an aviary of crows does not a spooky ghost tour make."

Jason opened the glass door, and when Kira stepped into the aisle beside the cage, the birds went nuts and flew in her direction.

Kira stepped back.

They landed on her side of the cage, extending their beaks between the bars, as if trying to reach her.

"Wow," Jason said. "I never saw them like this."

Kira stepped farther back, tugging unexpectedly on a black-and-white crow with its beak in her pocket.

"Yikes." She freed her jacket, and backed against the glass wall, leaving the pickpocket with a piece of tissue in its beak.

"Good goddess," she said, her hand on her heart. "What is *with* them?"

A black crow on the floor waddled to the bars, tilted its head, and winked at her. "Hello, Mommy."

Seven

KIRA escaped to the sitting room side of the glass, the safe side. "Now I know why it's illegal to keep crows. They'll scare you to death."

"We have a federal permit to keep them," Jason said, "though I think we should have been grandfathered in."

"Excuse me, but did you hear that bird call me Mommy?"

"Pretty cute."

"Pretty *weird*! Where did you grow up? I don't know why you keep birds. I mean, nobody lives here."

"Keeping them in the aviary was a stipulation in gifting the estate to the foundation," Jason said. "In order to keep the house, we *have* to keep the crows. The donor left a separate endowment. We use the interest to house, feed, and care for the birds."

"Now, that's spooky. Who takes care of them?"

"The Rainbow's Edge caretaker and his wife, the Deerings, you know, the couple who live in the gatehouse for life? They're older and treat the birds like their children. They're very into caring for them."

"Well, that's good, I guess. But we should make them work for us . . . the birds, I mean, not the Deerings. This *is* a neat setup," Kira granted, "when the birds don't go wacko." Still spooked, she regarded the room-sized cage. "Have you ever thought of making this a school-tour stop or something? Hey, have the kids at St. Anthony's seen it?"

"I don't know," Jason said. "Too bad the place is too small for their get-acquainted night, or whatever we're going to call the event for people looking to adopt."

Kira tilted her head. " 'Get Acquainted Night' might do, though I wanted something more meaningful. The play might give us a clue; Sister Margaret is in charge of that. I'm not sure we can schedule the event before December, though."

"Christmas would be a good time to bring kids and parents together. Maybe Sister should do a Christmas play."

"I'll mention it," Kira said, following Jason up the attic stairs. "Maybe we can bring the boys to see the birds some afternoon after hockey lessons?"

"The boys will fall asleep after hockey lessons, believe me. Sister will have to carry the little ones off the bus."

"Never mind," Kira said. "I forgot they're coming for a ghost tour on Halloween. They'll see the birds then."

"Right," Jason said, switching on the attic light.

"Oh, wow," Kira said. "Look at all this amazing stuff; it's fabulous. Look at that rack of clothes. I love old clothes." She threw a gold cut-velvet shawl around her shoulders, sneezing at the dust she sent into the air. "I buy most of my clothes at thrift stores, or at my friend's vintage clothing shop. Vickie gets a lot of her stock from attics. Look, a cradle someone painted flowers on, and a little baby slept in, like a hundred years ago. And this doll; her hair is probably real. Old books. I love old books. They're better than new ones, don't you think?"

Jason grinned. "Some of this is quite valuable."

Kira felt foolish for her rambling. "It's all valuable in my book," she said, standing to regain her dignity. "It's history. Somebody's past. That always has value."

Jason stroked the lines of a dusty bronze nude and allowed his appreciation to show. "This was done by Carl Bitter," he said with reverence. "One of the things I like best about this family was their interest in art and antiquities."

Jason shared his knowledge as they trudged through the rest of Rainbow's Edge, from attic to cellar.

Kira's respect for him grew. Not only did he know the house and its owners, he knew about the furnishings and bric-a-brac, even the stuff in the attic. Too bad he'd assumed wrong about the ghost.

"You *love* the history of the mansions," she said as she made her way down the main stairs, him with his cane descending slowly behind her. "And don't pretend otherwise."

He shrugged, as if he hated to admit it.

"You made fun of me because I read the mansion histories," she said. "Why?"

"Hey, you had just withered a man's penis. I didn't know what to make of you. I didn't know *you*. I thought maybe you were the enemy. Cut me some slack. I'll admit it, okay, I'm a closet historian. I especially love the Gilded Age and the Roaring Twenties, and I can be a real me-man/you-woman throwback, if I'm not careful."

"Well, yeesh, you were brought up in a Gilded Age household, what do you expect?"

"You understand now, but wait till I grab you by the hair and drag you into my cave. You won't be happy then."

Try me, she thought. "It's not a sin to be a historian, you know, though it's not consistent with the macho hockey-gorilla-type image, is it?"

"That's part of the problem, though I'd like to go on record as resenting the gorilla analogy. Part of it's because I have a reputation."

"To protect?"

"To live down. My grandfather's. He was the historian; *he* got Gram involved in historical preservation in the first place. Unfortunately, he was also a philandering old rogue trying to keep her occupied so he could spend his time chasing other women."

Kira stilled. "Oh, no. Poor Bessie. I didn't know."

"Well, don't let on. It'd kill her. She still thinks no one ever suspected. Here's the library. Find a comfortable chair and pull up a stack of history books."

"And I get paid for this? Cool."

Jason propped his cane against the wall and walked to the bookshelves under his own steam.

"Hey," she said. "No cane? Should you be taking that chance?"

"The doctor said I could start to wean myself off it, in controlled situations, and for short periods of time."

"Controlled?"

"Flat ground, nothing to trip me." He looked around the room. "This seems to fit the bill."

"Congratulations," Kira said, and for some reason, her words seemed to surprise and touch him.

That day the only information they found of any interest was about Nate Winthrop's wife, Addie, and the pet crow she carried on her shoulder.

The following day they planned to return to the Rainbow's Edge library, but when Kira got in his car that morning, he shook his head. "Black again?"

Kira looked down at her pantsuit. "I like black."

"No kidding. This is the third day in a row you've worn it."

"You have a problem with black?"

"You dress in black, but I'd be willing to bet the bank that you seethe with hidden depths of color."

"Get real."

"I like color."

"So do I. In quilts and stained-glass windows."

"Right," Jason said. "Coffee?" He pulled into a dough-nut drive-through.

"Diet cola," Kira said. "And a chocolate glazed, if you don't mind, to round out the nutritional value of breakfast."

"Good choice. I'll have the same."

They quietly ingested caffeine and sugar as they drove toward Rainbow's Edge.

"Here we are," Jason said.

"Let me at those history books." Kira got out before he could come around and open her door.

That day was also a wash, ghost-wise, though they learned about Addie's death, Nate's expensive taste, and his more expensive women.

On Thursday they continued their ghostly research, get-ting pizza for lunch, and eating in the mansion's big old kitchen, complete with Italian tiled step-in hearth and an-cient copper kettle.

Kira began to feel in sync with the hockey jock. Their shared enthusiasm for history was somewhat amazing, and made it all quite fascinating.

By one o'clock, after finishing every book they could find about Rainbow's Edge over the past few days, the spookiest event they had found was a prank played by a little boy in 1924. It had caused some notoriety at the time, and gave the impression, for a very short while during the man-sion's history, that Rainbow's Edge did have a ghost—a little boy crying for his mother.

"What if we were to recreate the prank, exactly as it happened," Kira said as they sat on the porch steps of Rainbow's Edge appreciating the Indian Summer day. "At least it would be true mansion history, not a misrepresenta-tion of facts."

"If we did that, wouldn't we have to find the hidden staircase the kid said he was locked in?" Jason asked. "We never saw one."

"We never searched for one." Kira looked toward the family cemetery on the property. "Odd how the crow thing keeps popping up. Both writers saw fit to describe Addie's pet crow. Her husband, the main historian, implied very strongly that she was thought odd and frightening by the general population."

"I hadn't realized that." Jason rubbed his nape. "But I chose the books about the house more than the people."

Kira already knew Jason's body language, and that neck thing was a sure sign of distress or exhaustion. "Are you worried about finding the hidden staircase," she asked, "or are you disappointed that we haven't found any real evidence of ghosts?"

"A bit of both I guess. And there's that obelisk of a gravestone. Look at it." He pointed toward the cemetery not too far distant.

The headstone in question lay facedown like a huge, bright white marble blight on an otherwise perfectly bucolic scene.

"Raising it is going to be a pisser," Jason said. "To make matters worse, the entire headstone seems to have been carved from one solid chunk. The pedestal alone must be four by five. We need to get it lifted and back into place. Gram says it's been tried over the years, with no success."

"Too bad you never looked at the place before you sent those inv—"

"Can it, Fitzgerald."

"Right. Look, there are seven crows on the obelisk. That's significant."

"Enough with the crows."

"Crow augury has been practiced for centuries. It's practically a science. Crows can have mystical significance in certain numbers. Do you know what seven means?"

"No," Jason said, "and I'm not certain I want to."

"Seven crows can mean that a secret is about to be revealed. In some cases, it's a sign of witchcraft."

The wind whistled eerily through the trees, like cheesy movie music when a dumb heroine descends a dark stair, candle in hand. Kira laughed.

"You're making that up," Jason said, looking at the trees as the whirlwind calmed.

Kira shook her head. "No, crow augury is taken seriously by some witches. I noticed right away that you keep four pairs. Four could mean the coming of a male child, or an event surrounding a son. Got anything you're not telling me?"

Jason barked a laugh. "No, no sons on the way."

Kira nodded, surprised by the odd flash in his expression as he denied the possibility.

"If we count the crows upstairs as two sets of four . . ." she said, pausing to spook him.

"Two sons? I don't think so."

"No," she said. "I mean if we count them as eight crows, we're talking about a life-altering experience to the good, a glimpse of heaven."

"Heaven?" Jason scoffed. "Though I wouldn't mind having someone return from there for a quick Halloween haunt, you know, to help our cause."

"It means heaven on earth," Kira said. "A *life*-altering experience."

"Yeah, right." Jason mocked her with his tone. "Give me a break. Wait. Is there a number of crows that portends the finding of a hidden staircase? Because I'll go out and find more crows, if I have to."

"Calm down," she said. "We've got weeks to look for the staircase and get Addie's gravestone raised."

"Wait a minute, what makes you think it's Addie's?"

"Hers isn't in the cemetery, that I could find. She was the wife of the house's builder, and since the fallen stone is the biggest monument out there, it has to be hers."

"Right."

"The cemetery's perfect for a ghost tour," Kira said. "And the house is quirky enough, with all its corners and gables, I'll give you that. I can see why you picked the place, though not why you didn't research it firs—"

Jason bristled.

Kira bit her lip. "Right. Been here, moving on. I'd like to create short stories about a couple of the characters beneath the cryptic headstones. You know, fictional pieces based on the epitaphs."

"Why the hell would we want to do that?"

"To *up* the spook factor," Kira said.

"But people would think the stories were real."

"Not if we made it clear that they're Halloween fiction," she said, "based on a few sparse facts."

Jason wasn't convinced. Kira could tell. "C'mon," she coaxed, "it'll be fun. After all this research, I feel as if we know the Rainbow's Edge residents pretty well, except for old Nate, who built the place and wrote most of the history books. He portrayed himself as such a great man, bragging about his women, that I've started to wonder about him. Something tells me that your grandfather wasn't the only philanderer in town."

"Gram always said there'd been rumors about Winthrop's version of himself." Jason chuckled. "You're right, fictionalized stories, admittedly based on fact and hearsay, will add another layer of ghostly depth to the tour." He picked a red-orange leaf from her hair, and grinned. "Same color. Almost missed it."

She snatched it from his hand. "That's not funny."

Jason grinned anyway. "We have to find the staircase, hire caterers, a decorator, and heavy equipment to raise and replace the stone, but I feel as if we're making progress."

"I'd like to decorate the house myself," Kira said. "I'd love to get my hands on the place, and I think I can do it for the cost of flowers and supplies, and save the foundation money. I might even be able to get some of the supplies donated. What do you say?"

"It would mean you'd have to put in more hours before and after the event," Jason warned her, "whereas the decorators would normally be responsible for setup and takedown."

"Yes and they'd charge big bucks for it, too. You've been

my boss for what, three days, and I've worked late on all of them. What would be different about this? And for that matter, what else do I have to do?"

"Fine, if you let me help."

"What, climb ladders and swing from chandeliers, like all gorillas with canes do?" She shoved his shoulder with hers to show she was joking, pleased when he shoved hers the same way, showing he'd taken her teasing as such.

"I forgot about the cane," he said. "Crap, I did forget about it; I left it in the library."

"I'll get it. Rest the knee."

Kira went upstairs, grabbed his cane, heard flapping, and thought a bird had escaped the aviary, but no, two crows were landing on the windowsill. They looked at her and preened their feathers in a way that made her think they were happy. Weird.

Two crows meant a surprise was coming, a change for the better. Joy. Mirth. Maybe that was it. Kira walked over to the window and touched it, thinking she might frighten them. But the birds touched their beaks to the tip of her finger, the glass between them. "Bye, little crows," she said, turning away with new hope for the success her job and the ghost tour.

A minute later she handed Jason his cane. "I think it must be a good sign for your recovery that you forgot it."

"I guess so."

"Just don't go home and try to play hockey this afternoon."

"This is bad," he said.

"What?" she asked.

"That you can read my mind."

"I wish," she said. "Let's go, I have a ton of paperwork waiting for me at the office."

"Okay, here's the plan in a nutshell," he said after he climbed into the Hummer beside her and turned the key. "Tell me if you agree. Canapés and champagne as people arrive, a theatrical of the ghostly prank, the cemetery tour with our ghoulish stories at a gravestone or two, then back to the house for a dessert buffet and cordials in the drawing room."

"Perfect," she said. "How about adding a live quartet in the music room, for after the cemetery, so people will feel free to dance or wander the house. We can wrap tiny white lights on the stair rail leading to the aviary."

"Brilliant," Jason said, as if he should have thought of it. "With the window behind their domed cage, the mischievous birds in their natural setting, the moon and stars behind them, will add to the eerie effect. Indirect lighting, music wafting up the stairs, and a visit to the aviary should round out our ghostly evening to perfection."

Kira shook her head. "I can't believe we've got the makings of a world-class ghost and graveyard tour at a mansion with no ghosts. Damned if you weren't right. And don't forget our real draw, our very own Ice Wolf, that famous kisser guy."

Jason checked the rearview mirror and made a right turn. "You know, I did forget about him. What was his name again?"

Kira was sorry she mentioned his kisses, because his lips suddenly looked perfect for the job. She opened her notebook, cutting her admiration, and their conversation, short.

Back at the office they both had paperwork to catch up on. By mutual agreement, they left their hall doors closed, and the door between their offices open.

Sometimes they spoke, office to office, a comment, a rejoinder, but mostly they worked in companionable silence. It was nice knowing he was there, Kira thought, to bounce ideas off, or simply for a smile. Who knew the jock could be amusing?

Her phone rang at four. It was Billy. "Shit," she said, hanging up.

"What?" Jason asked from his office.

"I forgot I had plans for dinner," Kira said. "Good thing

your grandmother suggested I keep my special events wardrobe in the dressing room off my bathroom. Always smart to be ready, Bessie said, and she was right. You don't mind if I leave early, do you?"

"Hell, no, you've earned it. Have fun."

"Thanks, I will."

Kira went into her bathroom to wash and change.

When she came out a half hour later, she went through her office and into Jason's, still putting on the finishing touches.

Jason turned when he heard Kira come in, and zing, like magic, she'd turned into a goddess radiating pure sex.

Her low-riding black silk hip-hugging pants were topped by a long, sleeveless black and white tunic, a deep vee at the neck, leaving only two buttons between her breasts and nakedness. Beneath the second button, the vee on the tunic inverted, presenting a naked triangle centered by Kira's belly button. But no worry, a nickel-sized cluster of multifaceted rhinestones filled the enticing well.

Fortunately for him, she'd come in combing back her cinnamon curls with a large Victorian fan comb and missed his ogling assessment.

Jason stepped away from the window as she looked up, zapped him with a man-hardening smile . . . and he walked into his desk.

"Ouch! Shit! Son of a bitch!"

Eight

"OH, no," Kira said. "Was that your bad knee?"

Jason looked at her with incredulity, and judging by her surprised reaction, his fury showed as well. And no wonder, this was all her fault.

"Oh, stop pouting and sit down," she said. "Really. *You* walked into your desk, not me."

She was right, damn it.

He sat, and God bless her, she knelt before him and rubbed his knee with her soft sensuous hands, while he looked down her tunic like a pervert. The view was so fine between her lush breasts that he could see all the way to her rhinestone belly button.

She wasn't wearing a bra, and *he* was going to need oxygen.

Shit, Jason thought as she continued rubbing his throbbing knee, her words soothing, her touch more so, his heat rising.

If Kira looked anywhere but at his face, or his knee, she

was going to be in for a surprise. "Where the hell do you keep your wand in that outfit?" he asked.

She whipped it from behind her. "In my pants."

In her pants; that's where *he* wanted to be.

Maybe he could pretend his knee was really damaged, so she would stay home and . . . tend him. "Where the hell are you going?" he asked her.

"To the country club for dinner with Billy. Why?"

"The Court Jester? He's nothing but a soft, candy-ass playboy."

"I know. That's what I like about 'Bewitching' Billy."

Jason ignored the "bewitching" part. "You like that he's a no-account playboy without an ounce of responsibility in his lazy blue blood?"

Kira raised a knowing brow. "And the difference between the two of you would be?"

"Shit!" Jason repeated.

"Suddenly you like that word?" she said. "When I used it, you thought I had a hormone problem. Do you have a hormone problem?"

Hell, yes! "I'm stifling my cussing instinct by substituting one four-letter word for another and cutting it short. Trust me, you don't want to hear the locker-room variety."

"For your information, Billy is not a jock, which is a definite plus in his favor, but I do realize he's an egocentric playboy, which is why I couldn't possibly fall for him. Honestly, he's a blast to hang with, and he's a great dancer."

That hurt. Jason pushed her hand away and rubbed his own knee.

She returned the favor by pushing his hand away and taking over again, thank the goddess.

"I'm sorry you can't dance right now," she said. "That was thoughtless of me."

"Yes, it was, and it ranks right up there with sucking me into coaching hockey. You have now rubbed salt in my every wound. You owe me."

"Hah," she said, rubbing higher along his thigh than was prudent. "What do you suppose I owe you?" Was she purring? Did she like her hands on him as much he liked having them on him?

Had she seen his boner? How could she not? Was she flattered? Tempted? She certainly didn't seem repulsed.

"Hey, hey, hey!" Billy said coming in. Then he stopped and frowned. "Am I, er, interrupting something here? I can go to the dance by myself, you know."

Jason wanted to barf at Billy's sad-little-boy look, perfected over years of practice at getting his own way.

"No," Kira said, standing. "No, I'm ready. Jason just smacked his bad knee."

"Helping him rub it, were you?" Billy kissed Kira's nose, chuckled, and gave Jason a my-win/your-loss pity-smile.

When the spoiled idler snaked a possessive arm around Kira's waist, Jason wanted to deck him, and jealousy was a feeling Jason liked about as much as a puck in the eye.

"Looks like you'll be the one going it alone tonight," Billy said to Jason. "Don't be too *hard* on yourself. Have some fun; play some couch hockey, and don't wait *up*."

Billy turned Kira toward the connecting door and looked back. "Tomorrow's Saturday," he said, throwing a wink Jason's way. "We'll probably want to sleep late."

Kira cuffed him. "Cut it out."

If she'd slugged him for the "sleeping late" comment, it didn't make Jason feel a whole lot better. She was still leaving with the jerk.

Like watching his team skate to a slaughter, Jason watched Billy and Kira in her office, all touchy-feely as they prepared to leave on their date.

"Hey, Princess," Billy said to her, "you're shivering." He placed a long black cape around her shoulders, hugging her from behind. "Maybe we should take a closed car," he suggested. "It'd be warmer, and more private."

Jason fisted his hands.

"No, I'm hot," Kira said. "I mean, I'm warm . . . enough.

Let's ride with the top down, like we planned." She extracted herself from Billy's embrace and turned Jason's way.

He knew by her look that she'd caught him watching them. His dislike for Billy—for her and Billy together—must be clear in his expression.

They made eye contact, sizzling eye contact, if he was any kind of judge.

"Night, Jason," she said, unmoving.

Jason wished he could ask her to stay, drive him home. He almost wished he wasn't up to driving.

Problem was, if she stayed, he'd want to take her to bed. Who was he kidding? He already wanted to take her to bed. "Night, Kira," he said. "Have a good time."

"What?" Billy pouted as only Billy could. "Not wishing *me* a good time?" The jerk laughed his way out the door and down the hall, and Jason remembered how he might once have stolen a girl from Billy on the spot.

But Jason didn't need a woman to complicate his life. Any woman. Life was complicated enough already.

He stood and looked out the window. When Kira and Billy got in the convertible, Billy patted the seat beside him, and Jason smiled at Kira's stubborn, negative head shake. That, at least, made him feel better. But damn it, his knee was killing him.

As Billy's sleek silver Porsche raced down the drive, a shock of red curls waving in the breeze, Jason wondered how a woman, any woman, could blindside him in one short week.

Bewitched was still the only word Jason could think of to describe the state he was in, besides blindsided and aroused. "Stupid fool," he called himself as he grabbed his cane and got ready to head for home. "One look at her jeweled navel, and you about walk into a wall. Smooth."

JASON took his grandmother to dinner that night. He honestly liked spending time with her, and they hadn't had a good chat since he started working at the foundation.

Besides, he didn't want to wait around and listen for the sound of Kira's door opening. He especially didn't want to hear the silence of it not opening.

"Why are you so sullen tonight?" Gram asked. "Eat your salad. It's delicious."

"Just tired, I guess." He sounded like a sulky kid, Jason thought, snapping out of it, for her sake.

"I guess you have a right to be tired. You and Kira put in a lot of hours this week. Where did you say she went tonight?"

"The Court Jester took her to a dance at the country club."

"Good for her," Gram said. "I like to see her having a good time, especially after that fiasco of a canceled wedding. She was so broken when she came to me."

"You wanna tell me what happened that was so dreadful?"

His grandmother patted his hand. "I think that's Kira's tale to tell. You like her, though, don't you? And she's a marvel at coordinating special events, isn't she?"

"Yes, Gram, you did well. Kira is definitely a find, though we *should* be paying her more. I looked at her contract the other day and I was shocked at her salary. I can't believe she took such a cut."

"Well, that's why the free rent dear, and free meals as often as possible. Wasn't that a stroke of brilliance on my part? I figure that makes up the difference and then some."

"Yeah, brilliant." And now he really couldn't do anything to change it, like move her out, though he wondered if he honestly wanted to.

"I know you like your privacy," Gram said, "but—"

"To be honest, Gram, I think I like having her around. She's good for a laugh, never mind a spell, though I really don't want her pointing her wand my way."

His grandmother laughed, because Kira had evidently recounted their first meeting, and Gram's happiness was worth everything.

"Kira is entertaining, isn't she?" Gram said. "Though I

hope she doesn't disturb you when she comes in tonight. Billy usually keeps her out late."

Usually? "She's dated him before?"

"Of course, dear."

Shit. "She looked tired," he said. "She might have come home before we left."

"No, dear, the flowers I sent Gracie upstairs with earlier were still sitting in front of Kira's door before we left. Gracie had just told me as much before you came down."

Jason remembered seeing the flowers earlier.

Much later, after dinner and a movie with Gram, Jason found that vase of flowers still sitting in front of Kira's door.

Were she and Billy still dancing at the country club, or were they doing another kind of dance? "Shit!"

By eleven Jason was pacing his empty suite. A ballgame, of all things, was playing on television, but he couldn't wrap his mind around anything but Billy's words. *We're sleeping late tomorrow.* The jerk.

Jason threw himself into a chair, channel-surfed, and kept track, more or less, of the damned game.

At midnight he started pacing again.

At one he left his cane behind and breached the sanctum known as the kitchen, which felt more like a lightning zone than a neutral one. He made an overloud creek with every stocking-clad step he took across the old wooden floor heading toward the door that led to Kira's suite.

Setting his ear against the red-enamel door made him feel like a freaking Peeping Tom. If he heard anything, he'd feel like . . . what?

A sick bastard.

Nevertheless, he grasped the crystal knob and tried to turn it, just to make sure it was locked, but it wasn't. Jason stopped short of opening the door, but he didn't let go of the knob. Should he consider the unlocked door in the way of an invitation, or a sign that Kira wasn't into details?

Crap, no, she managed details in a big way; she was getting every one straight for their events.

Hey, was this a come-on?

Did she want him to try her door? Wait a minute. Did she think he was a pervert?

Disgusted with his ridiculous speculation, Jason turned to move away, but his knee gave. He lost his balance, fell against her door, and pushed it open. He heard her key turning in her front door, which he could see from where he stood. Shit!

Jason pulled the door shut, him on the kitchen side, silent as a mouse, but he didn't dare let go of the knob, because she would hear it turn. He heard her in her apartment, dropping her keys, her footsteps coming in his direction.

What if she were on her way to the kitchen?

He got a mental image of the door opening and the two of them coming face-to-face, his hand on her knob. *He wished.* What would he say? "I was rubbing my face against your door because . . . I missed you?" *Yeah, that would work.*

Her footsteps stopped. She was standing on the opposite side of the door. He knew she was. Could she hear him breathing? He thought he could hear her.

Jason held his breath.

Kira turned the lock, swore when it must have seemed stuck, and bore down on it, hard. To keep from giving himself away, Jason went down on his bad knee, his wrist spraining to twist in the opposite direction.

The loose old-fashioned lock turned with the knob. If he let the knob go, the lock would turn fast, and click into place like a death sentence.

Sitting like a pretzel against her door, Jason counted three more steps, then nothing. He waited, his knee throbbing, his body aching for hers.

How sick was that? What the hell was wrong with him?

Where in the room had she stopped? What was she doing now? Just standing there? Why the sudden silence?

Her suite was a mirror image of his. It would take two dozen steps for her to reach her bedroom.

Maybe she stopped to remove her heels, the black ones with the white heart at the ankle strap.

Stocking feet on carpet could account for the sudden silence. Or she could still be standing there. He wondered if and when it would be safe to recross the creaking kitchen floor.

Her TV went on, making him jump, it sounded so close. Crap, he would never get out of here. If he did, without getting caught, he'd never step into this kitchen again.

After about twenty minutes Jason maneuvered himself into a semi-sitting position, to take the weight off his knee. A new show came on, a pops concert. Great. At the first crescendo, he took his hand from the knob and rubbed his wrist.

Suppose she fell asleep on the sofa and left the TV on all night? Suppose he fell asleep, and she found him here in the morning?

Man, he needed to take a leak.

What would be better, walking across the kitchen fast, or crawling slow on his hands and knees? He decided that trying to stand on his aching knee could cause a ruckus, so he started to crawl, every move painful.

When he was nearly to his living room, he thought he was safe. Then a sledgehammer hit the door from her side . . . and damned near gave him a heart attack.

Jason jumped a foot, banged his bad knee, shouted a succinct four letter word, and fell on his face.

He could have sworn he heard Kira chuckle.

Her TV went off and her footsteps faded.

They both avoided the kitchen, and each other, on Saturday. On Sunday at noon they came face-to-face at Gram's dining room table.

Despite remaining apart for nearly the entire weekend,

the pulsing heat between them, which had started when she soothed him after he banged his knee in the office, seemed to have risen.

She was wearing black—big surprise—and a bra, unfortunately, beneath a fitted V-neck pocket tee paired with black slacks. As usual, she looked neat, sedate, like nobody's fool, and sexy as hell.

Turned out that he, too, was wearing black slacks and a pocket tee. Gram noted their his-and-hers outfits with a matchmaker's delight, but neither of them appreciated the comparison or her enthusiasm.

"You're not yourself today, dear," his grandmother said to him. "Looks like you haven't slept as much as you should this weekend."

"I think maybe he stays up too late," Kira said.

"Oh, I hope he doesn't disturb you, dear?" Gram said.

Kira raised a brow. "Well . . . one of us is disturbed."

Gram frowned, looked from one of them to the other, smiled, and gave her attention to her lunch.

Jason did not appreciate the cat-who-ate-the-cream expression in Kira's wide bright eyes.

"I need skating lessons," she said. "Is that what's got you down?" she asked.

"Who says I'm down?"

She shrugged. "Just a feeling. How's the knee?"

Had she winked? "Where's the wand?"

"I've kept it sealed and out of sight since about one-fifteen Saturday morning, so I wouldn't be tempted to use it on any curious *Charlies*."

Shit! "Wanna go buy some skates this afternoon?"

"Sure, if you think you can teach me to use them."

"Let's talk about it on the way." Jason rose from the table. "We're going skate shopping," he told his grandmother as he kissed her brow. "Wanna come?"

"Hah, just what you need, a little old granny cramping your style."

They both stilled.

"No style, Gram. Nothing to cramp. We're coworkers prepping for a job *you* assigned us."

"Whatever you say, dear. Have a nice afternoon, both of you."

Kira kissed his grandmother's cheek. "You, too," she said.

In no time they were wending their silent way down the hill toward Sports Mania at the brick marketplace.

"So," Kira said fifteen minutes later as he laced her into a pair of women's hockey skates. "Why do I have to get on skates? I really hate making a fool of myself . . . unlike some people I know."

Jason figured that if he never acknowledged her taunts to draw him out about Friday night, she would never really learn how low he'd sunk. Good thing she hadn't seen him on his belly after she scared the crap out of him.

"Don't you think the boys wearing skates for the first time will feel less conspicuous with an adult as clumsy as them on the ice?"

"Great," Kira said. "So your plan is to humiliate me in public?"

"Not a plan," Jason said, "just a perk."

Nine

JASON made Kira stand on her skates in the store aisle as he walked around her, admiring her exceptional figure from all angles. "I can't say I won't enjoy watching you glide across the ice on your ass," he said, "but if you need first aid, I'll rub liniment on your bruised parts."

Her gaze rose, and they regarded each other, the heat between them subtle but remarkable.

"In your dreams," she said, with no conviction.

Cheered by her tone, Jason imagined running his hands over her every crest and hollow, forgetting he was supposed to be checking the fit of her skates until she raised a skated foot to remind him, and tumbled into his arms.

Jason cleared his throat and stood her up, then he made her flex her ankles and point each toe. "Sit," he said.

"I just realized that you're not using your cane," she said. "Why not?"

"Trying to break the habit in good weather on solid ground."

"Just see that you don't break the knee."

"I'm strengthening the knee, doctor's orders." He knelt, trying not to wince, and adjusted her laces before cupping her skate with both hands, checking the way her foot fit inside. He was looking for a fit as snug as a hand gloved in leather.

He had helped other people pick out skates before, but this was the first time he'd enjoyed the process so much.

"I'm gonna break my neck on these," she said, looking down at them.

"Nah, but watching you struggle will be the highlight of my hockey lessons."

She made a face. "How *is* the knee?"

"Bruised, like you're gonna be, after our lesson."

"Gee, thanks."

He cupped her chin. "You want to be a good example for the boys, right?"

"Yeah, but I didn't want it to hurt."

"I'll give you a preliminary lesson this afternoon, so you don't make a *complete* ass of yourself, but the kids *will* love that you're learning like them; they will."

"If I didn't think you were right, I'd be pissed."

"Actually, you're a pretty good sport," he said. "Let's go, and I'll give you that lesson." Jason brought her skates to the register.

"This is a work-related lesson," Kira said, as they left the store. "Not a date or anything remotely related, right?"

"Right," he said. "Absolutely. But speaking of dates, how did yours go Friday night with Billy?"

"He was right," she said. "We danced until dawn and slept late on Saturday."

Jason grinned despite himself, and she socked him.

IF this *wasn't* a date, Kira wondered an hour later, why were Jason's arms around her? Why was he snuggling his package against her bottom? Why were his arms crushing her breasts, and, more to the point, why wasn't she enjoying it more?

Because she couldn't stand upright, that's why.

"Try to keep your legs together," Jason said.

"Hah, I'll bet you never said *that* to a girl before."

"Stifle it, Wobbles."

Before he dropped her, which she expected him to do, he turned her in his arms, her feet doing a disconnected Highland fling kind of thing, as he rolled her against his body until they were breasts to chest, er, erection to . . . target, happy erection and happier target.

Okay, so she *was* enjoying this.

She looked up, right into Jason's sparkling silver wolf's eyes. She had never seen eyes with such clear, bottomless depths before, and in those sexy depths she could see that Jason knew that she knew that he wanted her.

What could she say to make him realize she felt the same? She could hardly believe she wanted to put into practice the meaning of the four-letter word he'd shouted when she scared the hell out of him Friday night. She tested it in the form of a sentence. *Fuck me.*

Then she remembered that Charlie had already done that, in more ways than she appreciated, and she gave up on the idea, even though her body was crying 'Wolf,' and Jason's was crying 'Here I am.'

She slid down his body and out of his grip, his erection grazing her chest. "Is that a hockey stick in your pocket?" Kira dared. "Or are you just happy to be back on the ice?"

Jason barked a laugh. "Sorry, sometimes Harvey has a mind of his own."

"How do you do, Harvey," Kira said, on her knees at Jason's feet, face-to-face with the big guy under wraps.

She looked up at Jason. "You dropped me."

"I got distracted." He watched her as if he could tell that, in her mind, she was fondling Harvey.

Harvey grew bigger before her eyes, proving her mental success.

She covered him with her forearms, as if she were trying to rise and was using Harvey as leverage.

"Shit!"

"Yeesh," she said. "I hope that felt better than it sounded."

"You caught me off guard. I didn't expect that, not from you."

"Me? Why am I so different?" She rubbed a wrist against that engorged area through Jason's thick man-scented sweats.

He said the word she'd wanted to use, only he said it with determination, and didn't use it in a sentence. Neither did he try to help her up, but she didn't mind being on her knees, because for the moment, she liked the view. "It's hot in here," she said. "You made me wear too many clothes."

"Take some off, by all means," he said, gazing heatedly down at her.

"I just might." She eyed Harvey again and licked her lips.

"Watch out," Jason warned. "The ice is hard."

"So's Harvey."

"I was thinking about your back, if you keep that up."

"Hey, I'm not doing a thing. He's keeping it up all by himself."

"You know what I mean."

"Promises, promises. Your knees couldn't take the ice any more than my back could."

"Hurts just thinking about it."

"I think the heat from *my* knees might be melting holes in the ice," she said.

"I don't mind," he said. "Get as hot as you want."

"Do you mind this?" She knuckled Harvey and felt a mini shock at her core.

"Doesn't hurt a bit. Do it again."

"Don't think I don't want to, but I'm starting to feel the need for equal attention."

"My pleasure," he said. "Let's get you on your feet."

He got her up and kept her from falling again by grasping her bottom in one hand as he slipped the other between them to cup her center, applying just the right amount of pressure.

Kira sighed while a series of mini shocks rocked her.

"Wow," he said. "You didn't just—"

"This is scary," Kira said. "We can't do this."

"You're right," he said. "Let's go upstairs. Your bed or mine?"

"Bed?" Kira said, coming out of her sexual haze. "You've sworn off women."

"Don't I know it."

"I've sworn off men, and we have to work together."

"I'm sure we'd work beautifully together."

Kira sighed. "I mean at the foundation."

"I don't think doing it there is such a good idea," Jason said.

"No more than here, or in a bed."

"Then we have to go our separate ways for the rest of the day at least."

"Right." Kira leaned away, looked down, and knuckled his length.

Jason touched her forehead with his.

"I'm out'a here," he said, but he didn't move.

When he started to back away, Kira panicked. "Wait, don't leave me here. I can't stand by myself."

"I won't be responsible if I touch you again. I'll turn my back while you crawl to the bench, because even that will turn me on."

Kira got to her knees the hard way, by landing on her ass. Then she did crawl, which was good, because it made her feel way less sexy. When she got to the bench, she used Jason's hockey stick to raise herself.

"Hey, watch out for Harvey."

"Wait! You call them both—"

"You got a problem with that?"

"You're nuts—"

"Are yours for the taking."

"Cut that out. As soon as my skates are off, I'm the one who's out'a here."

"That *would* be best," Jason said as he pulled her skates off. They walked back to the house with three feet between them, but ended up in the Cloud Kiss elevator together.

Kira wanted his world-class lips on hers, so she traced the dimple in his chin, hoping he'd bring his lips the rest of the way. Instead, he pushed her against the elevator door and ran his hands all over her, but he kept his lips to himself.

They shifted positions until she rode his good leg, the hard part of him teasing her center. Jason cupped her breasts and nuzzled her, from her neck to her breasts. Geez, she was gonna come just like—

The elevator door opened behind her, and she fell back, landing on her ass in the hall.

Gram's maid yelped and Jason stopped midlunge. He backed up and the elevator door closed. Kira saw the floor numbers go down, while Gracie gave her a hand up.

"I don't know where my mind was," Kira said to Gracie, aware that Jason had turned her on, and left her flat, just like Charlie. And in true Charlie-style, he'd brought her to the brink of orgasm and left her wanting.

FOR the first few days of the following workweek, Kira tried to pretend that none of it had happened, not Jason's midnight snooping, not their sexual interlude in the rink, not the heat lightning in the elevator, and especially not her abandonment afterward.

They were formal and polite, a boss and an employee, a bit snappish, pretty much like the week before, but with regret and frustration thrown into the game, in a weird and uncomfortable way.

Kira tried to figure out how many men in her life had brought her so close to surrender in so short a time, and she realized that no one else ever had, though plenty had dumped her, the way Jason dumped her on the floor outside the elevator.

Still, though he was no different from any other jock, her boss turned her on.

Great. She was such a loser, a toad could turn her on.

She tried to stay the hell away from him, caught up on paperwork, and set everything up with St. Anthony's to get the boys to and from hockey practice. She talked to Sister Margaret about a play for the boys to perform and suggested a Christmas theme.

She didn't speak to Jason and he didn't speak to her, except when strictly necessary for the sake of their jobs.

The first time he became the least animated was the day the box of children's hockey sticks was delivered to his office. She stood in his doorway watching him unwrap one of every size; like a kid beneath a tree on Christmas morning. "Having fun?" she asked.

He looked up guilty, as if he'd unwrapped every gift, his and everyone else's, and his half-grin enchanted the crap out of her.

"Come see," he said.

She went to sit beside him, and just like that, three dozen hockey sticks broke a week's worth of ice.

They visited every mansion after that, checking building- and fire-code compliance, scoped out ballrooms for dancing, patios for cocktail parties, kitchens and dining rooms, attics, billiard rooms, hothouses, doll houses, wine cellars, carriage houses and stables.

Kira tried to stay cool throughout, but when she saw the kitchen at Kingston by the Sea, her enthusiasm got the best of her. She knew exactly what event to plan around it.

"This kitchen is incredible!" she exclaimed. "We can't let it go to waste. What would you say to having Salem's *Kitchen Witch* show filmed here live? We could sell tickets to a pricey, elegant cocktail party on the night the show airs, and our guests could meet Melody."

"Melody Seabright? She can't come cheap," Jason warned. "I think getting her would eat up our profit."

"You think so?" Kira took out her cell phone, hit a single digit and Send. She listened to it ring while she eyed her boss with a "watch me" brow. "Hey, Mel," she said, enjoying Jason's stunned reaction, "I have a great idea for your show."

Jason listened to Kira talk with one of TV's hottest cooking-show stars, or to someone pretending to be Melody Seabright, of *Kitchen Witch* fame, for some time before he stopped gaping.

Then Kira spoke to someone named Logan, from whom she solicited a documentary about the mansions, then she went back to talking to Melody again, if her conversation was to be believed.

"Love to Shane," Kira said. "Really? Yes, please. Hi, baby. How's old Snoopy doing? He did?" She laughed. "Ink and Spot are what? No. Kittens? Both of them? You're kidding? What did your dad say? No, honey, you don't have to say the bad word. I get the picture. Love you, too. Give Mom a hug for me when I hang up, okay? Dad, too. Bye, sport."

Kira raised an arm in victory and did an enchanting little happy dance.

Jason shook his head in denial. "That was a joke right? Some family member was in on it."

"No joke. Mel's gonna talk to her producer tomorrow, but she said to consider it a go. She thinks the second week in November would be great. She says she has to reserve the third week for Thanksgiving, and the first is already planned."

"Now pull the other leg," Jason retorted, but Kira's enthusiasm seemed genuine.

"Melody suggested that a documentary about the mansions might be good promo. That's what her husband, Logan, does; he makes documentaries. He said he'd donate one for a tax write-off."

"I got that," Jason said.

"He'll shoot some of it when Mel's here to do her show. They'll film ahead, Mel said. They don't like to go live anywhere except in the studio. But she'll be happy to come back for our reception the night the show's aired."

"You're *not* kidding," Jason said. "About any of this."

"Of course not." Kira placed her hand on her heart. "Witch's promise. Mel wants to work the show around a Gilded Age Society menu. She asked if I could send her info on the dinners they served. She was thrilled."

Kira walked around the kitchen, touching everything as if she imagined her friend was there. "Mel likes to stay with New England themes as much as possible, so Newport is perfect. I knew it would be. I'll bet we hook some great promo with this. Mel will plug us in her 'upcoming show' credits for weeks before our show airs."

"Is she really a witch?"

"Melody has always worked some pretty amazing magic," Kira replied with a wink. "We grew up together. She's from the Boston Brahmin side of the tracks; I'm from the poor Irish side."

"What? Same school?"

"Hell, no. Mel went to boarding schools, the poor thing, but the summer we were five, we met in Boston Common, Mel's nanny and my mom looking on. About a week later we met Vickie there, and the three of us have been best friends ever since."

"Is Vickie the friend who sells vintage clothes?"

"Right," Kira said, somewhat surprised. "I can't believe you listened that closely. Anyway, Mel grew up in a mansion, but she always liked our small houses better. Vic's mother spread affection like icing, so that was understandable, but Mel liked my house, too. Not sure why. It was the smallest, the noisiest, and had the most kids running around. Busting at the seams, literally. Still is, most days."

"Sounds great to me. I think I would have liked your house better as well."

"Poor little rich boy." She patted his cheek.

Jason grabbed her wrist and held her hand in place, loving the feel of her skin against his face, the two of them eye to eye for the first time since the rink, neither of them giving, neither looking away, for too long to be comfortable, but he didn't care.

"Hockey lessons in less than an hour," Kira said, sucking the heat right out of him.

"Right." Jason rubbed his nape, so flummoxed, so freaking beguiled, he felt bewitched.

He watched her write a few more notes in her day planner, the hoops in her ears swaying with each shift of her pen.

He wanted to shock her out of hiding, which is what he feared she was doing by wearing nothing but black.

"I'm looking forward to hockey practice," she said.

"Figures. Most hockey players who turn to coaching are considered to be washed-up, you know."

Kira raised a brow, as if he'd made her point, and he was pissed. "I am *not* washed-up! The NHL wants me back, and I'll be there before you know it. You'll see. Meanwhile, I *hate* the idea of coaching, just in case you didn't know."

"I saw you with those hockey sticks. My ass, you hate the idea."

"Don't talk to me about your ass," he said. "I'm trying not to remember how good it felt in my hands."

"Can it, Ice Boy. If my ass is so hot, why did the Penis get the grope on every female with a pulse?"

Jason tried to take her arm, but she pulled away.

"For that matter, why did you let me fall out of the elevator and leave me there? Talk about rejection. Yeesh."

Ten

JASON couldn't believe Kira thought he'd rejected her. He took her by the shoulders. "If I had stepped out of that elevator, Gracie would have known what we were up to. I stayed out of sight to save your reputation."

"My what?" She mocked him with a laugh. "Get serious."

"I am serious. A staff as big as ours would have been talking about you, looking down at you."

"But not at you?"

"Well, no. I'm a Gilded Age throwback, remember? They expect me to—"

"Hit on anything that moves?"

"Speaking of hitting, Tillinghast must have been hit with a few too many fast balls, if he couldn't see what he had in you."

Kira looked as if he'd insulted her intelligence.

"What?" he challenged. "No comeback? Good. Damned if you haven't been shocked silent, and about time. You don't even know your own worth. That deadbeat ballplayer hurt you and I'm sorry, but stop hiding behind all that black. I like the real you."

She stood so still, Jason was able to run his hands through her crown of copper curls, the way a kid tests a candle flame to see if he can touch it without getting burned. "Tell me the real reason you always dress in black," he said.

"The real me wears black," she said so softly, he barely heard, but her eyes spoke a different language, one comprising heat and desire, "to look professional."

"You do look professional, but you also look sexy as hell. I see sex in those straps you call shoes, in defiance of everything, including the weather. I see sex in your black outfits, even if you don't, but I can't help feeling you're hiding under there."

"Get real. What you see is what you get."

"Do I?"

When she didn't answer, he continued. "Why are you trying to play down your natural sexuality? You're not a nun. You're a . . . a—" He looked at her sandals. "Inside, I think you're a butterfly, colorful, flamboyant, and you should be proud of it."

She turned away, crossed her arms, and gazed silently through Kingston's wall of pocket windows to study the sea.

"Tell me the truth," Jason said, coming up behind her and daring to run his hands down her arms. "Do you wear black because you're a witch? Do you wear it because you're hiding your true nature? Or are you actually mourning the loss of that lousy scum-sucking relationship?"

Kira turned on him so fast, Jason stepped back.

"I like black, damn it! It's nobody's business but mine what color I wear." She went around him and grabbed her purse off a marble-top console table. "You're my boss, not my fashion consultant. I dress in a businesslike manner for my job, and that should be enough. I believe I'm allowed to wear whatever color I choose, thank you very much." She checked her watch. "We'd better get a move on; hockey practice started five minutes ago."

"Shit!"

Jason's ire cooled as she ran through an icy rain toward the Hummer. If his feet were cold, hers must be freezing in those sandals. He got in, shut the door and swore beneath his breath as he divested himself of his raincoat. He threw it over her lap and tucked it around her feet, then he placed his suit jacket over her shoulders, fighting her for a minute to keep it there.

When she pulled it closed at the front and shivered inside it, he was satisfied she'd keep it.

"A sweater's not warm enough!" He started the engine, put the heat on high, and broke the speed limit getting them to the rink.

"It's a sweater coat, but . . . thanks for the . . . extras," she said, her belated gratitude barely tempered by her resentment.

Jason figured she had a right to be miffed. He didn't know which of them was acting weirder. Her, for shrouding her true nature in black, and failing to protect herself from the elements. Or him, for trying to protect her . . . from what? Herself?

She'd gotten this far without him, hadn't she? Why should she listen to someone she'd just met? And why the hell should he care whether she listened or not?

A shiny yellow bus—St. Anthony's painted in royal blue letters on the side—sat waiting at the door to the Cloud Kiss rink.

Unfortunately, some aspiring artist/delinquent had painted a huge *sucks* beneath St. Anthony's in bold red letters.

"Don't tell me he drove it through Newport like that?" Kira said, sitting up, the first sign of life since they'd argued.

"Betcha it's only on the driver's side. Those nuns are gonna croak," Jason said, trying not to show his amusement.

Kira must have sensed it, though, because she gave him a double take, before looking back at the bus in appalled horror.

Most of the twenty-some boys who had signed up were hanging out the windows cheering their arrival. The bus rocked as if the rest were bouncing off floor, walls, and ceiling.

Jason stroked the Hummer's leather-covered steering wheel. "This baby is loaded with soundproofing," he said. "I can't wait to hear those boys up close."

Kira tossed his raincoat over his head. As Jason pulled his coat down to clear his vision, he felt an icy draft and saw her door slam. When he spotted her, she was running between the raindrops toward the rink, his suit jacket wrapped tight around her. Good thing they'd left their arena gear in the dressing room this morning. He'd feel better when she was wearing more clothes.

Had he ever had a weirder thought? That witch was distorting his perspective on everything.

Jason cursed, locker-room style, and left the quiet safety of his truck. Kira had screwed him up, and down, and all around, because she left him to quiet the boys by himself. "Screw me," Jason said, raising his collar against the icy rain.

He was right; the door side of the bus had *not* been desecrated, so no one in St. Anthony's garage could have seen it. Jason knocked and the door swung open, old Mr. Peebles, the school's janitor-driver ready to weep in gratitude.

Jason barely said hello before he was forced to step gingerly aside, as the boys flooded out like the bulls on the streets of Pamplona.

"They'll calm down when they're not so confined!" Jason yelled to the driver.

"Yeah, right," Peebles said with a laugh. "Have fun. I'll be back at five to pick up the pieces."

"Wait," Jason said. "You might want to pull into that big garage and get my caretaker to see if he can scare up some body paint for the other side of the bus before you get back on the streets. Do Sister Margaret a favor and hide the evidence."

Peebles swore before he ever got out to view the damage.

Two long agonizing hours awaited him, Jason realized as he followed the boys into the rink, sending them to the benches where they'd put on their skates.

He'd told Sister Margaret that if she dressed them for two hours on the ice, he'd provide their skates and hockey sticks. Since Kira hadn't emerged from the dressing room, he might end up having to sort shoe sizes and hand out skates by himself as well.

When he opened the lockers, new skates and sticks inside, the boys hushed, as if in church. Jason sighed in appreciation and let the silence wash over him.

Kira appeared, dressed warm, praise be, and stopped when she saw the gazes on the boys' faces, and the relief on his.

With a nod and almost a grin, she took immediate charge of the boys, and of him, truth to tell, and began taking off shoes and checking sizes in her usual efficient manner.

Instead of the edge she showed the rest of the world, she gave the boys smiles and hair strokes, as if she were a Kira Jason hadn't known existed. One minute she was the wand-wielding witch, the next, the staid businesswoman, but this Kira was painted in soft pastels and existed on a plane somewhere between the butterfly he longed to meet and the witch he liked sparring with.

Did he like sparring with her? Who knew?

He only suspected she hid a bright side, of course, and he'd seen the witch side, but now this. How many more layers did she possess, he wondered, and why did he want to know them all?

In the first ten minutes, before lessons had even begun, half the boys fell in love with her. Jason studied their faces. In each of them, excitement and adoration were tempered by a kind of preservation instinct he was sorry they'd already learned to employ.

He hadn't spotted Travis, not yet, but he remembered how the boy's grin about buckled his knees.

He'd dealt with kids at every rink he played in. Why had that one child affected him, even before he'd asked to be adopted?

A small hand slipped into his, and Jason knew before he looked, because he remembered the unwelcome chest tug.

Prepared to be strong, Jason looked down, set to smile, but he got a shock, because he saw double. "Two of you," he said. "There are two?"

Except for the dimples on opposite cheeks, they were identical: their grins, their cowlicks, their freckles, the red hair . . . the jelly on their chins. Jason chuckled.

Travis nodded, one hand in Jason's, one clutching his twin's. "Zane wants to play hockey, too," Travis said, and the tug on Jason's chest became an all-out clutch.

Zane was wearing a leg brace.

JASON and Kira managed to get all the boys on skates, except for Zane, whose brace was connected to a special shoe, so it wouldn't work with a skate, and without it, he couldn't stand.

Zane was a trooper and took it with good grace, especially when his twin hesitated to take advantage of his own perfectly fitted skates. "Go skate, Travis," Zane said with an excited smile. "I wanna see *you* do it."

"No," Travis said, looking wistfully down at his skates, "I'm gonna sit with you for a while."

Kira came over and took them both to the bench. Like a hen with her chicks, she tucked Wizards stadium blankets around them and gave them hot chocolate and cookies.

Jason shook his head as he turned toward the rest of the crew. Before he could give them hockey lessons, they needed skating lessons. He was really working from the bottom up, here. But they were supposed to be having fun, weren't they? So maybe he'd hang loose and let that happen.

He turned to coax Travis on the ice, just in time to see the boy throw himself into Kira's arms. Uh-oh.

When she gazed his way, Jason gave her a sympathetic look, realizing her expression must mirror the one he'd worn that day in the schoolyard. She was as shocked and hooked by the boy's adoption request as he'd been.

The difference was that Travis had managed to knock his latest mark on her fine little ass.

Jason grinned and gave her a salute much like the one she'd given him on her first day, but she scowled at the gesture, rose, dusted herself off, and pulled the boy close, as if to protect him.

Jason knew exactly how she felt.

Wishing he could be out there skating with the boys, he wasn't satisfied until two-thirds of them were steady on their feet, some actually skating, some putt-putting along like Model T's on a bad road, others grinning just to be standing, one or two with their arms spread like wings.

At any given moment a third of them went down, face or bottom first. Good thing they'd stocked up on ice packs.

Jason found himself grinning a great deal more than he expected.

"Tell Travis to come and skate," he called to Kira, and she nodded, grudgingly, and spoke to the boy, because she knew as well as he did that Travis should take every opportunity given him.

It took her quite a while to convince the boy. Jason watched the series of stubborn headshakes and glances Travis gave Kira and his brother, an indication of his stubbornness. But finally Kira took Zane on her lap and urged his twin sternly forward, sending one of her chicks from the nest. Travis had no choice but to turn and come in Jason's direction.

"Is Zane gonna be okay?" Travis asked, pointing his thumb over his shoulder in his brother's direction.

"He sure is. Kira's gonna keep him company, so they can watch you together. See how happy Zane looks?"

Travis did look, and he turned back to Jason with a grin.

"He looks like her little boy. See, their hair is the same color. And they both gots freckles."

"Yes, I do see," Jason said, surprised and warmed by the observation, until Travis tugged on his sleeve to regain his attention.

"Ready to skate now?" Jason asked, putting on the pair of climbing boots he'd bought himself.

"Okay," Travis said as he stepped onto the ice, wobbled for half a beat, and caught his balance. With a grin he put one skate in front of the other, caught the rhythm, and kept going, a natural on the ice.

At the beginning of the second hour, against his better judgment, but caving to the boys' begging, in the name of fun, Jason emptied a bag of pucks on the edge of the ice.

Kira and Zane handed out sticks, according to Jason's instructions, based on the size of each child.

He studied the boys—faces eager, stance at the ready, and was almost, almost, glad Kira had suggested the lessons.

Only one problem: He had quite the range of players— Mites, Squirts, Pee Wees, Bantams, and Midgets. Talk about an informal mix. How he would eventually separate them into teams, he had no idea.

"Right now I want you to test the feel of the stick in your hand," he told the boys. "No, no swinging the stick. That's right, blade to the ice. Now see if you can skate with the blade. Whoops!"

Jason helped a couple of the boys get back up. "Travis," he said, "you've got Gordon's hat at the end of your stick. That's why raising the stick is dangerous. Give Gordon his hat back and put the blade to the ice now. That's it. We wouldn't want to see Gordon's head hanging there, now would we?"

The boys' mirth gave Jason a chance to regroup and re-organize. "Now," Jason said, "a man's hockey stick is one of his most prized possessions." He couldn't stop himself from glancing over the boys' heads at Kira when he said it.

In true Kira fashion, she stroked the hockey stick she

was holding suggestively, just enough to make him a little bit uncomfortable, then she raised it in challenge, as if it were a sword.

Jason rolled his eyes and turned back to his "team," watching the boys find their levels as they skated, blades down, mostly. He'd let them get the feel of the stick for a while.

If he found them tripping over it, he'd choose something else. He needed to be certain each stick was the right size for the height and weight of the boy.

When he looked back at the bench, Kira and Zane were, literally, sword fighting with their hockey sticks. "Kira, no!" Jason shouted. "That's not a good example—"

Sure enough, a couple of the monkeys on the ice had turned to swordplay. Others tried jousting, charging each other, sticks straight, body parts in dire peril.

Jason blew his whistle. "Cut that out! This isn't a medieval tournament, it's a hockey lesson."

Too late. A jousting skater took a stick to the gut, went flying backward, and took out three others in the process.

Jason took it slow crossing to center ice, helping everyone up, making certain no one was hurt. Steady on his feet, he got them all standing, and made it to the red line without a fall, glad he'd purchased the climbing boots for their grip alone.

In the neutral zone he broke up the sword fights. "Sticks to the ice," he ordered, and the boys complied. "Now find a puck," he said, "and do what I do."

Jason showed them how to control the puck with the stick, walking it, working it, then the hard part, doing that while skating.

Travis saw his brother sitting with Kira, playing cards, and finally let himself skate, stick and puck under full control. Wow. He was more than a natural; he was a winner. Funny how he'd held himself back, as if he couldn't have fun unless Zane did. What a great kid.

Twelve-year-old Brad, the oldest and professed leader,

jumped the gun and tried a shot to goal. He scored and the boys cheered, a dangerous precedent to set. Jason tried to say so, but the boys were too noisy to hear him because they were smacking pucks in all directions.

Shit!

A puck bounced off the wall near Kira's head, and she pulled off a smothering save. Rather than throwing her body on a puck, she threw herself on Zane to protect him.

Jason grabbed the rising blade of a stick before it made hard contact with Travis's head, and yelled, "Freeze!"

As a puck hit Jason in the temple, and a runaway skater hooked his ankles with his stick, and pulled his feet smack out from under him, the boys froze . . . and Jason hit the ice.

Eleven

WHEN Jason's focus returned, he found himself flat on his back on the ice, with at least two dozen pairs of eyes looking down at him.

A screech and a curse from Kira made him turn his head. Running in his direction, she slipped, tried to regain her balance, fell forward, and bellied his way, breaking the land-speed record for beached witches on ice.

On her way, she took out half the team.

It rained freaking hockey sticks. "Oomph." Jason took one in the shoulder, and one in the gut, before he stopped Kira's forward surge with his prone body.

She landed across him, which felt pretty good, until she elbowed herself up by crushing his nuts.

"Geeeezzzzzuhhhh." Jason cupped himself.

The boys stopped laughing and winced.

"Cups," Jason groaned. "Cups . . . next time."

Kira turned so red, holly berries would be lost in her blush. After a two-second moratorium, honoring the loss of his manhood, a distant giggling echo in the huge arena became infectious.

Zane was literally rolling on the floor, laughing so hard, he was holding his belly. Jason chuckled at the sight, and the boys did, too, except Travis, who looked as if he'd been hit by a puck.

Zane's laughter was the happiest sound Jason had ever heard, but Travis had tears in his eyes.

On her knees Kira hugged Travis and kept an arm around his waist. "You okay, buddy?"

"I never seen him do that before."

Kira turned to Jason, and she didn't even have to say a word; he knew what she was thinking. "I know," he said.

"Some things are just worth doing," she said, before she focused on his throbbing temple and reached toward the bruise.

"Don't touch," he snapped.

She retrieved her hand. "Bet you say that to all the girls." She laughed at her own joke. "Does it hurt?"

"Is it blue?"

"Well, yeah."

"Then it hurts."

"How's your back?"

"Wait, geez," he said, softening his words with a hand on her arm, and sitting up. "Boys, I said freeze. Move one more muscle and this is your last day at the rink."

They stood like statues, one or two poised to whack pucks, or each other.

"Good," Jason said. "Stay that way. Just give me a sec and we'll do a controlled warm-up. From this moment on, you will not make a move on this ice until I tell you."

He sat up and realized that Kira had an arm around his shoulders as if she were helping him. He tapped her cold nose with a finger. "You can go back and sit with Zane. I'm fine."

She rose with difficulty, so he held her ankles to help steady her, which turned out to be an extra treat.

"You sure you're okay?" she asked.

"This is nothing, believe me. Be careful walking back. Don't try to run this time." He quirked a brow to remind her of their first time in the rink. "Ice is . . . dangerous."

"Yeah," she said, "I remember."

"Try wearing skates next time," he said.

"Yeah, yeah, yeah." She waved his words away, as she walked gingerly back across the rink.

Jason didn't look at the boys until Kira was safe on the bench. Zane covered her with the stadium blanket she'd used on him earlier. Then he brought her a hot chocolate.

"At ease," Jason said to the boys, and when they relaxed, he told them to freeze again. Then he took Brad, the boy who'd made the unauthorized goal, by the shoulders, and walked him to the edge of the ice, away from the others.

He needed Brad Davis, oldest, professed leader, and troublemaker par excellence, on *his* side.

"Whasup?" Brad said, defensive stance in gear, excuse at the ready.

"The boys look up to you," Jason said. "I can see that, and you seem to know your way around a rink, so I'm thinking you might be the team captain. But . . . that means you're their leader; it means that you have to lead by example. Do what I say. Show them the meaning of rule-following and teamwork."

Struck speechless, Brad's expression could only be interpreted as amazed, and up for the challenge, maybe. He finally nodded, likely after deciding he wasn't getting screwed.

"Good," Jason said, clapping him on the back. "Let's say I make it official in a week or so, after I see how good a leader you really are."

Another nod and Brad turned away.

"Hey," Jason said, "is that red paint on your sleeve?"

Brad covered the spot with his hand, his expression saying he'd known this was too good to be true. He raised his chin.

Jason raised his. "I'll have no more of that. You're almost a team captain now. I'm gonna trust you to lead by example . . . in *everything* you do. Got it?"

Almost a smile, almost a nod, definite relief. "Got it."

Jason had Brad help him put the rink rats in line for warm-ups, little guys first, so they wouldn't be intimidated by what the big guys could accomplish.

"When you get to the front of the line," Jason told the boys, "you're gonna tell me your name so I can learn it. When I tell you to move," he said, "and not a minute before, that's when I want you to skate from the red line, sticks to the ice, while you walk the puck toward that goal. When I yell 'shoot,' I want you to try to get the puck into the net.

"Whether you succeed or fail, after you shoot once, and only once, I want you to skate back here and get at the end of the line. No punching, shoving, spitting, or cussing. Just wait for your next turn in an orderly fashion. Got that?"

Brad nodded, so the rest did, but Jason shook his head. "I want more enthusiasm than that. Say, 'Yes, Coach' nice and loud."

Jason grinned when they did, so did Brad, and so did Kira and Zane. "Louder," Jason said, twice more before he was satisfied and all eyes were bright, all hands eager.

He'd tried to make them feel like real hockey players, but damned if he hadn't made himself feel like a real coach, instead.

He had Brad collect the scattered pucks, put them in the bucket, and bring them over.

Warm-ups took the rest of practice.

Jason was so tired that night that he passed on supper with Gram, grabbed a muffin, and headed upstairs. Kira grabbed an apple. Neither said a word in the elevator.

Bone tired and sore, in both cases, Jason was sure, they parted to go to their respective doors in silence.

Jason took a couple of aspirin and went right to bed, but

the pain in his knee, and his empty stomach, woke him around ten. He hurt like a bastard, and his knee was roughly the size of a soccer ball. He'd overworked it, and there was only one thing that would help. He needed to ice it.

"Fuck," he said when he stood and tried to straighten. Not only his knee, but his ass, his shoulders, the back of his head, his temple, and the ankle where he'd been stick-hooked hurt like a son of a bitch.

Unable to bend enough to reach his robe, he gave up. "Screw that," he said. "Hurts too much."

Who would see him anyway? Kira had surely been asleep for hours.

Stooped like a ninety-year-old, Jason made his plodding way toward the kitchen, flipped the switch, and found Kira standing before the open fridge.

She turned her startled gaze his way, a jar of chocolate sauce in one hand, the spoon she was licking in the other.

Wearing turquoise silk lady-boxers and a matching half top, her midriff as bare as her breasts beneath, her naked torso was outlined by the fridge light behind her, in tantalizing relief, down to the pebbled nubbins on her beautifully lush breasts.

Jason memorized every line, as finely sculpted as a French bronze, every crest and hollow so well put together, she rivaled a work of art. He wished he dared kneel before her to trace the curves with his fingers.

He ached to palm the globes of her breasts and taste her darkly shaded center until she came, just there where she stood, just for him, the cool air blessing them, nothing and no one to come between them.

"Are you okay?" she asked.

"No," he said, moving her way, having trouble walking now for a whole new reason.

"I'm sorry," he added. "I didn't know you were in here."

"Are you limping? Oooh ouch, look at that prune on your forehead. It's as big as a plum. It's not blue anymore, though. It's purple and yellow with dried blood on it." She replaced the cover on the chocolate sauce, put it back in the refrigerator, and shut the door. Then she saw his knee. "Cripes," she said, opening the freezer. "You gotta get off that leg."

"Yeah, well, I needed to get some ice first. Thanks." He accepted a couple of frozen gel slabs and turned to go.

"Wait a minute. Come here," she said, taking his arm and leading him toward her suite. "You need some serious first aid. Oh, for pity's sake, stop being so macho and lean on me, will you?"

The fact that he was wearing nothing but a pair of boxers made Jason hesitate, though at least his were black and opaque, never mind that she was wearing, well, not a whole lot more, and he could see through hers.

But his knee, and a wide range of other parts, hurt so much, he gave in and slipped his arm around her bare waist and let her help him. Her naked midriff felt incredibly soft against his hand. He splayed his fingers to see if he could reach her breast. Close enough. Nice.

At least one part of him hadn't been damaged. The most important part. Harvey was in fine form.

When she got him to her sofa and bent to raise his foot to a pillow on her coffee table, Jason got a glimpse down the front of her top. Same naked breasts as date night with the candy-ass, same lovely navel, though her belly button ring was small and less flashy. And he caught sight of a few new freckles he'd like to explore.

He could, in fact, see every incredible inch of her, including her nipples and the wide band of rose surrounding them. He covered his pounding heart with a hand. After a sight that awesome, he was surely doomed to going blind.

When she put a pillow beneath his knee, and ice packs above and beneath the swelling, he thought he was gonna pass out from relief. As a matter of fact, he had to lay his head back and close his eyes for a minute as some kind of weakness flooded him. He knew that seeing something that glorious was gonna kill him, and he didn't care.

When he opened his eyes, Kira was watching him with . . . concern? Wow, that would be different, plus he didn't deserve it, pervert that he was.

Had he passed out, though? Because she was tying the belt on a soft figure-hugging turquoise robe.

Jason raised a brow. "Turquoise?"

"You're hallucinating," she said, swabbing his throbbing temple with some kind of stinging antiseptic.

"Ouch?"

"Sorry," she said. "I didn't think you would feel pain during a hallucination."

"Right. So I'm *not* covered with a beautiful handmade quilt?" He fingered the perfect stitching. "And these are not jewel-toned butterfly pillows on a *red* sofa? And you were not just wearing the most amazing see-through—"

She straightened. "See through?"

"I didn't see a thing."

"Right," she said. "Because you've fallen down a rabbit hole. Nothing will be the same when you wake. You'll forget you had this dream."

"I will *never* forget this dream."

"Shh," she said, lighting a white candle, releasing the scent of vanilla and something flowery into the room. "Take a deep breath, hold it, let the pain go, relax, breathe out, and heal."

And damned if Jason didn't feel enchanted enough to believe he was doing exactly that.

He watched her lift the quilt off his leg, felt her cup his knee, the heat of her hand going deep, bringing a measure of relief.

Move your hand a bit higher, he thought, Harvey coming to life in anticipation of the wish being granted.

Kira shook her head and checked his ice packs. "I'll be right back." She returned to the kitchen. "I'm going for a couple of fresh ice packs. Anything else ache?"

"Everything else aches . . . especially Harvey."

Kira's answering chuckle was both enchanting and . . . promising.

"Don't worry about a thing," she said, returning. "Kira will make it all better."

Jason sat straighter. "All of it?"

"Harvey, of course, will fall asleep."

"He doesn't *seem* sleepy— Wait! Where's your wand?"

"Don't worry. Harvey's safe. But you need to rest and heal more than anything."

He wanted to say he needed to get laid more than anything, but maybe that was too blunt, even for a rabbit hole. After all, this was only their first rabbit hole. Maybe in their second. If there ever was a second.

She cupped his knee through the quilt and he could almost feel a warm healing energy infusing him. "Are you some kind of healing witch?"

"I'm a solitary white witch just trying to ease your pain. Do you feel soothed?"

"Horny. I feel horny."

Kira laughed.

"What does 'solitary' mean?"

"I don't belong to a coven. I'm not Wicca."

"In other words, you're on your own."

"Right. I do my own thing."

"And 'white' means you're a good witch?"

"Define *good*." She wiggled her brows, intriguing the hell out of him.

She took the first ice pack away, slipped a new one behind his knee and another on his fat kneecap. "Are there any meds that you should take? I could get them for you."

"You're a goddess," he said. "Nobody has ever taken such good care of me. I'm used to somebody tossing me an ice pack and walking away."

"You're kidding?"

Jason shrugged, refusing to be pitied. "On the whole, guys don't show much sensitivity in a locker room. I don't know why."

She smiled the way he hoped she would.

"Can I get your meds?"

"I don't take anything but aspirin."

"You want me to get you some?"

"I'm okay for now. How come you're still awake at this hour? I thought you were bushed."

"I fell asleep at six and woke up starving."

Jason nodded. "I did pretty much the same. I might still be sleeping except for the knee. I am hungry, though, but if chocolate sauce is all we've got, I'll pass."

"Oh, the chocolate sauce was just an appetizer to hold me over, until I could find real food."

"As in?"

She tilted her head. "A grilled-cheese sandwich."

"Trade you for the Hummer."

"Deal," she said, heading for the kitchen. He heard her knock some pans around, open and close the fridge, while he examined her living room as if he'd never seen it before.

His parents had furnished it with earth tones, but Kira brought it to life by picking up the honey gold, crimson, royal blue, and emerald green in the Gothic arched stained-glass window.

Then she'd turned the window into the focal point of the room by hanging a clear glass shelf beneath it, topped with bright candles and clear compartmentalized glass tubes layered with herbs, seeds, and spices. He saw that her wand rested there as well, atop its purple velvet pouch, beside a crystal salt cellar.

His living room's matching stained-glass window looked lifeless compared to this one. His entire living room seemed without life compared to Kira's. He liked it better here.

He read the spines on the books between the pineapple bookends on her coffee table. *Prince Smarmy; Boyfriends into Frogs and Other Fun Spells.* Jason chuckled. *How to Charm Your Way Out of a Bad Relationship. Mastering the Naughty Witch Inside. Never Cross a Witch with PMS. Sex and the Single Witch.*

Jason bent to choose one, until he heard Kira's bare feet padding his way.

She appeared in the doorway, a dishtowel over one soft turquoise shoulder, and he wondered if *mastering* her naughty witch meant making good use of it or keeping it at bay.

He grinned, suddenly up for finding out. Literally "up."

"What?" she asked.

"You look . . . snuggable?"

"Then think of me as an electric fence. Do you like tomato juice?"

"Yes," he said, watching her go, fantasizing about electric charges of another sort.

He shivered and pulled her quilt over his shoulders. With the ice packs lowering his body temp, a power surge this intense could put him into shock.

Jason sought a diversion and found it in the quilt she'd thrown over him, a work of art bearing every color of the rainbow.

He picked up a similar unfinished square from the coffee table. Judging by the needle and crimson thread, Kira must be the artist.

She returned with a tray of quartered grilled-cheese sandwiches and two glasses of tomato juice.

He held up the quilt square. "Pretty bright stuff for a woman in black. This *is* your handiwork, isn't it?"

"Doesn't matter," she whispered, covering his mouth with a finger. "Shh. We're in a rabbit hole. Nothing is as it seems and neither of us will remember any of it."

Twelve

"EAT," Kira said, shoving a wedge of cheese sandwich into his mouth. She switched his ice packs for fresh ones and returned the originals to the freezer. When she came back, she sat in the corner of the sofa beside him and raised her legs to tuck her bare feet beneath his thigh.

He looked down at her exposed ankles, her legs bare to the hem of her robe, then up at her, his temperature rising.

"My feet are cold," she said with a grin. "And you're toasty warm under there." She grabbed a sandwich and took a bite while he got a picture of her toasting her feet on some of his warmer parts.

"You made enough," he said, dragging a corner of the quilt over her ankles before taking another quarter sandwich.

"I worked up an appetite this afternoon, and I wasn't even on the ice. I figured if I could eat two sandwiches, you could eat four."

"Bless you."

"How long has it been since your parents lived here?"

"I don't think they ever really *lived* here," he said. "Mostly, they just stayed here when they visited. Gram's the one who raised me. My parents came more often when I was small, of course, but never for more than a few weeks at a time, and only to issue orders about my upbringing that Gram thankfully ignored after they left."

"That's . . . that's—"

"The way it was. It did suck in a way, but at least I had Gram, unlike the boys we worked with today. Gram was the constant in my life, and I was the constant in hers. We're the lucky ones."

Jason wished he hadn't revealed so much. On the other hand, Kira had invited him into her rabbit hole, tended and fed him. The least he could do was tell her the truth. Not that it felt comfortable, this sharing shit. "Nothing *leaves* the rabbit hole, right?" he confirmed.

She placed her hand on her heart. "Witch's promise."

He nodded, only half thrown by the sorcery in the promise, and grabbed another sandwich. "Tell me about *your* family," he said. "Siblings?"

"Five." She licked a piece of warm cheese from the corner of her mouth.

"Five? That's a big family these days. Must have been fun growing up."

"You're being facetious, right? I have five siblings; we're six children, plus grandpa, so that makes us a family of nine."

"No shit? Small house, you said, right? How many bathrooms?"

"One and a half now. Used to be just the one."

"You're kidding?"

She grinned. "Strengthens the bladder."

Jason nearly choked on his sandwich. "Girls? Boys? And where do you fall into the scheme? Not in the middle, I presume. Already you strike me as more like a first child, a bossy overachiever."

"Hah. Good call. My brother Michael is the oldest in

the family, but I'm the oldest of the three girls. I'm the second child, so I try harder."

"Three boys and three girls. Cool. Good odds. Always somebody to play with."

"Hah. Or fight with, or lose your toys to, your friends, your dessert, your clothes—you name it. Hell, I even lost the Penis to one of my—"

She bit her lip. "Forget I said that."

"Tell me you're joking."

Kira rubbed her arms. "A big family is not all it's cracked up to be."

"Which sister?" Jason asked.

"Rabbit hole secret?"

He placed his sandwich to his heart. "Gimp jock's oath."

She chuckled, and he felt pretty good about making her smile, under the circumstances.

"My sister Regan."

"How did you find out?"

"I got a visual," Kira said. "Up close and personal."

Jason winced. Shit. "No wonder you canceled the wedding."

"To my parents' horror."

"They thought you should marry the jerk?"

"I could hardly tell them about my sister, now could I?"

"Sure you could."

"And hurt my parents? There had already been enough hurt. It had to stop somewhere."

Jason leaned over to wipe a tear from the corner of her eye with the tip of his finger. "They hurt you, didn't they, your parents, because they didn't trust you to make the right decision?"

Kira caught her breath, closed her eyes, and leaned into his hand at her cheek. He'd salted an open wound and her pain infused him.

She regained her composure before he did, shrugged, and took another piece of sandwich. Feeling like a robot,

Jason did the same, her pain too raw inside him to think of anything else. The vanilla scent of her candle surrounded them.

They became quiet, in harmony, munching grilled-cheese sandwiches while a life-scarred door leading to a deeper, more sacred rabbit hole—a cocoon where butterflies of new dreams warred with ghosts of slayed dreams—lay open and inviting between them.

Jason felt as if Kira stood on one side of the door, while he stood on the other, both of them afraid to cross, despite an attraction as unrelenting as the moon's pull on the sea.

He wondered for a minute if Kira's enchantment stirred these wild fantasies he was having, and he realized it probably did, but not the kind of enchantment she made with her wand.

Hers was a natural kinetic force that had hit him the first time he saw her. He'd denied it then; he'd deny it again tomorrow, but right now, in the rabbit hole, there was no mistaking it.

Kira shrugged again, as if to prove that her parents' doubts, her sister's betrayal, and the cheating Penis didn't matter, which told him otherwise.

She offered him a napkin. "Didn't your parents hurt you by leaving you for your grandmother to raise?"

"I didn't care. I still don't."

"Like hell you don't."

"Look, just because you've got ghosts to face, don't go making me dig any up."

"Hah! You *have* to dig some up. Remember the ghost tour?"

"Hey," he said. "I'm calling rabbit hole privilege here." And shutting that other door as well, he thought.

"Rabbit hole privilege?" she asked.

"Reality has no place in the rabbit hole, especially job-related reality."

Kira nodded. "And never the twain shall meet?"

"Deal," Jason said, extending his hand.

"Deal," she said placing hers in his, and on the strength of the faith in her look, and the need in her touch, Jason pulled her close. "I'm sorry you were hurt by the people you love," he whispered in her ear.

The shock of her tears seared, then chilled him as they hit his collarbone. Though Kira made no sound, her throat convulsed, as did her chest. Her fingers closed into fists at his back.

Jason held her close, showing her, as silently as she wept, that she could trust him. Had he ever wanted another's trust so much?

What was it with this woman? How did Kira Fitzgerald imprint her emotions on his soul, and why did he feel privileged to receive them?

He kissed her brow, her eyes, afraid and awed by the whole mystical experience.

KIRA wanted to climb inside Jason's skin, as if she would be safe and secure there in a way she could be in no other place, not even the rabbit hole.

Instead, she held herself together.

When the pain began to subside, she was shocked to discover that she also wanted to straddle him and let him make the pain go away. She wanted to know she was desirable, lovable.

She wanted . . . the oblivion of sexual fulfillment.

She *wanted* her first, real honest-to-goddess orgasm, and she was pretty damned sure Jason Pickering Goddard was the man who could give it to her.

Her boss. No, he wasn't her boss in the rabbit hole.

He was, however, still a jock.

As good as she felt in his arms, nobody knew better than she did that Jason was a player like Charlie, a care-for-nobody-but-himself kind of guy who'd publicly screwed his way through half the Free World. Hell, he was *better* at it than Charlie. He was so good, she fell for it, despite her hard lessons.

Unlike Farm Team Charlie, however, Jason was first string, top of the game, with everything he could ever want, every woman he could ever want, and no reason to be faithful to one.

That alone should make her run, and fast, in the opposite direction. So why was she clinging so hard? And why was it so difficult to let go?

Kira moved from Jason's protective embrace, his silver eyes piercing, predatory, his arms not letting her go as easily as she'd wish. Then she discovered that she also needed to move from his lap—not sure when she'd landed there.

She sat back in her own corner of the sofa, wiped her eyes, curled her feet under her, and took a sip of her tomato juice. "I'm sorry," she said. "That was unforgivable."

"No," he said, standing, his ice bags hitting the floor as he unconsciously wrapped her memory quilt around himself like a shield. She knew it, if he didn't.

"It was completely forgivable," he said. "Thank you for the TLC, the great sandwiches, and the peek into your rabbit hole. I think I'll be able to sleep now." He moved awkwardly toward the door, his antiwolf toga bringing hearthside snuggling and sweet slow sex to mind, despite her need to stay the hell away.

He looked down at the direction of her gaze and saw that he was still wearing her quilt. "I think some of my great grandmother's quilts are around here somewhere. You'd like them. Can I borrow this until tomorrow? I'm feeling a chill from the ice packs."

"Keep it. I have plenty."

He looked uncertain again, as if he might step back into the rabbit hole, then he scooted into the kitchen, a toad once more, seeking fast freedom from the dangers of the warren.

"Night," she said.

"See you at work," he said.

She watched him shut the door between them, leaving one of them in, and one out, though she didn't know which was which. She saw the light around her door go dark, and still she sat there stunned.

If she didn't know better, she'd worry she chased him away, that she'd scared the bejeebers out of the Big Bad Ice Wolf . . . no, the slimy little toad. He was definitely back on that lily pad.

She guessed they weren't riding in to work together anymore because he said he'd see her there.

"Well, fine," she said, picking up her remote. "Fine. That's what you get, Fitzgerald, for revealing yourself to a male of the jock species. Idiots. All of them. Scared of emotion, of commitment." Like her, she thought.

To hell with it, then.

She spent the rest of the evening punishing herself by watching the highly publicized *Best Kisser in America* series, one segment after the other, the entire set of DVDs courtesy of Bessie.

No wonder Jason had won. It certainly looked as if his kisses were as amazing as the sex dolls he kissed claimed they were. The girls named the kisses, and rated them and their instigators, like in the Olympics. A nibbling kiss, a romantic kiss, a trying-too-hard kiss, a wet kiss—always a low rating—a shooting-star kiss, a looking-for-sex kiss, an out-of-the-ballpark kiss, a sincere kiss.

Watching him on the show was like watching a disaster take place; she knew she should turn away, but she couldn't bring herself to hit the Off button on the remote. She was both repulsed and mesmerized, though it was killing her watching Jason kissing all those women when she wanted so badly for him to kiss her.

Past tense. Had wanted. Screw him.

If only she didn't want— Shit. Why *did* she want him so much? Why him, of all men? Why did she keep choosing the wrong men? Did she do it on purpose?

"Screw commitment!" she said, tossing a butterfly pillow at the TV. "Why can't I just find a man who can give me a freaking orgasm?"

Kira sat up. Maybe that was it. She'd always thought sex meant commitment. Maybe *she* was ready for sex without commitment. She grinned. Okay, so she was no different from Charlie or Jason. But that was good, right? Safe.

She thought about the vast world of possibilities that had just opened up to her. Sex without commitment. "Yes!" Good sex, no hang-ups, no hurt. Wouldn't that be liberating?

What a hoot. What a temptation.

Kira sat back and rewound a particularly great kiss to watch Jason in action again, and she smiled.

This time she might get into the game to have some fun. She could play as hard as the jock—no strings, no emotions, no fouls, no penalties . . . no pain. Talk about a turn-on.

Sex for sport. How kinky was that?

Kira chuckled and wondered what Jason would think of her idea, providing she ever got up the courage to . . . propose it.

She wondered what he'd do if she went into his room now and told him she wanted hot, no-strings sex.

She laughed as she imagined the look on his face.

Except tonight she'd probably hurt him, he was so sore, and it had been so long for her, so she turned off her lights and went to bed to sleep and dream of one man's world-class kisses.

She didn't see him again for the entire weekend and she wondered if he was avoiding her the way she was avoiding him. Since she hadn't gone down to Bessie's to eat once, she'd never know.

On Monday morning it was raining when she got to the office and her feet were soaked. She supposed she should give up on the sandals for the season, but the more Jason hounded her about them, the longer she'd wear them.

He came into her office, his expression thunderous, and

her dream of his great kisses and no-strings sex disappeared like so much vapor.

"Your feet are wet," he said.

"Thank you for stating the obvious." She wiggled her toes, admiring her barely there peach nail polish. "They're cold, too."

"Serves you right for wearing straps instead of shoes. The suit's nice," he said. "Too bad it's black."

"Black is a professional color. It's also slimming. And classic. Black is always in style."

"And perfect for a witch."

"Right." Kira slipped her wand from her pocket and toyed with the tip, stroking it the way she'd like to stroke Harvey. "Don't forget it."

Jason quirked his brow at her gauntlet as if he were trying to subdue his curiosity. "Do you keep any socks in that special events dressing room closet of yours?" he asked.

"No, but I have an old pair of slippers that got brought over in a box of Halloween decorations."

"Go dry your feet and put them on. I've just looked at our schedule, and frankly, we don't have time for you to be sick. When you're ready, come into my office; I want to go over the details of our upcoming events."

"Good idea." Kira headed for her bathroom and turned at the door. "Thank you. Nice prune by the way."

He touched the lump on his temple and winced. "I liked you better in turquoise."

She put a finger to her lips and shook her head. "Rabbit hole. Shh."

Jason shook his head and went back into his office.

Ten minutes later Kira felt pretty stupid. Nevertheless, her feet were warm, and that's what counted. She picked up her special events notes, her wand, her cola, and went into Jason's office.

He was staring up at the portrait over his mantel when she did, and he came around to sit across from her on the matching sofa.

When he saw her crossed ankles, he barked a laugh.

"What?" she asked in all innocence. "Oh, these?" She turned an ankle as if she were showing off the most delicate of glass slippers, instead of a pair of playful witch-face slippers, complete with nose warts and pointy hats. "Don't you like them?"

"They're you," he said.

"Thank you, dahling."

"They're more you than the black suit."

She stiffened. "Don't go there."

"Where's your wand?"

She took it from her pocket and placed it on the coffee table between them.

Jason reached for it.

"Touch it," Kira said, "and Harvey's a cocktail frank."

Thirteen

JASON froze, looked sharply up at her, left her wand alone, and placed his reaching hand in his pocket.

"Smart move," Kira said. "Hey, Bessie," she added as Jason's grandmother came in. Kira patted the space beside her. "Sit. Want some coffee or cola? We were just about to discuss our upcoming events."

Bessie took off her cape and sat, which suited Kira fine. "Something to drink?" she asked, rising.

"No, sit, dear, oh—" Bessie saw the witch slippers, and her laughter filled the office.

Jason's grin was incredible. Now Kira knew how he looked at someone he loved. Wow. If she'd thought he was handsome before, she'd been wrong. The love in that man's eyes made him drop-dead gorgeous.

He'd been right; he didn't care that his parents had all but abandoned him. Bessie had done a fine job raising him, and she'd given him all the love he needed.

Bessie wiped away her tears of laughter, chuckled a couple more times, whenever she looked down, then cleared her throat and became chairman of the board again. "Special events," she said, a last chuckle escaping. "What's on the agenda?"

"Actually," Kira said, "I was about to ask Jason how many of his famous buddies he's gotten to volunteer for the celebrity bachelor auction. We need to set a date and location so I can order the invitations."

Jason growled, not quite beneath his breath.

"Jason?" Bessie said. "Do you have any prospects for the auction?"

"No," he said, uncrossing his legs and sitting forward, "because I was hoping you'd forget that ridiculous scheme, which I believe you might have without this cauldron-stirring witch beside you."

"Maybe I should let you two talk," Kira said, going into her office and shutting the door.

"That woman can be a real pain," Jason said.

His grandmother grinned. "She is cute, isn't she?"

"I didn't say she was cute, I . . . never mind. I'll give hockey lessons to the kids, Gram, but please don't let that witch auction me off. You don't know what it's like to be treated like a piece of meat. I'm telling you that reality show really put a sour taste in my mouth for some of the things I used to enjoy a great deal."

"You mean it helped you grow up? Glory be."

Jason shook his head, because dealing with his grandmother could be such a lost cause. "Sometimes I don't know which of you is worse," he said. "But at the moment, the witch is in first place."

"Is she the one who gave you that bruise, dear?"

Jason touched his brow. "All but. I got it at hockey practice yesterday. I have bruises that would make you cry." He stooped down in front of her. "Feel the lump on the back of my head; it's twice as big," he said, turning so she could. "Feel. I smacked it and every other part of me on that ice yesterday."

His grandmother found the lump in his hair and made

some cooing noises. He turned, expecting sympathy, and she dutifully patted his cheek and shook her head as if the bump was a crying shame. "I hope you heal fast," she said. "You have hockey practice again in a couple of days."

Jason regarded her with disgust. "You're all heart, Bessie Hazard."

"Call Kira back in, will you?" his grandmother asked. "I want to talk to you both."

Jason rose and hit the buzzer. "You can come back in now, Mizz Fitzgerald."

Jason noted that Kira tried to act dignified when she returned, but with her eyes filled with merriment, and her feet covered in green wart-nosed witches, she failed.

"Sit, dear," his grandmother said. "We've come to a decision about the auction. Jason is still going to get some of his famous friends to volunteer to be auctioned off," she said, taking Jason's breath away, "but we're going to let *him* off the hook."

Jason relaxed for the first time since the rabbit hole.

"We're going to put a ringer in the audience," Gram said. "I'll bankroll you, Kira, so you can bid as much as you want for Jason, so long as you're the one who gets to take him home."

"What!" They were both on their feet.

"Whatever you cost, dear," the old meddler said to him, "will be my contribution to the event. It's the only solution," Gram said, standing, sliding on her leather gloves and buttoning the tan cashmere cape she'd worn for as long as he could remember. "See you both at supper."

After his grandmother left, Jason stared at Kira and she stared back, both of them in shock.

"Special events?" she suggested, her voice a squeak, and Jason nodded, dumbly, he was certain, and picked up his notebook.

Kira chewed her pen. "She's a tough old bird, isn't she?"

"The toughest."

"Tough love. Probably why you're not a spoiled brat *or* pining for your parents. She's good."

"She's certifiable."

Kira giggled.

"You think it's funny to have to dance to her tune. She's not easy to live with, you know?"

"Yeah, and I'll bet you're a barrel of laughs. But I wasn't thinking about your grandmother. I was thinking of the ways I might make use of you after I win you."

Jason looked up at her, his pen halfway to his paper. "What do you have in mind?"

"Does the word *slave* ring any bells?"

"As in sex slave?"

"Yep."

He sat forward. "Can you give me any idea what that would involve, from your perspective."

"Ask me again the next time we're in a rabbit hole."

"Shit," he said.

"Nice talk," she echoed.

THAT evening, to keep himself from thinking about how much he'd like to be Kira's sex slave, Jason focused on keeping her from catching pneumonia—so she wouldn't have to call in sick and leave him to manage the boys at the rink by himself.

First order of business. Shopping.

The next morning he came to work bearing gifts—well, one gift. Not that he knew how she'd take it, but what the hell? He had good intentions. After his glimpse into the rabbit hole, he'd had it wrapped in butterfly paper with a huge turquoise bow and hoped she'd accept it in the spirit with which he was giving it.

Fact was, there was a chance she'd use her wand on him when she saw what was inside.

He found her at her computer, in deep concentration, her fingers moving on that keyboard faster than he'd ever seen anybody type. He felt awkward and stupid just standing there holding a fancy box with a fancy fat bow, worse because she was ignoring him. "I thought maybe you—"

She screamed and jumped a foot.

He jumped, too, and dropped the box. "Geez. You scared the crap out of me."

"What do you think you did to me?" She held a hand to her heart.

"I figured you heard me come in."

"You figured wrong."

Jason took the box from the floor, set it on her lap, and stepped away, wishing he could disappear.

All she did was look down at it, an inscrutable expression on her face.

Waiting for her to acknowledge its existence unnerved him. "Open it."

She examined the bright package, top, bottom, sides. She jiggled it, then she fingered the bow and the wings on the silk butterfly in its center. "It's . . . beautiful, but why?"

"Why is it beautiful?"

"Why the gift?"

"You'll see. Open it."

"It's too pretty to open."

"Open the damned thing or I'll rip the paper off myself. I'm going nuts here."

Kira stifled a grin. "You don't give too many gifts, do you?"

"What was your first clue?"

"Your hands are shaking."

Jason swore, grabbed the box from her hand, went into his office, and shut the door between them. "Enough of that crap."

A minute later Kira came in, remorse in her demeanor. "I just wanted to treasure the moment," she said. "I don't get many gifts. It felt like Christmas, you know, the awesome part, when you look at all the beautiful gifts and hope one might be yours, and then one is."

"Geez, I didn't mean for you to go all mushy on me," Jason said, shoving it back at her. "Just take it."

"Is it breakable?"

"No."

"Good." She smacked him with it. "Now stop sulking, sit down, and watch me *enjoy* opening my gift."

Jason did as he was told.

On the sofa opposite him, Kira untied the ribbons and set them, with the bow, aside as if they were as priceless as a rare French clock. She removed every sliver of tape with careful and slow precision, smoothed the perfect sheet of butterfly paper, and folded it.

At about the fifth piece of tape, Jason was so uptight, he was gritting his teeth, so he made himself relax and accept that she would take forever.

If he'd known a gift would mean this much to her, he would have gotten her one sooner.

When she removed the cover from the box, he held his breath. When she parted the tissue, she gasped, and he nearly came off his seat.

Then she went silent again.

"They're Wellies," he said, a little too fast. "Very trendy . . . so your feet stay dry . . . and you stay healthy."

She removed one of a pair of red-and-yellow Argyle-style boots from the box and regarded it, a hand to her mouth for too long. Then she ran her fingers over the shiny-smooth surface and traced the argyle design.

He'd never seen her wear anything but black, except in the rabbit hole, and she was right about that night, it did seem like a dream. But boots were different, weren't they?

He couldn't tell if she liked them or not, if the wild-patterned colors insulted her or not. He *could* tell that if she didn't say something soon, he was in for a case of heart palpitations.

When she finally looked up at him, she had tears in her eyes.

The palpitations stopped. "Geez. Now what? I didn't

mean to piss you off." He reached for the box. "Hand them over; I'll take them back. Stupid idea."

Kira squeaked and pulled the box from his reach.

Jason stopped and straightened. "I can't read you," he said. "Say something, please."

She swallowed. "They're beautiful."

"They're just boots."

She held them closer. "They're *my* boots."

"So wear them, damn it!"

She frowned, bit her lip, put the Wellies back in the box, covered it, and set the paper and ribbons on top . . . at which point Jason expected to have them shoved down his throat.

But she set them aside and picked up her notes. "Want to go over a couple more events?"

"Okayyyyy." Jason followed her lead and picked up his notes, still not sure if the boots were a good idea or a bad one, though he knew that snapping at her had been lame, and he was grateful he wasn't barfing boots about now.

"I have some thoughts regarding our 'Get Acquainted' event," Kira said, all business again.

"Shoot," he said, watching her sneak peaks at the box of boots, as if she were suddenly vulnerable, which was odd, considering how strong and determined she really was.

"I have two possible titles for the event," she said, turning in her seat to face him . . . or to face away from his gift. "How about 'Empty Arms' or 'Waiting Arms'?" she suggested. "Or even 'Open Arms,' " she added, "now that I think of it."

"I think Empty Arms has a negative connotation," Jason said, "and we want the event to be festive. I'm afraid that Waiting Arms will remind the prospective parents of how long a wait is involved with an adoption, plus both might be reminders that they can't have children of their own. But I do like Open Arms," he said. "It's . . . open, honest, hopeful, positive . . . something to come home to."

"Wow, you're good at this."

Jason shrugged. "In the nonprofit arena, I'm a junior-varsity player and you're in the national league. The call may have been mine, but the game is all yours."

"Okay, but you're insightful. I had already seen the negativity in Empty Arms, and I didn't think of Open Arms until I started talking. I like it."

"That's why we discuss these things. Get them out in the open."

"Okay, next: We have to set the date for the Open Arms event and discuss Sister Margaret's theatrical ideas."

"Which do you want to do first?"

"A date will automatically narrow the list of possible plays."

"A date first, then." Jason opened his day planner.

Kira did the same. "Given the fact that October is half over," she said, thinking out loud, "and figuring in the time to design, print, and mail invitations, I see Saturday November twenty-sixth as the earliest possibility, though I'd rather have the extra week we gain by going with Saturday night December third. We have to pick an auction date, too, by the way."

"I have a brilliant idea," Jason said. "Let's auction off the kids!"

Kira raised her day planner to hide her face, but her shoulders were shaking.

"Okay," Jason said, "not such a brilliant idea, but why does Open Arms have to be on a Saturday night?" he asked. "This is a kid thing, right? How about we make it a Sunday afternoon? How does Sunday December fourth sound to you?"

Kira slid her calendar slowly downward, revealing herself in increments, her gorgeous cinnamon curls first, her speaking emerald eyes next, and ah, there was her smile—as potent as her wand, and able to achieve the opposite effect.

"That's bloody brilliant," she said.

"When did you become British?"

"I may have watched *Love Actually* and *Bridget Jones's*

Diary too many times this weekend. They're two of my favorite movies."

"Never saw them."

"You poor deprived male. I'll have to make popcorn one night and invite you over for a chick-flick fest."

"I'd rather give hockey lessons. No, scratch that. I'd rather get hit with a puck."

"I wish Travis and Zane could be lobsters in a Nativity play."

"What?"

"You wouldn't understand."

"Maybe that's a *good* thing?"

"Come and sit by me," Kira said, patting the space beside her, "so we can look at what plays the boys might perform. Sister gave me a good-sized list."

Who was he to argue? Jason thought, happy to settle in beside her. She smelled great close up, better than toxic perfumed smoke, his first aromatic memory of her, and better than grilled-cheese sandwiches, his last and favorite, until this moment. At this moment she smelled of berries again, ripe summer berries, and again, he wanted a taste.

"Sister Margaret put down the usual child-type plays," she said, showing him the list. "See, and, frankly, they're all boring. I want the boys to give a performance with an up-to-the-minute edge, something to make them shine."

"Yeah, well, then, don't set it in a hockey rink. Do *we* get to pick the play?"

Kira nodded. "With Sister's approval."

"Okay, what have we got?"

"Since it's in December, let's eliminate the autumn plays and the boring ones." Kira scratched some titles off her list. "I see potential in . . . Scrooge and the Nativity."

"Either, I guess, though they seem as boring as the rest to me, or should I say they've been overdone, at any rate."

"That's almost the beauty in them, so I've been trying to come up with ways to combine them," she said, pencil to her teeth, gaze focused inward. "Instead of *Ghosts* of Christmas

Past, Present, and Future, we could have . . . angels—edgy, today angels." Her smile tightened Jason's chest. "Won't the boys make great little angels?" she asked rhetorically.

"Hah!" Jason touched his temple. "Sure, and I suppose Zane would make a perfect Tiny Tim?"

Kira patted his cheek, which he liked, and his body agreed he liked. "That's the spirit," she said. "For instance, we could make one of the angels a hockey player."

"Yeah, well, don't give him a stick and a puck, because he'll knock out the cast and half the audience in one swing."

Kira giggled. "What if . . . we ended the play with the angel of Christmas past at the Nativity . . . and the kids give parenthood a not-so-subtle plug using Mary and Joseph as examples."

That was the kicker, Jason thought. She'd hooked him. She'd freaking knocked him on his figurative ass. She didn't get paid enough was his first thought, but he couldn't afford to admit that, so he simply grinned, and high-fived her, a compliment she seemed to appreciate, judging by her eyes.

She'd only ever looked at Zane or Travis that way, he thought, humbled.

They remained, palm to palm, her verdant eyes bright, electricity sparking between them, his blood hot and heading south. But when he stroked her fingertips with his . . . he broke the spell.

She reclaimed her hand, as if from a fire.

He was sorry he'd spooked her.

She stood to leave, almost at a run.

Kira was running scared, or so it seemed to Jason.

Fourteen

"I'VE got volunteers coming in to get the *Kitchen Witch* invitations into the mail," Kira said from beside the door to her office. "I figured I'd invite only female donors, then it occurred to me that men think Melody's hot, so I invited them as well." She had worked her way back into his office.

"That's about two hundred and fifty invitations and a potential five hundred attendees," Kira added, "but Kingston's grand ballroom opens to an enclosed swimming-pool patio, so we'll have plenty of room. If everyone we invite attends, which *never* happens, I can still do it."

Jason was beginning to think she could do anything, though some of the things he imagined her doing could get him into trouble.

"I know this is not your favorite topic, but . . ." Kira distracted him by walking away, so he focused on her fine ass, which she removed from his view by leaning against his desk.

She faced him, crossed her arms, and skewered him with a determined look.

"Uh-oh," he said.

"You guessed it," Kira said. "At this point we have no choice but to hold the celebrity bachelor auction on the last Friday night in November at Summerton. So . . . unless you say different, I'm designing the invitations today and getting them to the printer tomorrow afternoon, at the latest. Which means, you need to get on the phone—this afternoon, if not sooner—and get your famous buddies to volunteer their time for a good cause. I'd like to be able to put a couple more hotties on the invite."

Jason stood. "You think I'm a hottie?"

"That's not what I said." Kira's blush rose, but Jason kept his grin to himself. He wanted her to read his interest as he approached her.

She looked like she might want to run, but his desk at her back, and his hands braced on either side of her, stopped her retreat. The position also allowed him to rise over her, so to speak. "I think you're hot," he said, "especially in filmy turquoise boxers."

She stomped on his foot. "Rabbit hole!"

"Ouch! Right. Sorry. Admit it; you think I'm hot, too."

"Like hell, you're hot."

"Thank you," he said, warming her ear with his breath. "Hell *is* a pretty hot place."

Like a shot, she left him with an armful of air. She'd ducked from beneath his arms and stood again at the door to her office. "Get on the phone, Goddard."

Jason wondered for half a beat which of them was the boss, but he remembered that she'd thrown him a boss-type bone: "unless you say different," she'd said.

He sighed, straightened, went around his desk with as much dignity as his boner would allow, sat down, and picked up the phone.

"Wait, you need to know that your grandmother said the bachelors can stay at Cloud Kiss, if they're flying in. Plus they should know in advance that they have to plan a date, a great date for the following day or evening."

"Okay. Right." Jason made notes as she spoke.

"We'll announce their date plans as we introduce them," Kira added. "We'll also send them a questionnaire about their interests for a program bio within the week. They can call me if they have questions."

Jason had to put the phone down and regather his enthusiasm. Everything she'd just said applied to him as well. Son of a hockey puck, but that woman was a take-charge kind of girl. Then again, he got to plan the date, didn't he? And since she was a ringer, and would absolutely, without a doubt, win him, he began to think about where he'd like to take her.

But hadn't she once said *no* dates, and later, hadn't she mentioned using him as a sex slave? Jason grinned. Okayyyyy!

"Oh, one more thing," Kira said, sticking her head back into his office. "They should know that this is a black-tie event, though the dates they plan can be as casual or as fancy as they want. And as much as I hate to say it, I think you should take out your little black book and invite some of your bottle-blond babes to come and join in the bidding."

Kira pulled her head back into her own office, like a turtle retreating into its shell, and left him fantasizing about getting into her shell with her.

Jason started to dial as Billy sauntered into her office, threw his arms around her, and planted a long, hot, familiar kiss on her lips.

"Kira!" Jason shouted, and when she disentangled herself and came in, he blanked.

"What?" she said after a minute.

"Can you read me my rights again?"

She ticked off the auction rules on her fingers, and while she did, her volunteers arrived to give Billy some competition for her attention.

When Kira left, Jason grinned with satisfaction and dialed.

"Hey, Seth," Jason said. "How's the Company of Rogues doing, and how would you like to donate yourself and a few of your rogues-for-hire to a good cause?"

While Jason was on the phone with baseball's famous Santiago the Stealer, he could hear the Court Jester entertaining in Kira's office, making her volunteers giggle like schoolgirls.

Kira looked in, saw his distraction, and shut the door to cut the noise, but not without a moment of electric eye contact between them.

It was enough . . . for now.

Jason smiled as he continued talking to his best friend.

Kira left work before him that night, didn't come to Gram's for dinner, and got to the office before he did the next morning.

He leaned on the door between their offices and watched her deep in concentration. She was wearing black again today, a svelte seventies-looking one-piece jumpsuit, with a sailor-suit collar and a familiar pair of black sandals, but the weather had warmed and cleared, so he didn't suppose she'd be wearing the Wellies yet anyway.

He already knew that if he spoke before she saw him, she'd jump a foot, so he waited patiently for her concentration to break.

It never did, not in the ten minutes he enjoyed her every expression and facet, so he moved closer to her desk so she could see him in her peripheral vision . . . and she jumped and screamed.

"Well, hell," he said. "What do I have to do to get your attention without scaring you to death?"

"Sorry, I kinda get into what I'm doing and turn off the world around me."

"No kidding."

"What's up?" she asked.

Wouldn't you like to know? "By my calculation, we have

less than two weeks to find that hidden staircase at Rainbow's Edge, and I want to see how the crew raising that gravestone is faring. The stone is so big, it keeps breaking their equipment. Are you up for a bit of stairway hunting this morning?"

"God, yes, get me out'a here. I'm sick of doing paperwork."

"You read my mind. Want to come in the Hummer?"

She raised a brow.

He chuckled when he caught the double meaning. "I like the way you think, Fitzgerald."

"You'd be *shocked* if you knew the way I think."

"Nothing can shock me. I'm a hockey player."

"Let's give your shock-meter a test sometime, shall we?"

"Just say the word." He grabbed the doorknob.

"The word."

He stopped, turned, and regarded her, silently asking for an explanation.

She shrugged. "Just making sure you were paying attention. We should travel separately, if we want to end up at home tonight with both vehicles. Hockey practice after school today."

"You *had* to remind me."

She took a black all-weather coat from the mission-style coat rack, and he helped her into it. Not that he minded. He appreciated any excuse to touch her and he approved the excuses she used to touch him.

"Sister Margaret says the boys have talked about nothing but you since hockey lessons," she said, pulling a wealth of curls from the neck of her coat. "Three of them wrote papers about you and several wrote about hockey lessons in their religion journals."

"What was so religious about the experience? I'm probably going to hell for the things I was thinking that afternoon."

"You're an adult who gave them your undivided attention. That matters to those boys. Give yourself a pat on the back."

"I can't. I'm still too bruised from the experience. I'll tell myself that *you* said I did good, and I'll be satisfied, okay? Where'd you park your broom?"

•

DID it matter to Jason, Kira wondered as she drove her Jetta toward Rainbow's Edge, that she thought he'd done well with the boys? And what was that ear nuzzling in his office yesterday? She shivered and grinned. Could Jason possibly want her as much as she wanted him?

She turned up the heat. If she hadn't been able to keep the Penis interested, how the hell did she think she could interest the Ice Wolf? Even if she did interest him, for a time, how would she survive when he got tired of her?

She was definitely *not* up for that again.

Jason was waiting for her at Rainbow's Edge. They headed toward the Winthrop Family cemetery, where six ham-fisted men with shoulders as wide as doors, and arms as thick as tree trunks, stood around talking about why they couldn't lift Addie's gravestone.

"They're efficient," Kira said as they approached the strapping crew.

One of the bruisers took a drag on his cigarette when he saw them, then he used the coffin nail to direct their gaze toward the recumbent marble giant. "Did you know this sucker's been facedown for more than eighty years?" Smoke poured from the man's nose and mouth as he spoke, a derelict dragon with bad breath.

Kira shivered in repulsion.

"Yes," Jason said. "My grandmother said it's been like this since she was young."

"It didn't budge then," the guy said, squaring his shoulders and spitting into the grass. "It won't budge now. End of story. Sorry. No can do."

"Try again!" Kira snapped. "It's not rocket science."

A bird in the tree above them cawed several quick times, like a crone laughing.

The Neanderthal stepped away, said something that made the cretins around him chuckle, and the crew went back to work.

Jason led Kira away.

"What'll we do if they don't raise it?" she asked. "Maybe we should call a bigger company?"

"Good idea," Jason said. "If these guys don't raise it today, we'll tell them to forget it. By the way, *that* was a gorilla."

She snapped her fingers. "Right; now I see the resemblance."

Jason stopped. "Is that a dig?"

"You think I'm mocking you? Me?"

He stroked the back of her neck with his thumb and forefinger.

"Mmmm." She hunched her shoulders to trap his hand, so he continued as they walked.

"Promise you won't pay them, if they fail," she said.

"I'll do my damndest not to," he said, "but if it comes to a showdown, you're my man."

"Gee, thanks." She shrugged his hand away.

"Hey," he said, "I thought you were gonna bite the guy."

"I thought about it," she said, "but I have a strong gag reflex."

"Remind me not to piss you off."

"Too late."

Kira realized, if Jason didn't, that they had somehow become a team. He needed her, and he didn't even seem to mind. Her step got lighter. Her new job, and maybe even her new boss, was working out great.

Okay, so he could have any woman he wanted, but he seemed to want her, at least on the job, and that was enough. For now.

"Let's walk around the perimeter of the house," he said, "see if we can spot any jogs in the construction that seem odd or big enough to hide a staircase."

He pointed out each room as they went, and they both

agreed that the outside seemed to conform with the inside. "The stairway must sit in the center of the house," he said, talking to himself. "It's possible."

"Where do we start?" she asked, once they were inside. "Did you find the architectural drawings in the archives?"

"I went through tons, but I never found any on this place. How about we start in the attic and work our way down to the basement?"

"Sounds like a plan."

Kira waved to the chaotic squawking birds in the aviary before heading for the enclosed stairway nearby and making her way up to the attic.

"Those birds are never as noisy as when you're around; you know that, don't you?" Jason climbed the stairs behind her.

"Maybe they're trying to speak to the witch in me," she said with a trembling voice and fake cackle. She turned, making claws of her hands, to wrap them around his neck.

With her on the step above him, they stood eye to eye, everything meeting as it should, the potential high for a kiss, and then some. Kira allowed herself the sensual pleasure of toying with the curls at his nape.

Jason's sigh spoke of desire, and as he covered her hands with his, she felt something like a spark rising between them, making her wish again for the touch of his lips against her own.

"Don't witches always have pets? Special ones?" he asked, eyeing her lips but appearing to seek a distraction at the same time. Conflicting body language. How odd.

"What *do* you call a witch's special pet?" he asked.

Kira sighed and pushed his hands aside, pulling herself physically away as he'd pulled mentally away. "A familiar."

"Right. Where's your familiar?"

"You think I should walk around with a crow on my shoulder like weird old Addie Winthrop?"

"That might bring some notoriety to the foundation."

"No." Kira was adamant. "One crow does not bode well for the wearer."

"Excuse me?"

"One is for sorrow," she said.

"Seriously," he said. "No pets?"

"I had a dog, Spooky, but I gave him to Melody's son, Shane, when I moved to Cloud Kiss. I didn't even want to ask your grandmother if I could have a pet. Cloud Kiss has 'no pets' written all over it. But Shane lets me visit Spooky, because I miss him."

"I thought witches kept cats."

"I'd like to have a kitten, someday, but I haven't found the right one, or maybe I should say, it hasn't found me. My sister Regan has a cat that needs an exorcist," Kira said as she searched for the light switch.

"And my brother Aiden has a lizard that looks like it's wearing a green Breathe Right strip, but it still sounds like an obscene phone call."

Jason did a double take.

Kira shrugged. "We seem to end up with the pets nobody else would want . . . and it's not like we go shopping for them."

"What about your dog, Spooky?"

"He just showed up at my door one day with a bark like an owl on steroids.

"Sounds spooky," Jason said.

"Right. Hence the name. What are you *doing*?" He was feeling up the wall, making Kira wish his hands were all over her that way.

"There *has* to be an entry to the hidden staircase somewhere," he said.

"Good point. But I thought you said it must be in the center of the house. That's an outside wall."

"We can't afford to overlook anything. Come here, start beside me, and go that way. I'll go the other way," Jason said, "and we'll meet in the middle."

Kira winked. "Meet you in the middle."

They separated, him shaking his head.

Halfway there, she turned and screamed.

"What?" Jason said, coming over.

Kira shook her head. "A woman."

"It's a dress form."

"For a minute, I could have sworn it was a woman with dark hair wearing a long, black dress from years ago. It— *she* . . . lurched in my direction, as if . . . in need, desperate need, of my help."

"It's a dress form. Have you had enough to eat today?"

"Why?" she said. "Afraid I'll take a bite out of you?"

"I should be so lucky."

Kira swiped the hair from her eyes. "What did you say?"

"I said, you're lucky she didn't have a crow on her shoulder."

"Who?"

"The lady who needed your help."

"You think it was Addie, don't you?"

"No, *you* think it was Addie. I think it's a dress form. Back to work."

Three hours later they had tested every wall, floor, panel, bookshelf, hearth, mantel, closet, and cubby in the place, Kira thought, and, still, no hidden staircase. "That's it," she said. "We're done. "This house doesn't have a hidden staircase. The Deerings were right."

"They never looked for one; they simply never stumbled across one."

"I know, but she cleans this place and he's done all the yard and repair work, for what, twenty years? You'd think if there was a hidden staircase, one of them would have stumbled across it at some point in time."

Jason firmed his lips as they neared the stairs that led to the aviary. "You know where we didn't look?"

"We didn't miss an inch. Give up. The story of the fake haunting was fiction and that's how we'll have to play it."

Jason shook his head. "We didn't check the walls inside the aviary."

"You're joking."

Jason motioned for her to precede him up the stairs, and Kira went despite herself. "Those birds are not happy," she said. "They hear us coming and they know, they *know*, we're going to invade their space. I don't like it. We're gonna get pecked to death."

Jason chuckled and tugged on her hair from behind. "We might get crapped on, but I don't think their peckers are big enough to kill us."

Fifteen

"YOU'LL be sorry," Kira warned as Jason undid the latch on a birdcage bigger than her bedroom.

Jason went in anyway, despite the ballistic birds, and despite her warning, but when he dragged her in, against her better judgment, the birds calmed down.

The flirty black winking crow said, "Hello, Mommy," again, and took a literal flying leap to land on her shoulder.

Kira yelped in surprise, and the bird on her shoulder laughed like the crow in the cemetery, and though Kira wanted to get it off, she could feel the crow's claws in her skin, almost like a threat, so she didn't push it. From her perspective, that beak looked plenty big.

The second black crow had waddled over and stood looking up at her, its head tilted consideringly.

"Geez, they like you," Jason said.

"Yeah?" she said. "What was your first clue?"

All eight birds were suddenly surrounding her, on perches above and beside her, and on the floor at her feet. The one on her shoulder began running its beak through her hair, as if combing it, in an affectionate or soothing motion.

Kira did not feel either cherished or soothed.

"I wish I had a camera," Jason said.

"I'd beat you with it," Kira said. "I'm kinda freaked, here. You think you could check the walls so we can get the hell out? I'm sorta tied up right now."

Amused, but biting his lip, the smart man, Jason began a painstaking search of the two walls that made up the cage back and half of one side. A floor-to-ceiling window met the half wall, to give the birds a sense of the outdoors.

"Oh, crap," Kira said. "One of them is eating my shoe."

Jason turned and saw that the black crow on the floor was indeed nibbling the flowers on her sandal.

Two black-and-white crows sat at the edge of a perch, one pecking at her sailor-suit collar, the other pulling a loose yarn from her sweater, like a worm from the ground.

When a gray crow flew her way, Kira removed her hand from her hip and clamped it to her side, as if she were afraid it might land there. It settled on a low perch and went for her pocket.

On her right shoulder, the black crow that seemed to have fallen in love with her continued to play with her hair.

Much as Jason tried to hide his amusement, he chuckled. Once.

Kira looked up, eyes narrow. "I am going to kill you."

"Trust me," he said. "This is worth dying for. They think you're a statue, and you know what that means."

"Dead," she said. "You are so dead."

When the other gray abandoned her nest to fly over and settle gently atop Kira's mat of lush red curls, her shock alone was enough to do Jason in. He lost his breath trying not to laugh. "Relax," he said, biting his lip. "They won't hurt you."

"I'm getting my wand," Kira said, stamping her foot, knocking the shoe-munching bird on its tail. "You're toast, Goddard!"

Jason couldn't fight his laughter any longer. He lost his breath trying, tripped on a bird, and fell against a wall that groaned, heaved, and gave . . . then he was tumbling, ass over head, down a real rabbit hole.

This was gonna hurt, he thought during the free fall.

Jason opened his eyes on a grin when he heard Kira tell a crow to shove its beak where the sun don't shine.

He had ended sitting on a landing, at the base of the stairs, where it was cold, dark, and damp, a wall at his back, and one at each elbow. The dim cubicle, as square as the stairs before him were wide, harbored cobwebs, spiders, and dry dead bugs, draped, caught, and sprinkled everywhere.

He'd found the hidden stairwell.

He swiped a web from his face as Kira called his name, but he didn't have enough breath yet to answer. The next thing he knew, she was running down the stairs.

When she got there, she knelt before him, and as she did, a chill draft encircled them, like an invisible rope tying them to a tree, before it rushed up the stairs, caught the door at the top, and slammed it shut.

"Shit," Kira said. "Shit." She ran back up. "There's no handle." She tried prying at the edges of the door with her fingernails. "I can't get it open. Shit, I broke a nail."

Jason rolled his eyes.

"Geez!" Kira said on a shriek.

"What? You broke two?"

"The birds are trying to get us out. The space between the bottom of the door and the top stair isn't big enough for my fingers to slip beneath, but I can feel the tips of their beaks in the crack. Can you hear them? They're shrieking like scared old women."

Jason stood, rolled his shoulders, and flexed his bad knee, which took the fall pretty well, considering.

The rising sound of fluttering wings near his ear made him duck. It sounded like a bird was dive-bombing his head. "Son of a—"

Kira ran back down. "What? Are you hurt?"

"More or less. Did you hear that bird? I think one of the crows got in."

"Very funny." Her fearful darting gaze denied her statement.

"No, really, I heard a bird fly by my ear, and I thought— I suppose it could have been a bat."

Kira ducked, squeaked, and stepped into his arms, which was fine by him. "Are you sure you're all right?" she asked, stroking his brow. "You hit your head, didn't you?"

He slipped an arm around her waist, as much to steady himself as to cop a feel. "My bruises have bruises."

She ran her hands over his arms and he stood there, hoping for more, but she quit too soon.

"I'm okay," he said. "Honestly."

"Your knee?"

"I came down pretty much on my backside."

"So you're okay?"

"Pretty much."

"Good, now I can kill you."

"Before you do, I don't suppose you could wiggle your wand, say something sexy, and get us out of here?"

She went for her man-drooper like the fastest gun in the East. Jason covered Harvey with his hands. "Never mind!" he said. "Geez. Ask for one little favor."

"I'm pissed at you for laughing at me."

"I apologize, sincerely."

"You should."

He thought about how funny she looked and bit his lip to keep from making a fatal mistake. He regarded the stairs and the sealed door at the top and tried to look needy.

Kira sighed in resignation. "The best I can think of is to try and make someone miss us."

"Thank you, yes, please. I'll kiss your feet."

"Kiss my ass, and we've got a deal."

"Yes! Deal."

"Shut up and let me think."

Jason shut up, but the fantasy lingered.

Kira tapped her chin with her wand for a few thoughtful minutes as she examined every facet of the stairwell, including the door at the top of the stairs.

The she swirled her wand upward and began her chant.

> *"Not at work, not at play.*
> *Wonder why we went away.*
> *Find the birds,*
> *Hear their song.*
> *Enter where you don't belong.*
> *Look here, look there.*
> *Find us in the hidden stair."*

She nodded and slipped her wand back into her pocket.

"That's it?" Jason said.

"What? It's not good enough? You want I should turn you into a beetle so you can crawl under the door?"

"Those birds eat beetles."

"Yeah, I pretty much knew that."

"Sometimes you scare me."

"You're a smart man, Jason Goddard."

"We have to get out of here."

"I'm with you on that one."

Jason palmed the three walls at the base of the staircase, but he could find no opening. "No exit here," he said.

"No fooling, Sherlock."

"I'm surprised there's any light in here at all." He looked for the source and saw a window about fifty feet up. "Damn," he said. "I saw that window from outside. It's on a center peaked dormer."

"I'm so relieved," Kira said, swiping at cobwebs, "that we know where we are!"

"Are you being sarcastic?" he asked.

"Not at all," she snapped. "But watch my mouth, because an ugly creature with slimy teeth is gonna come out and eat your head!"

Jason coughed, sensing this was not a good time to reveal amusement. "What are you doing?"

"Nothing!" she snapped again, then she shoved the top of her head into his face. "Do I have bird poop in my hair?"

He snickered, and she whipped out her wand and held it to his crotch. "One more sound, and your pecker's a tootsie roll."

"My pecker's a steel rod," Jason said, "and it's your fault. I have never been trapped, amused, and turned on, all at the same time. Please tell me this counts as a rabbit hole."

Kira trailed a finger down to his belt and traced the design in his buckle. "Where nothing is as it seems?"

"Yeah," he said. "An amazing anything-goes dream we'll both forget."

As if channeling her fury into desire, Kira about knocked him over trying to climb him. Her wand clattered to the floor as he caught her by the ass and lifted her high against him. Her legs clamped around him like vises, turning his pecker into one big, happy camper . . . looking for a place to park.

With her clinging like a monkey, he turned and sat them on the bottom stair, her straddling him, the way she'd damned near done the other night in her apartment. If only there were as few pieces of clothing between them now.

She rode an erection she'd pretty much stirred to life the first time he saw her. Funny how he'd worried all this time that she would destroy Harvey, when frankly, nobody had made him quite so happy in years.

Of course, the fact that he'd been celibate since his accident might have something to do with Harvey's anticipation.

"I can't think of anyplace I'd rather be than in a rabbit hole with you," he said against her hair. "I hope my nuzzling your ear doesn't remind you of the crow, by the way."

She smacked the heel of her hand against his shoulder.

"I'm never gonna forgive you for laughing," she said, rocking against him, contradicting her ire, causing some incredible big-time friction and Harvey happy-dancing.

"I can tell," Jason said. "So what would it take," he asked, "to make you forgive me?"

"You can let me have my wicked way with you," she said, pushing his suit jacket off his shoulders and going for the buttons on his shirt.

Jason tugged the corkscrew curl over her left eye and watched it spring back. "Have at me, Glinda. Your wish is my command."

"Kiss me," she said.

Jason's head fell forward. He met her brow with his, and sighed. "How about you put your wand where I can see it."

"You afraid I might want to zap the pecker, Ice Boy?"

Jason raised his head and grinned. "Yeah . . . cause my kisser's kaput."

"Say what? The Best Kisser in America can't kiss?"

"Those limelight wind-up dolls fried my lip-to-lip circuit. It's toast. Nothing. Nada."

"Yeah, you acted totally miserable on that show."

"Operative word: acted. I might as well have been kissing rotten rutabagas."

Kira smiled, but Jason caught her sympathy and concern. He tucked an unruly lock of her hair behind her ear. "You deserve better than an act."

She cupped his cheek and stroked his chin with her thumb, her touch like a blessing. "You had to disassociate yourself, didn't you?"

"Yep." Jason sighed, regret heavy on his chest. "And now I'm ruined."

A light entered Kira's eyes. "But you can still do, er, everything else?"

"I didn't play at anything else. When the fake kisses sucked, excuse the pun, I couldn't risk my favorite sport."

"On the show, they implied you did."

"The implication was in the contract. Sleeping with the windups wasn't, though I had my chances, believe me."

"My luck," Kira said, knuckling his lips. "I get a free rabbit-hole card and a gimp jock with no kisses."

Jason smiled. "If my lip-to-lip instinct returns, you'll be the first to know. Gimp jock's promise."

"Promise noted."

"You're not disgusted, or angry, are you?"

"No, but I feel bad, for your sake," Kira said, kissing his brow, his eyes, his chin, nibbling her way from his neck to his chest.

She made him believe *he* was important to her. Her sounds of appreciation were a real turn-on.

Jason *wanted* to touch his lips to hers, but he was afraid he'd be repulsed, and she'd think it was her fault, especially after Charlie. She'd already been hurt by one of his kind. He was not about to add to her pain. Kira Fitzgerald was a goddess. She deserved . . . everything.

They had something special going, and he'd be damned if he'd ruin it with a kiss.

Right now he'd take what she offered. And her offer was generous. He absorbed every nuance of her every touch. His body roared to life at the way she moved her hips against his.

Jason felt caring and affection in the touch of Kira's lips against his chest, and he began to remember how that used to work from his end. How he could worship a woman with his lips . . . except that he had never quite understood the meaning of the word *worship,* not until he entered Kira's rabbit hole that night.

That's what scared him away that night, he thought. Attraction. A very strong attraction. Strong and scary and sitting here making him hot.

"I just want to play," she said.

Jason translated that to mean that she didn't want to go all the way. "I'm pretty sure we can satisfy each other," he said, "though I wish we hadn't reached this state in a musty stairwell."

"I've seen nicer rabbit holes," she said, "but right now I don't care.

"Where's your sweater?" he asked.

"I left it to the birds. They wouldn't let it go."

He undid the zipper on her jumpsuit, pushed it off her shoulders, and the light beamed down on them as if in blessing. Her crimson bra raced his blood, pounding it through his chest, and points south.

He undid the clasp at the front of every man's fantasy, but when her luscious breasts fell out, Jason forgot fantasy and embraced reality. "Beautiful," he said as he nuzzled her, each breast overflowing his happy hands. "*You're* beautiful," he said.

He changed positions, reclining Kira in his embrace, so he could feed off of her, suckling like he'd never done, using his lips in a way that was still sacred and special, and only for her. "Kira," he whispered as she moved her hands in his hair.

He'd been in lust with her since he caught her wielding her vengeful wand, and now she was his, at least for a while.

She arched as he suckled, until she began to writhe, and call his name.

That easy, she came, with his mouth on her breasts and their clothes between them.

As she rolled into him and caught her breath, her heart pumping like after a race, Jason felt pretty powerful, mighty hard, and damned near to exploding.

He held her close, rubbed her back, nuzzled her hair, and thought about all the ways and places he'd like to make her come again.

Kira Fitzgerald was the most sensuous woman he'd ever been with. In black and white or in color.

"You did it," she whispered against his ear.

"Did what?" he asked, sliding his fingers from her naked back to her silky bottom.

"You gave me an orgasm."

"I figured that out."

"You're the first."

He settled her so she faced him. "You're not saying that was your first orgasm?"

"Of course not. I'm just saying that you're the first *man* who ever gave me one."

"Wait. You've been with women?"

She laughed and fell forward, exhausted, against him. "Sorry to disappoint you, but no." She spoke against his neck, kissing it between words and bites. "I've only ever come with . . . mechanical devices."

"If I had protection on me, I'd put your mechanical devices to shame."

"Protection . . ." Kira went for his belt buckle. "Just for the record, I'm on the pill, and clean," she said, "safe-sex wise. I felt the need to check after the Penis. Haven't been with anyone since."

"Clean here, too," Jason said. "Got checked in the hospital after my accident. Haven't been with anyone since, either. What are you doing?"

"Tit for tat," she said.

"Stop that. Pull the big guy out and I guarantee you, a twenty-man rescue team will rush down these stairs."

"Come on, I wanna meet Harvey, give him a hello kiss."

"And he sure in hell wants to meet you."

"Well?"

"I'm better in a bed."

"Is that supposed to turn me off?"

Sixteen

JASON barked a laugh. "Are you nuts, Fitzgerald? It's *not* supposed to turn you off. It's supposed to turn you on, make you hop in the sack with me the minute we get home. But, no, you can't wait."

"And that's bad how?" Kira asked.

"Location, timing . . . leg room."

Kira scoffed. "Screw that."

"Okay, I didn't want to do this," Jason said, "but you're forcing my hand. Now I have another confession to make."

Kira stopped, her hand on his zipper, and looked up. "Uh-oh."

"Yes," Jason said, "you *do* have bird poop in your hair."

Kira whooped and fell against him, charming him out of his mind with her unabashed laughter.

"You're just getting it, aren't you," Jason said. "How ludicrous this whole thing is? You with the birds? Us, in a hidden staircase? How bad I want to turn you on, not off?"

Kira squeaked a yes, rolled out of his arms, hiccupped, and kept on laughing.

Jason sat on the landing beside her and let her merriment carry him away. Before he could think straight, he had her laying across his lap, her head on his arm, as he watched her laugh.

He had never seen such open merriment on her face. Kira Fitzgerald laughed the way she worked, the way she made magic, putting her all into it. Jason wanted to know if she made love the same way. He wanted *her*.

Sliding his hand inside her red bikinis, he found her warm wet center, and when he began his intimate quest to bring her fulfillment once more, she rose, hips and all, and followed where he led.

She wept her joy, against his fingers, against his face.

He'd been branded, Jason thought, branded and bewitched.

Their play went on while the slant of the light changed position and their rabbit hole became too dim for Jason to see the stairs or much of anything else.

Kira fell asleep, her head on his shoulder, the warmth of her breath, her fresh berry scent, flooding his senses, as he continued to caress her warm slick center.

When he started to pull away, she whimpered, and he grinned. How amazing would she be, if they ever really did . . . have sex. They *would* have sex, or at least he hoped they would. Maybe he should hope they wouldn't. He'd have to think about that. He had a feeling that sex with Kira Fitzgerald would be as addictive as a drug. Madness.

But right now, sanity was returning, and with it the harsh reality of voices and footsteps.

Jason sat up, confirming the echo of sound. He didn't call out because he needed to do a fast reorganization of Kira's clothes. "Wake up, sweetheart. We're being rescued."

He raised Kira enough to slip her arms back into the top of her jumpsuit, but her eyes remained unfocused.

"Button my shirt," he said. "Help me, please. They're coming closer."

"Who? What?"

"Our rescuers. We're about to get caught half naked."

That woke her up. "Yikes!" She went to work on his buttons. He had less than a minute to stand and tuck his shirt into his pants before the door at the top of the stairs banged open, and Deering nearly fell down the stairs, himself.

A policeman, standing at the top, invaded their rabbit hole with his flashlight, the beam hitting Jason square in the eyes.

Jason stepped away from the light. "How'd you find us?" he asked, letting Kira precede him up the stairs.

"The birds," Deering said. "They were screeching fit to wake old Addie, and pecking at the base of the wall, almost as if they were trying to get you out themselves. One of the blacks was pecking so hard around the door, it chipped its beak."

Jason touched Kira's hand from behind.

She shook it off. "I don't want to talk about it," she said, and he didn't know if she meant the birds . . . or the other.

The crow with the chipped beak, the one who had landed on Kira's shoulder, said "Shiver my liver" when she emerged into the cage from the stairs.

"Shut up," Kira said, then she saw its beak and stopped. "I hope you didn't do that for me." She stroked the damage. "Poor baby."

The crow tilted its head. "Nice, Mommy."

Kira rolled her eyes and left.

Deering chuckled. "Wait till I tell m'wife. She read that crows talk like parrots years ago, and she's been trying to teach this lot ever since. Now here they go and say their first words to somebody else."

"That explains their vocabulary," Jason said, following Deering and the cop downstairs behind Kira. Though it didn't explain why they chose Kira to communicate with.

"What made you look for us?" Jason asked. "I thought my grandmother would have to report me missing before somebody—"

Deering smiled. "Your granny says there's a busload of

kids waiting for hockey lessons and you'd better get there fast, if you know what's good for you."

Jason laughed, and Kira groaned and fell against him, which meant she wasn't upset with *him*, precisely.

A mostly white mite of a kitten, with one black ear and a black tail, scooted in, went right to Kira, and mewled plaintively, its paws on her foot.

Deering scooped it up. "You wanted inside bad, didn't you, Misty?" Deering shook his head. "She's been over here scratching at the doors all day. I keep bringing her home and she keeps coming back."

Kira took the kitten from the caretaker, rubbed its fur against her cheek, and got a lick on her nose.

Jason recalled Kira's cat theory. "She looks too young to be away from her mother," he said.

"She is, the scamp. And I don't know why her mama can't keep track of her. She's an only child." Deering took Misty from Melody. "M'wife keeps calling her back, she says, but Misty's either deaf or stubborn. Hey, look at the time. Your granny's gonna have my head, if you don't get out'a here."

"Hockey practice, Glinda," Jason said. "Let's go."

During practice, Kira played a board game with Zane and handed out hot cocoa to the kids who took breaks, more for her hugs than her hot chocolate, Jason suspected.

Kira wouldn't look his way. Therefore, Jason kept looking her way, so she could continue to ignore him, which is why Jeff, the brat, managed to poke him in the eye with his stick blade.

Jason moved more slowly around the ice as the boys' ice time was coming to an end. His slowing stride reflected the newest beating he took tumbling down the stairs. Every bone and muscle in his body hurt, except, oddly enough, his bad knee, which felt better than after their first hockey practice.

Despite the soreness, Jason realized that he was, in fact, enjoying himself. The musky frosted air unique to a rink, the swish of skates shaving ice, all of it invigorated him, and gave him hope for the future.

The woman entertaining a child in a leg brace instigated a different emotion, one similar to hope, perhaps, a little more frightening, but nonetheless invigorating.

He thought of her in the stairs, coming like fireworks in his arms, and realized that what he might actually want from Kira scared the crap out of him.

They parted the minute they stepped into Cloud Kiss. She took the elevator; he went to the kitchen.

Later, he went downstairs for dinner with his grandmother, holding an ice pack to his eye, hating that the chair opposite his sat empty.

"Kira went where?" he asked when everything was served, not sure he'd heard correctly the first time.

"Home to her family, dear," Gram said. "They only live in Boston. I could give you her cell phone number, if you need to get in touch with her. Or her address, if you'd like to go and—"

"Of course not," Jason said, trying not to snap. Something had spooked Kira enough to send her running home to the safety of her parents' house.

Granted, she had plenty to be spooked about: infatuated birds; his amusement over same, which made him smile even now; and him making her come all afternoon, which made him hard even now.

Jason had never witnessed such sensuality in his partner before, and, frankly, the way his . . . captivation escalated in those few short hours scared the hell out of him. He moved a meatball around in his plate, while his body calmed enough for him to rise, with dignity, and go upstairs.

"Yes," he said, looking at his grandmother. "Give me Kira's number. I'll program it into my cell phone, in case."

Later that night, after hours of talking himself out of calling her, he lay in his bed, in the dark, and hit speed dial.

Kira answered on the first ring.

"What are you doing?" Jason asked.

"Trying to sleep," she snapped.

"It's only eleven."

"What do you want?"

"I wondered if you made up with your sister."

"She's a witch."

"Like you?"

"No. I stand corrected. She starts with the letter *B*."

Jason smiled. "Did you have another fight?"

"No. She's not here, or I wouldn't have come home."

"I'm calling from my rabbit hole," he said. "Are you in yours?"

"My very first," Kira said.

"Describe it."

"I'm safe in an enchanted glade," Kira said, voice soft, "where pastel butterflies sleep on lush green leaves, bathe in buttercups, and sip from dewdrops. Yellow organdy curtains form a canopy for my bed and my window-seat."

"Anything hanging on the walls?"

"A copper moon. Crystal stars."

"No quilts, nothing red?"

"No, this is the ultimate rabbit hole; it's like climbing back into the womb."

"And you needed that tonight?"

"Why did you say you called?"

"Do you want me to describe my bachelor rabbit hole?"

"Let me guess," she said, "chrome and glass?"

"Wrong. Aged honey-gold wood and an ancient brass bed four feet off the floor."

"I'm impressed, but I'm betting you have a brown or tan bedspread."

"Afraid you've got me there," Jason said running a hand over her quilt—the window into her soul—with which he'd replaced his tan bedspread, though he wasn't ready to confess as much, especially to her.

"Why did you really call?" Kira asked.

To be, or not to be . . . honest? But Jason decided to blow the bankroll on truth. "I'm hot."

"I told you, I didn't mean that, I meant—"

"Not that. I mean I'm laying in my bed thinking about you coming like a rocket in my arms today, and I'm hard-as-a-rock hot and . . . wishing you were here to make *me* come."

An indrawn breath, then silence. Jason waited for the inevitable click and dial tone, but then he thought he heard her shift in her bed. "Kira? Are you still there?"

"You should have let me take Harvey out this afternoon."

"I wanted to be there for you. If Harvey got involved, if I got carried away, I didn't want to make a mockery out of . . . what might have taken place, so I . . . didn't take the chance. I wanted better for us."

"I can't decide if that was thoughtful," Kira said, "or stupid."

"In hindsight, me, either."

"Hindsight; I hate that shit."

"Me, too. Why did you run? Wait, let me rephrase that," Jason said. "I'm sorry if I did anything to make you r—"

"I'm hot, too."

Jason closed his eyes, half in relief, half in ecstasy. "Yeah? Want to tell me about it?"

"My mechanical device doesn't work as well as it used to," she confessed.

"You tried? Just now? Tonight?"

"Yeah."

"Today wasn't enough?" Jason wiggled out of his jockeys to give Harvey room to grow.

"I tried to tell myself that what you did wasn't such a big deal. That I could, you know, any time I wanted."

"And you failed?"

"Yeah."

Jason felt like beating his chest, or beating his saluting soldier, at any rate. "I think maybe you came about thirty-three times this afternoon. Could be that you reached your limit."

Kira chuckled, her voice wobbly, her laugh throaty, as if he'd more than entertained her, as if he'd made her hotter.

"I wish I was there," Jason said. "Or you were here."

"Yeah, me, too."

"Because you want me to make you come again?" he asked.

"I . . . yeah."

"You're greedy, Fitz. You'd have to give me a turn, you know. The big guy's crying and moaning here, looking for a warm place to go, and he's really disappointed you're not here."

"That's your fault. You wouldn't let me take him out to play when I wanted to."

"More fool me. I wish you hadn't gone home."

"I think it's best that I did. I'm not ready for any kind of . . . anything right now, and if I had stayed—"

Jason knuckled his erection. "I know what you mean. I'm not ready for . . . anything like that, either. We both gave that up, remember?"

"Yeah, I do. How long since you actually got laid?" she asked, a note of amusement in her voice.

The lighthearted question made him smile. "Since my accident nearly a year ago."

"Yeesh, it's a wonder you haven't exploded."

"I have actually, a couple of times. What about you?"

"Since the Penis screwed me over. Couple months now."

"So now you're having a fling with a mechanical device?"

"Hey, my devices never let me down, and they don't cheat on me, either."

"I hear you. Er, did you say devices, plural? You have more than one?"

"I have . . . an assortment," Kira said.

Harvey did a little happy dance. "You are incredible," Jason said, grinning.

"What? That's not allowed? Guys like to have a lot of women."

"Kira, sweetheart, I'm grinning here. I'm proud of you for taking your sex life into your own hands . . . so to speak."

"Are you making fun of me?"

"No, damn it, you're making me hot. I'm getting hard just thinking about you using those things. Geez. Calm down and enjoy a little vocal stimulation, will you? Talk about uptight."

She was quiet for a minute, and Jason thought he'd lost her, and he was sorry. That was when he realized that he'd be happy, if she were happy. Serious stuff.

"So . . . say something stimulating," she finally said.

What he wanted to say scared the crap out of him. "Harvey is really hard. How fast can you get home?"

"Tell you what," she said.

"What?" Jason asked, the big guy "up" for anything.

"Why don't I turn on one of my devices and tell you how it feels to me, while you take Harvey in hand and tell me how that feels to you?"

Jason's hips came off the bed with her words. "You nearly finished him off with the suggestion," he said.

ON Monday Jason anticipated an awkward workday, perhaps worse than Friday after the hidden staircase. Not only had they talked sex on the phone Friday night, she'd called him Saturday night for more, and he'd called her Sunday night.

Funny how you could say things on the phone that you weren't ready to say in person.

Jason ran from the Hummer, through the biting rain toward Castleton Court, glad Kira's car wasn't in the lot yet, wondering exactly what he'd say to her when she arrived.

He'd no sooner hung his raincoat on the rack than he heard her key in her lock and went through the adjoining door to wait in her office for her.

"Shiver my liver," Kira said, coming in and leaning her

wet umbrella against the wall in the corner. "I hope it's not like this on the night of the ghost tour, or we won't be able to visit the cemetery."

"Sure we can," Jason said, charmed and disarmed by the sight of her in her bright new Wellies, "we can hand out black umbrellas. It'll add to the graveyard ambience."

"Oh, I almost forgot. Look," she said, showing him her red-and-yellow argyle umbrella, opening and closing it with several soft, effective clicks. "I found one to match."

"Damned if you didn't," Jason said, wishing he could take her into his arms, a reckless inclination.

After her argyle raingear was stowed, she still wore unrelieved black, her simple dress fine and figure hugging, but Jason was still turned on, so for the sake of self-preservation, and to give Kira space to bloom, he went to his own office.

She had worn the argyle boots he gave her. This was big. They'd come to some kind of crossroad, made some kind of peace, and perhaps Kira herself had taken a first tentative step out of hiding.

As the two of them had become emotionally and physically intimate, at least in their rabbit holes, Jason thought, their minds and libidos were getting closer in the real world, which meant they could very well be rushing headlong toward either a merger, or an explosion.

Time to tread wary.

On and off the job, he realized, they'd been pushing each other's buttons, literally and figuratively, testing boundaries, goading each other into outrageous behavior and daring wordplay, speaking and touching just to raise the heat between them.

He had never felt so exhilarated.

Seventeen

*
 * *
* *
 *

THE night of the Rainbow's Edge Ghost and Graveyard Tour, Jason arrived just after dark and saw the house decorated for the first time. Kira had aced it.

Tiny white lights outlined Gothic peaks and gables. Grisly bright jack-o'-lanterns hung from the trees nearest the house. The spotlighted front entrance, black enameled double doors, with matching bittersweet wreaths, stood bright and welcoming.

Outside, behind the house, and off to the side, distant spotlights made the family cemetery, its bright white stones bathed in shadow, look stark and eerie, setting the perfect stage for the event.

It was All Hallows' Eve, Kira had reminded him on the phone, the night spirits roamed free. Oddly enough, tonight, at this moment, he believed her.

Kira met him at the door, looking like magic herself.

"The house looks great," Jason said, kissing her cheek. "You did a wonderful job."

"I'm glad you like it," she said. "I have a surprise."

Jason tilted his head. "Do I have to close my eyes," he whispered. "Does it involve a rabbit hole?"

"A surprise that will excite our guests," Kira said. "Not us."

"Bummer," Jason said. "Okay, shoot. What's the surprise?"

"Milford Marble and Granite raised Addie's gravestone this afternoon. I had the gardeners stake a tarp over it, and tonight during the tour, we'll have an official unveiling. I have news crews coming."

Jason high-fived her. "Have you seen it? Is it really Addie's? What does it say?"

"Jim, the owner, confirmed that the gravestone was Addie's when he called to say it had been raised. After that, I had barely enough time to alert the media and go home to change, so, no, I haven't seen it yet."

"You're right. After all these years, seeing Addie's stone for the first time will excite our guests," Jason said. "And raise the spook factor big time."

An hour later, as the noted host, Jason welcomed their guests. Beside him, in a floor-length black strapless gown and cape, a gold-starred black net scarf over her fiery hair, Kira added to the mystical aura of the evening. Her black lace Victorian gloves left her fingers bare, making them seem forbidden to the touch.

Jason found that he needed to touch them often.

Though the evening had barely begun, more than a hundred people, at a thousand dollars a clip, made it an instant success. Waiters in the formal livery once worn by the original staff of Rainbow's Edge served cocktails and hot canapés.

Inside the house lit jack-o'-lanterns sat high and low, on mantels, bookcases, and tables, while corners held huge vases brimming with Chinese lanterns and bittersweet.

To allow their guests to view the theatrical of the fake haunting, they were forced to use the stairway that opened into the drawing room, the largest room. Therefore, by virtue of its location, the hidden stairway remained hidden.

In the guise of little Davie Winthrop III, Travis aced the portrayal of the child closed in the hidden stairwell for hours, who claimed to have been captured by a ghost.

Zane made a scary-cute ghost, almost frightening, Jason thought, with his filmy white gauze layering, as he moaned and limped in his brother's shadowed wake, haunting him by stalking him.

At the end of the play, everyone turned toward a bejeweled matriarch jabbing the floor with her cane. Like a painted china doll, with her rice-paper face and circles of blush on each cheek, Gram's old friend Doris Putnam continued the jarring noise until she captured every eye. "That's not the whole story," she cackled. "I was there, six years old and ears wide open."

Uh-oh, Jason thought. *This can't be good.*

Doris pointed a finger Kira's way. "You got the story from the last book about this place, didn't you? Davie's uncle wrote that, and he never did get the story right. It was the birds, Davie said. He told me the ghost was after getting the crows back."

"Are you sure, Doris?" Gram said.

Doris pulled her arm from Gram's hold. "Yes. The aviary had been closed, you see, and the ghost said to get the crows back, or everyone would be "kissed." Silly, I know, but that's what Davie said. They got the birds back; he was that scared. Got 'em and kept 'em, and Davie put it in his will that they had to stay, forever."

"Yes!" Kira said, her eyes so bright, Jason could fall in and drown happy.

Everyone applauded, as if Doris's revelation were part of the show.

Jason offered Doris his arm and escorted her to the refreshment table, probably to quiet her ramblings while they were ahead of the game, Kira thought.

Wherever Jason went, their attendees rallied around him. Jason Goddard in person was pure charisma, a rare diamond of a charmer, flawless, his smile alone worth the million he'd won on the reality show.

He was flirting for dollars, and he was a natural.

Kira felt as if she'd fallen in the deep end of the infatuation pool where he was concerned, which made her nervous as a cat.

She wondered now if he had been using his million-dollar charm for her benefit in the stairwell the other day, except that she was the only one who benefited from that performance.

If he had honestly been attracted, which his erection plainly said he was, it must have been because she was the only warm body available. Because when he really had his chance, he'd run away.

And on the phone? Well, what man wouldn't be turned on by phone sex? What woman, either, for that matter?

Kira gave credibility to her rising blush by announcing that it was time for the cemetery tour, pretending embarrassment for her interruption.

No sooner had she announced it than Jason took her arm, as he had taken Doris's a while ago, but this time he placed his hand over hers and squeezed as they led the way to the cemetery. The evening was comfortably cool, enough for just a sweater. No coats or umbrellas necessary.

Four gravestones would be spotlighted, as needed, three whose epitaphs lent themselves to fictionalization, and as a grand finale, the headstone most of them had never seen, the monument to Addie Winthrop.

They decided to save Addie's for last, because the fact that it had been raised after so long was big news. Crews were standing by to film the story, great coverage for the foundation and its causes.

The news crews had asked to film segments of the cemetery tour, as well, which would surely raise the prestige of the event in the eyes of their philanthropic attendees.

Kira led them to the first stone, and when that spotlight went on, she read the first fictionalization into a portable mike, a lusty tale of Nathan Winthrop's third cousin, Kathleen, age eighteen years, who died in a suspicious carriage-house fire in 1919. Kira ended by reading the stone:

> "KATHLEEN HARRINGTON
> Vain in beauty,
> Siren in song,
> Perished in shame.
> Nevermore do we speak her name."

Jason read the second story, of a young dressmaker, a stranger who died at Rainbow's Edge in 1920, after residing with the family for three weeks, while fashioning a new wardrobe for Addie. Jason read her stone:

> "LYDIA GODEY SPIRE
> Sewed by the fire,
> Caught her skirts
> And made her a pyre.
> 'Twas it that warmed her,
> Also claimed her."

Gram told of a sixteen-year-old servant girl who'd killed Addie's beloved crow with a rock in 1921. The girl did the deed, ran, tripped, and fell into an inferno of autumn leaves. Gram read the last epitaph:

> "LIZZIE WILLIAMS
> As if an unseen arm
> Propelled her in,
> The fire she swallowed,
> And the witch did win."

"What gruesome stories," Jennie Ellers, heiress and busybody, said as she preened for the cameras. "And all of them young women."

"Well, what do you expect to find in a cemetery?" Gram

asked. "Happy endings? Besides, this is a ghost tour. How frightening would a normal death be?"

Jennie harrumphed. "Did no one in this place die of old age? Of anything but fire? Did none of the *men* die young?"

All morbidly valid questions, Kira thought.

"Thirty-five was old back then," Jason said, capturing a few grunts of assent. "There are plenty of people buried here who died of natural causes," he said, "but their gravestones weren't as interesting."

"Now for Addie's mysterious gravestone," Kira said to capture their attention as she signaled for the spotlight, then the unveiling. The cameras moved closer as Jason took the mike to read the stone:

"ADDIE WINTHROP
Her words:
At the edge of the Rainbow
In the void of the mist,
Accused of witchcraft,
Her accuser, she kissed.
With a beak and a claw,
And the flap of a wing,
She sent him to Hades
For the fire to sting.

Beneath this stone,
She does not lie.
Do not question;
The birds know why.
She's at the edge of the Rainbow
In the void of the mist,
Waiting to kiss you,
And you will be missed."

A stunned silence was followed by murmurs of speculation.

Doris Putnam poked Jason in the side with her cane and cackled like the crow in the aviary. "Didn't I tell you? She had a love for the birds, did old Addie."

Still laughing, Doris shook her head. "Davie, you old bugger," she said, waving her cane toward the heavens. "You were right all along."

Kira realized that her fingernails were cutting into Jason's arm and that he was holding her waist in the same gripping manner.

"My God," Jennie breathed. "There really is a ghost at Rainbow's Edge."

"Of course," Jason said, not looking Kira's way, since she was as surprised as him, and they both knew it.

"Why do you suppose Addie let her stone be raised now, after more than eighty years?" Gram asked.

"Perhaps it's because we brought everyone here to witness her plight," Kira said.

"Plight?" Jennie said with a laugh. "Old Addie reveals a pretty clear *threat* on that stone."

"Or a great deal of fear," Kira said.

"Yes," Jason said. "She had to have written it when she was alive and frightened, perhaps in an attempt to intimidate her accusers?"

Kira shook her head, denying her belief in his statement. "Perhaps *Addie* didn't even write it. Look at the dates on the stones we chose—1919, 1920, 1921—and in 1922 Addie gets accused of witchcraft, then she's found conveniently dead?"

"What are you getting at?" Gram asked.

"The epitaphs on those three stones are poetic, different from the rest, making them stand out," Kira said, "similar to Addie's stone. That was the reason we chose them for tonight. If we could take a trip back in time, I'll bet we'd find that old Nate, Addie's husband, had the stones engraved," Kira said. "It looks like a setup to me."

Jason nodded. "Who else but the head of a family would order the gravestones in those days? Not a woman," he said.

"And what's with that additional line: 'Her words'? Why was that necessary?"

"To point the finger her way?" Gram said.

"Right. Maybe old Nate *wanted* Addie out of the way and under suspicion."

"The philandering sot," Gram snapped, firming her lips.

"That's what I suspected," Kira said.

"Some people still didn't take kindly to witchcraft back then," Jason said. "It's likely Addie was accused for foolish reasons, the pet crow, for one, or these fiery accidents . . . if they were accidents. Maybe the squeaky-clean old Nate was behind them all."

"But there's no mention in the family history," an attendee said. "I believe I've read them all."

"Of course there's no mention," Gram said. "Nathaniel wrote most of them, didn't he, except for the one by Davie's uncle, thirty years later. Nate let us know that the women died here and how they died, but not much more, except to cast a shadow on his wife."

"I may have been a girl back then," Doris said, "but I heard talk. Old Nathan did like the skirts. He always had a different woman on his arm, sometimes two, before and after Addie passed."

Kira shivered and Jason brought her close, the closest they'd been since the week before in the hidden stairs.

"I have to tell you," the president of a local bank said, "I feel as if I've actually seen a ghost on this tour. Good job, Goddard. Excellent!"

Applause followed the man's words, but Jason gave Kira the credit before Gram hustled their attendees back toward the house, all of them highly entertained, ready for the dessert buffet, a visit to the aviary, and dancing.

The news crew remained and interviewed Kira and Jason, then they packed up the news van and left.

Still standing there, stunned by the way things had come together, Kira turned to Jason. "Why do *you* think Addie let her stone be raised now?"

"Because you're here?"

"That's not funny."

"No, I mean it. Maybe it's because you're a witch, too, or because you befriended her birds, or because you made everyone see what she faced. I have a feeling that you might have set Addie free tonight. Cleared her name. Given her closure."

"I like that theory."

"Good," Jason said. "You should be pleased. Our first event was a success, because of you."

"Well, you're the one who picked Rainbow's Edge on All Hallows' Eve. How bizarre is that?"

Jason took her into his arms and nuzzled her neck, her shoulder, the edge of her strapless gown, there, under the pale quarter moon, and Kira loved it.

As their play became heated and sensual, the wind rose, sighing as if in contentment, swirling the leaves high about their ankles, then higher into the air until the turbulence caught their attention.

When Kira and Jason looked up, a murder of crows flew from the trees in a vee, dipped their wings, cawed as if in approval, and spiraled into the black starless sky.

"We've never seen that many before," Jason said. "How many were there? I know you counted."

"Twelve," Kira said.

"Which means?"

"I think Addie got what she was wanted."

Jason nudged Kira's bodice with a finger, traced the edge, slid his finger beneath, and distracted her.

"What was it that you think Addie wanted?" he asked some time later. "What *do* twelve crows augur?"

"Closure."

Eighteen

JASON led Kira back to Rainbow's Edge after a ghost and graveyard tour neither could have imagined, one that left his heart racing as much for its magic as for the witch who brought it about.

Jason chatted up their guests and gave house tours, and later, to his amazement, Kira agreed to get into the birdcage and show off the crows.

Once inside, she patted her shoulder, and the crow with the chipped beak jumped up to perch there.

"Nice Chippy," Kira said, naming the bird as she stroked its feathers, and it stroked her hair.

"Nice Mommy," Chippy said, and Kira winked mischievously at Doris Putnam, who gasped and would have lost her footing if not for Jason, who righted her, winked, and offered his arm.

Jason let the development director introduce him to as many potential major donors as she could find before he caught Kira on her way by, excused himself, and escorted her to the music room. There, he took Kira into his arms to dance until Gram came to say that their guests were leaving.

Jason bid them a good evening, basking in the magical afterglow of success and congratulations. *Bewitched* was the only word to describe his evening, his emotions, his pleasure at having Kira beside him, his satisfaction with where he stood at this moment in time, all of which should scare him, but didn't. Not tonight.

The next afternoon, after school, on Halloween, they repeated the event, in costume, with seven nuns, two hundred boys, unlit jack-o'-lanterns, Halloween treats, outdoor games with prizes, an amusing visit with Kira and the birds, and no graveyard tour. Those gravestones would have scared the boys, Jason thought. Hell, they had scared him.

He'd condescended to wearing his famed hockey jersey. Kira wore a witch's hat, her gold-starred scarf around her neck, flowing to the floor, front and back, over a *modest* black dress, fortunately or unfortunately.

Tuesday morning Jason drove Kira to Rainbow's Edge, each of them trying to get enough caffeine into their systems to jumpstart their fried brains.

"It was an amazing event, both times," Kira said, while she helped him unstring the lights from the stair rail leading to the aviary, the birds screaming as if they knew she was there and could hardly wait for her arrival.

"I think they want a command performance," Jason said, looking up the stairs.

"I'll give you a—"

He grinned. "Anytime, babe."

"Babe?" Kira said, hand on hip. "You call your employee *babe*?"

Jason pulled the curl over her brow. "I thought this was a rabbit hole."

"No. The hidden stairway is a rabbit hole."

"Let's go, then." Jason grabbed her hand and started in that direction.

Kira stopped and pulled him up short. "We have to clean this mess."

"Right." Jason sighed, honestly disappointed. "Sometimes I have trouble distinguishing black holes from rabbit holes," he said. "Was Sunday night a rabbit hole?"

"Oh, yeah," Kira said, "on an entirely different plane."

She climbed to the stair above him and bent to whisper in his ear. "We were on the edge of the rainbow in the void of the mist."

"You're turning me on," Jason said.

Kira shoved a string of lights at him, and chuckled at his surprise, enchanting him the more.

"Sunday night's rabbit hole," she said, "was a hell of a lot bigger, deeper, and scarier, than even I could have imagined."

"No kidding," Jason said. "Not half bad, for a ghost tour with no ghosts. Don't I have an apology coming?"

"I don't think so, but Addie might."

"Hey, I object."

"Beginner's luck," Kira said, patting his cheek, putting his systems on alert.

He patted hers the same way but ended up caressing her cheek, because he *needed* so badly to touch her, and when she didn't object, he slid his fingers downward, stroked her collarbone and knuckled the spot between her breasts. "The ghost and graveyard tour wasn't a success because of my luck anyway," he said. "It was yours. The luck of the witch."

"So," came a familiar voice, "Kira told you she was a witch, did she?"

Jason snatched his hand from Kira's cleavage as Melody Seabright entered what suddenly seemed like another rabbit hole. "Major TV star giving me the evil eye," Jason said.

Kira squealed and threw herself into Melody's arms, both of them holding tight. Jason could see the tears in Melody's eyes, and hear them in Kira's voice.

"What are you doing here?" Kira asked. "You're hours early, not that I mind, but, hey, what's—" Kira stepped back, ran a hand over Melody's slightly rounded middle, looked up, and grinned. "Is that what I think it is?"

"Yep," said the man coming up and clasping the shoulders of the Kitchen Witch. "She ate a pumpkin whole. I told her to be careful."

Kira squealed. "Oh, my gosh, a baby? We're gonna have a baby?"

"Oh, good," said the man Jason presumed was Melody's husband. "That must mean that *we're* paying for her to go to college."

"Her? It's a girl? A girl?" Kira high-fived Melody and did a happy dance that woke Harvey right up.

Jason shifted his stance.

"Why didn't you tell me?" Kira asked, hugging Melody again.

"I wanted to see the look on your face, which was worth the zillion times I bit my lip to keep from telling you. And I have another surprise."

A beautiful blonde, in clothes as dated and classic as Melody's, came in.

"Vickie?" Kira screeched, and another emotional embrace took place.

Vickie welled up. "I couldn't let you two try on those vintage gowns without me, now could I?" she said. "It's been too long since we played dress-up."

During their squeaky, weepy, three-way hug, Jason and Logan shrugged, shook hands, and introduced themselves.

"Not that I need an introduction," Logan said to Jason. "I watched that reality show in a haze of pure green."

"It wasn't all it was cracked up to be, believe me. Besides, you married better than anyone I kissed during that nightmare."

Logan grinned. "I did, didn't I? Better things to do than watch TV now."

Jason watched as Logan regarded that tiny mound, then

Melody herself, with possessive pride, and unadulterated love. Wow.

Kira turned his way, her big green eyes mischievous and pleading, as she went for, and toyed with, a button on his shirt.

"Oh, this should be good," Jason said.

She gave him a hundred-watt smile. "Bessie said we could raid the preservation vault for outfits for Mel's show, and we can't wait," she said. "Do you think you can finish cleaning up here without me?" She went for that button again. "Please?"

Jason listened as if for a distant echo. "Let *me* decorate for the ghost tour," he mimicked in a high voice. "I'd *love* to get my hands on the place. I won't mind cleaning up after. What else do I have to do?"

Kira laughed, as he intended, and placed her cheek against his, speeding Jason's heart and making him work at keeping his hands to himself. "Give me the keys to the Hummer," she whispered, "would you?"

Her request warmed his ear . . . and places best ignored. He shifted again, as surprised by her action as her request. "Are you out of your mind?"

She stepped back, frowning. "You'd let me drive the Zamboni, but not the Hummer?"

"Damn straight."

"I'll drive," Logan said.

"No," Melody said. "You'll stay and help Jason—it is Jason, isn't it?"

"Gosh," Kira said, "I forgot to introduce you all, I was so excited."

"You're Melody and Vickie," Jason said. "I got that. I'm Jason Goddard." He extended his hand.

"Oh," Vickie said, shaking it. "You can be sure we got that, too."

Melody took Jason's hand, but instead of shaking it, she kissed his cheek and turned to her husband. "Just for the record: I just kissed the Best Kisser in America."

"Just for the record," Logan said, "I'm it for you, and don't forget it."

Melody raised her chin. "Maybe you are, and maybe you're not."

Jason gave a bark of laughter while the girls did a three-way high-five, and Logan shook his head, looking terminally bewitched.

Melody let her fingers glide across her husband's cheek. "You *will* be my favorite, if I can drive the girls in your Mercedes."

Logan flinched at the request.

Jason grinned, fished the Hummer keys from his pocket, and tossed them to Kira. "Drive safe."

"Precious cargo," Logan said, stroking Melody's waist as he caught her in a lip-lock. "Your kisses are mine, Seabright." ·

Kira watched, pleased and . . . wistful, and Jason wished he'd saved his kisses for her, that he'd never participated in that blasted reality show.

After the kiss Melody looked besotted, and in complete agreement; her kisses were Logan's.

Jason didn't think he'd ever met a couple who were married *and* in love, an oxymoron in his book, until now.

"What does Shane think about having a sister?" Kira asked.

"Shane would rather have a gerbil," Logan said. "My luck. The rodent would be pregnant, too."

Kira grinned. "You do have a fertile household at the moment, don't you?"

"Tell me about it."

Mel nipped her husband's ear with her teeth. "I didn't get this way by myself, Kilgarven."

"I remember it well." Logan grinned. "But you *are* the one who brought those felines into the house."

"As kittens, yes, but you're the one who said, 'Put 'em outside. We don't need 'em underfoot all the time. Give 'em some fresh air. Give 'em room to get frisky.'"

Logan winced. "I didn't think they'd get that frisky." He pulled Melody close. "Have fun playing dress-up."

"Wait," Kira said, coming to a full stop. "I just realized that sleeping arrangements have changed. I was going to put Melody and Logan in my guest room, Vic. Do you mind taking my room? I can sleep on the sofa."

"Sure. No problem," Vickie said, "but I can take the sofa."

"Nobody needs to sleep on a sofa," Jason said. "Kira, you can sleep in *my* guest room while your friends are here."

Melody and Vickie raised their chins as if they'd caught a radar signal Jason didn't realize he'd sent.

"But we wanted Kira with us," Vickie protested.

"She will be," Jason said. "We share an apartment."

"Do tell," Melody said, as if all her suspicions were confirmed.

"Kira is living with you?" Logan asked after the girls left. "That doesn't seem possible," he added, "not after the way she left Salem. Are you sure it's wise to—"

Jason raised a hand. "We share the family suite in my grandmother's house, well, my house, actually, but our separate, *private* apartments are split by a kitchen and two doors. Kira lives on my parents' side, where she'd already been staying for a month, before I moved back home."

"Ah," Logan said. "That makes sense. Listen, Goddard, I know we just met and all, but . . . don't hurt her, okay?"

"Not to worry; we've both sworn off the opposite sex, vows made before we ever met, actually, but we've discussed it and we're cool with it."

"Been there, failed that," Logan said, "and when we walked in, I could have sworn that you had your hand down her—"

Jason cupped his nape and rubbed it. "Yeah, well, there is a small flaw in our plan."

"Which is?"

"I can't explain it," Jason said. "It's like . . . I'm a magnet and Kira's . . . true north."

Logan raised his brows. "It's worse when the two of you are alone, right? Especially in confined spaces. Like if you don't touch her, you're gonna jump from your skin?"

Jason stepped back and almost tripped on the stairs behind him. He had to catch the banister to keep from falling on his ass.

"Take it from a man who knows," Logan warned. "Kiss her once and your vow's history, not that I'm complaining."

"I haven't kissed her, not once."

"Good; you're strong. Stay that way."

Right, Jason thought. *Strong. I've made her come forty times, but I haven't kissed her once.*

Logan glanced up the stairs. "Wow, that racket quieted fast. What *was* that?"

"Birds," Jason said. "Crows. We keep them in the aviary upstairs. They're in deep mourning at the moment. Their inspiration just left. Help me with this, would you?"

Logan removed his coat and draped it over the banister. "By the way, I can start shooting the documentary whenever you want. Can you spare the time for a tour of this place later?"

"Sure," Jason said.

"Good. When we're finished taking down the decorations, I'll get my video equipment."

"Thanks . . . for helping me clean up, and for donating the video. Can I ask you something?"

"Sure."

"How much for a separate documentary about a boys' home?"

KIRA clasped the Hummer's supple leather-covered steering wheel. "Oh, man, I like driving this," she said. "It's a powerful beast."

"So's your wolf, honey," Melody said from beside her. "Grrr."

Vickie leaned forward from the backseat and flicked Mel's shoulder. "Melody Seabright, are you looking at other men?"

"I'm not blind," Mel said, looking back at Vic, "just pregnant."

"You'd have to be blind not to look at eye candy like that," Vickie said. "Jason's yummy."

"With icing you could lick right off him," Melody said.

Kira turned a raised brow her way.

"Hormones," Mel said. "Lots of them."

"Open the windows," Vickie said. "Cool her down. Oh, the mansions are amazing," she said as her window slid down. "Can we take a tour?"

"After we tour St. Anthony's, which we'll do after we raid the costume vault," Kira said. "Are you up for a couple of tours, Mel?"

"Sure. Why not?"

"Good. As for the mansions, I live in one and work in another, Vic. You found me in our smallest. The Edge was once called a cottage, even though it had more rooms than a hotel back when it was built. We also have a traditional French chateau and two Italian villas."

"Sheesh, talk about moving up the ranks," Vic said. "Which one do you work in?"

"Castleton Court, where the foundation's temperature-controlled costume vault awaits."

"I hope I find something to accommodate little Suzie Q here," Mel said.

"Do you have a *real* name picked out yet?" Kira asked.

Mel chuckled. "Shane wants us to call her Hermione, right now, but I figure that when he gets home from Florida, he'll want to call her Minnie."

Kira chuckled as well. "Is he having a good time with his grandparents?"

"He's in heaven," Mel said. "I don't think they've missed an attraction. You want to know what's really funny? My father's having a blast, too."

"It figures," Kira said. "And you don't mind that he only just started acting like your father?"

"Can't change history," Mel said with a shrug, "but he's good to Shane and he loves Logan's mom, so I'm okay with it."

"You have a real father-daughter relationship now, don't you?"

"The best," Melody said. "I'm his little girl, Shane is his adored grandson, and Logan's mother is his pampered wife, plus I have a mother for the first time ever." Mel sat forward. "Oh, and you should see Logan when his mother takes my side in an argument."

"How's the judge?" Kira asked. "Still retired and giving graveyard tours?"

"Jess is Jess. After selling us her house, she married her DA, and they're thriving. We're actually thinking of naming the baby Jessica, after her, since she saw the good in Logan when he was a kid and eventually brought us together. But never mind me," Mel said. "Tell us about Mr. Melt-My-Ice. How *are* those world-class kisses, the real ones, I mean, not the peck-on-the-cheek kind I stole?"

"I don't know," Kira said, ignoring her friends' shocked silence.

"Here we are," she said, parking the Hummer in Jason's prime spot. "This is the mansion where I work."

Nineteen

VICKIE and Melody admired Castleton Court from the outside and marveled at its opulent beauty all the way up the stairs.

Kira introduced them to Bessie, then they went up to the vaults to look through the late-eighties, early-nineties gowns on the racks from which Bessie said they could choose.

Melody found a gown right away, tried it on, and stepped onto a dais before a three-way mirror. She viewed herself from all angles. "You really think this hides my condition?"

"Mel," Kira said, "it's Empire style and you're barely, what, four weeks pregnant?"

"Eighteen, and *you* noticed."

"Your hormones *must* be raging, because you usually just throw something on and know you look great. Of course I noticed. You have a perfect figure, tall, thin, sexy— breasts and butt not too big—whereas I"—Kira regarded her bottom in the mirror and sighed—"would not need to pad my bustle."

"We're talking about my *waist*," Melody said.

"Which is more than twenty inches around for the first time in your life, ergo, I noticed. Get over it. People are going to figure it out, hon," Kira said, trying to be gentle. "Do you know how lucky you are?"

"Yeah," Melody said, and Kira handed her a tissue and laughed.

"Weren't Empire gowns from an earlier period, though?" Mel asked, smoothing her skirt.

Kira read the dress tag. "It says 1892 and petunia crepe. The color looks great with your dark hair and tan skin. I love it on you. Don't you love it on her, Vic?"

Vickie passed them by, arms full, headed for the dressing room, but she stopped to examine Melody and shake her head in exasperation. "It's gorgeous, Mel. Chill."

"Your grandmother will kill us if we get them dirty," Mel said.

"*Jason's* grandmother," Kira corrected. "Bessie's glad they're being used. She thinks they're going to waste up here."

"They are," Vickie called from the dressing room. "I have buyers who would kill for some of these. Do you think Bessie would be interested in doing a fashion-show auction at some point? My Immortal Classic customers would come in droves and bring their collector friends. We could charge admission, and the foundation could profit from both."

"I think you should talk to her," Kira said. "Sounds like an awesome idea to me. Mel, stop fussing over the gown. It'll be perfect for the reception. Now show us the dress you're wearing to cook."

"Here," Mel said, showing her a red, low-waisted saque dress on a hanger. "It's French to go with the menu I chose."

"It's perfect," Kira said.

"I want Jason to be a guest on the show," Mel said. "He can stir a sauce or something." She wiggled her brows. "It'd be a shame to waste such a hunka-hunka manhood."

"Fine," Kira said, "but no kissing."

"Okayyyyy," Mel said with a huff. "How many people are coming to the reception?"

"Nearly three hundred. You're a real draw. We didn't get half as many on the ghost tour, which was fine, because the house is small, so we only invited a certain level of donor."

Melody turned to the mirror again and grinned, accentuating her belly by hugging the dress against it.

Logan and Jason came in, and Logan went over to admire his wife's tummy as well.

Kira's heart did a flip. She yearned for such an intimate experience, but knew she would never have one. She turned to Jason. "Already finished cleaning up?"

"Long time ago," Jason said.

"We make a good team," Logan added. "Mel," he said, "Jason took me to St. Anthony's Home for Boys. It's the institution the foundation supports. I'd like you to see it, if you're not too tired."

"I'm fine," Melody said, "but don't stop fussing over me. I like it. Vickie are you ever going to show us what you picked out?"

"Hey, I'm savoring. You know how much I love old clothes. Calm down, Seabright, or that kid's gonna pop out and salute you."

Kira sent Jason and Logan out to see Billy's cars.

"Yeah, like that's my favorite pastime," Jason said, but Logan voiced an interest, so they went.

Vickie came out looking like an icon of the Gilded Age.

"Good goddess!" Kira said. "Is that you in there?"

Vickie shrugged. "It's a redingote dress by Felix of France, 1898." She fingered the hand-printed tag.

"I love the pale blue pinstripes," Mel said, "and the way the triangle bodice buttons on your left shoulder while the skirt buttons on your right hip."

Vickie nodded. "All this vertical braid fakes a slimming line, too. Exactly what I need," she said.

"I wish my sleeves weren't poufy," Mel said.

"You've got a figure that adores pouf," Vickie said.

"Kira, what are you wearing?" Mel asked.

"Bet she searched widow's wear for black crepe," Vic said.

"I picked out my gown last week," Kira said. "I wanted to make a statement."

"Well, put it on," Vic said. "We're waiting to hear what you have to say."

A few minutes later Kira mounted the pedestal before the three-way and placed her hands on her hips, tossing her hair off her shoulders. "Well?"

"It's black," Vic said, "but it's sure in hell not a mourning gown."

"I love the leg-o'-mutton sleeves," Kira said.

"I love the scarlet-edged black braid," Vic said, "the way it runs up each side of your skirt to kiss at your tiny waist, and make a vee up your bodice. It's simple and stunning."

"You're a knockout in it," Melody said.

"There is something about it that makes a statement," Vickie said. "It's a baby step forward, isn't it? You *are* getting over Charlie, aren't you?"

Kira huffed. "I don't know why everybody thinks I'm wearing black because of him. I wore black before."

"But not every day for months," Vic said.

Kira wondered what Jason would think of the dress.

"The Best Kisser in America *is* helping you through this, isn't he?" Melody asked.

Kira hated to think so, because she and Jason had no future, but Vic and Mel knew her too well for her to pretend, even to herself, so she nodded.

"So . . . why hasn't he kissed you?"

"That's not my story to tell. Let's go meet the guys."

AN hour later at St. Anthony's, when Melody saw the boys playing in the old brick gym, she grabbed Logan's hand with a white-knuckled grip.

Vickie got into a game of basketball with the older boys.

Travis took a running leap into Jason's arms while Zane limped over and slipped his arm around Kira's leg.

Kira introduced the twins to Mel and Logan, aware they were about Shane's age.

Melody lowered herself to a child's chair to talk with them. She smiled at Zane's hockey chatter, but her eyes were full. Kira took the Lilliputian chair beside her.

"I'd ask *you* to 'dopt me," Travis told Melody, sliding to the ground from Jason's arms, his small voice a mock whisper, "but I already asked the coach here, and I don't wanna hurt his feelings."

Kira's heart skipped at the shock mixed with pride in Jason's expression.

Logan ruffled Travis's hair and asked him to lead their tour. Later, Melody asked Sister Margaret about everything from tucking the little ones in at night, to dental care, to bad dreams.

Back at Cloud Kiss the doors to the neutral zone were opened, as if the two apartments had become one, the kitchen its epicenter.

Logan and Jason chilled in Jason's living room, in stocking feet, with open collars and rolled-up sleeves, drinking beer from bottles, and watching hockey on Jason's big-screen TV.

Kira, Vickie, and Melody got into their nightclothes, curled up in Mel's parlor, and talked until Melody fell asleep on them.

Kira went for Logan. "She's a goner, Logan. I think it's time to put our little mother to bed."

Logan rose. "I'm surprised she lasted this long."

Kira got her guests settled and came into Jason's apartment, her squishy pillow under her arm.

"Game's nearly over," he said, tugging on her pillow. "C'mere."

When she stepped closer, he took the pillow, placed it on his lap, and urged her down. Kira clearly remembered stretching out on his sofa and snuggling into her pillow.

She vaguely remembered Jason's arm coming around her waist, and later, she dreamed he had his hand on her ass, then before she knew it, he was placing her in a bed.

"You snore, Fitzgerald," he said, lips to her brow.

When Kira woke, she expected to find him beside her and was disappointed. So disappointed, she couldn't fall back to sleep. It was only four A.M., so she got up, grabbed her pillow, crept toward his door, and nudged it open.

Jason looked peaceful in sleep, her quilt his only cover, which warmed her, but he was so tangled in it, she knew he'd had a restless night.

She wondered if he'd been using her memory quilt as his blanket since the rabbit hole. Now, more than ever, she wanted to climb beneath it with him and make new memories.

Too sleepy to fight the urge, Kira lifted the corner of the quilt and started to slip beneath it when Jason sat straight up. "Huh?"

"You look as if somebody used an eggbeater on your hair," she said on a giggle.

"What?"

"Brilliant morning vocab," she said, sliding in along his length.

Jason looked quizzically down at her, a light coming into his eyes. "Rabbit hole?"

"Go back to sleep," she said, pulling him down and turning on her side to face away from him. "I'm gonna do the same. I just wanted a morning snuggle," she said, backing into him, ass against his groin, and pulling his arm over her. "I won't bother you."

"The hell you won't," he said, throwing a leg over her, and sliding his hand up beneath her camisole to find a handful of tingling breast. "The hell you won't."

Kira snuggled against his erection, her center warm, moist, and ready for . . . anything.

As if he knew as much, Jason made a southward journey with one capable hand and slipped a finger between her warm wet folds. She opened to him on the instant, growing him harder against her, Harvey riding her backside, as she rode Jason's talented hand to a rising plane filled with starlight and promise.

"I . . ." She sighed, gasped, bit her lip. "I . . . really . . . only . . ."

"A cuddle, I know, and we will," Jason said. "Right after we both . . ."

Words were not necessary as pleasure bloomed in her, glowed bright, and brighter still, splintering like fireworks with every beat closer to the pinnacle, until she shattered completely.

When she caught her breath, she turned and searched for Harvey.

"Oh, man," Jason said. "He's been dreaming of this, of your hands on him. Better watch out 'cause he's been cocked and crying for your attention since the first time you threatened him with your wand."

"That fast?" she said.

"He's precocious," Jason said on a gasp as Kira closed her hand on a cock bigger than she'd ever held or imagined.

"I'll say he is, and huge, too."

"Well, he's been . . . plenty . . . stimulated." Jason released a long slow breath when Kira started to slide her fingers along his length.

"When was he 'plenty' stimulated?"

"The first rabbit hole; he wanted you bad. Then in the arena, then the 'wow' in the hidden stairs. Then . . . the . . . phone calls."

"He liked the phone calls, did he?" Kira was on all fours now, giving Harvey her full attention.

"Yeah," Jason said, his eyes closing in ecstasy. "Your voice when you come makes him . . . yeah."

Kira made Harvey last, and last some more, though he wept a little because she didn't quite make him come.

She let Jason make her come again, twice, before she let him give himself up to her torture. He came like a rocket, and Kira was proud.

Together they sighed, snuggled, and drifted into a sated sleep.

Kira woke to Vickie calling her name.

"She's in the shower," Jason called in reply, covering Kira's mouth, and she licked his hand.

"Oh," Vickie replied. "Just tell her we're up."

"Yeah," Jason whispered. "I'm up, too."

"Oh," Vickie added, "your grandmother has invited us for breakfast. We're going down when we're ready. See you there."

"Okay," Jason called.

Kira raised the quilt to check beneath it and see if Jason was telling the truth. "I'll say you're up. Impressively . . . up . . . considering."

She gloved him and he groaned, raised his ass off the bed, but he covered her hand to stop the pleasure. "Shower," he said through clenched teeth. "You're in the shower, remember?"

"I am? Oh, right." She rose and tugged him up by his Harvey. "Let's shower together and save time."

Jason allowed himself to be led into his bathroom like a docile pup on a hard leash, and Kira loved having this power over him.

"You're a *bad* influence on me, Fitzgerald."

"Like this is all my— Your shower is as big as my parent's bathroom."

He turned on both showerheads in a gold-fixtured cream marble stall so big, it didn't need a door.

Inside the shower he kissed his way from her breasts to her center, knelt before her, and let her revel in the talent of his mouth, until all she could hear was the pumping of her heart, the thunder of the spray, and the echo of her whimpers as she rose on a crest almost too perfect to be borne.

She came in such a rush of pleasure, he had to hold her steady, and when he let her go, she slid like liquid soap down the side of the stall, to land knees up and breathing hard. She could barely speak.

Concerned, Jason bent down beside her. "Okay there, Fitz?"

"Yeah, I think my heart is pumping again. I can't believe you did that."

"Damned near drowned." He wiped his face, his grin as huge and proud as his cock.

"I don't think I have the strength to stand," Kira said, "never mind shower and reciprocate."

"You'll owe me," he said, raising her to hold her up and soap her up.

When they arrived in the dining room, Kira wondered if anyone suspected why they were so late, but one look at Vic and Mel, and she knew that they were both suspicious and amused.

Though everyone was full of energy and looking forward to filming Melody's show, Kira just wanted to take a nap. In a haze of afterglow, she let the caffeine kick in and listened while the others discussed the shooting.

"I went to Kingston by the sea the other day," Jason said to Melody. "Your crew tested the cooktop and preheated the oven. Looks like they got everything set for an easy shoot."

Logan chuckled. "After a year Mel's crew is prepared for disaster. Easy would shock them."

An hour later Melody stroked the huge red metal coffee grinder on the marble peninsula countertop, beneath two rows of copper pots. A tureen sat beside a pressed-glass canister set and a rack of matching spice jars.

"Your crew had our caretaker set bamboo privacy screens before a few of the windows," Kira said, while Melody preheated the oven and prepped pots with chicken stock, milk, onions, and butter to turn into French sauces during the filming.

Half an hour later the cameras started rolling. Melody, in a scarlet marvel of covert folds and overt sensuality, waltzed onto the set to the strains of "Do You Believe in Magic?"

"Welcome to Kingston by the Sea in beautiful Newport, Rhode Island," Melody said. "Before I begin the show, I'd like to introduce my special guest, Mr. Jason Pickering Goddard."

The applause track came on as Jason walked in, wearing a cappuccino turtleneck, matching slacks, and a black apron, his sleeves rolled up. Every woman's dream hunk.

"Though he's an NHL god and America's very Best Kisser," Melody said, "to which I can personally attest . . ." She sneaked a kiss, so Jason took her in his arms and bent her back for a real kiss, and the canned laughter rose.

Back on her feet, Melody fanned herself. "Jason is going to take a break from hockey and kissing, and he's going to help me cook for you today."

"I cook good." Jason wiggled his brows.

Logan laughed at their antics, but Kira was jealous. How stupid was that? Jason didn't belong to her. They were consenting adults playing a rabbit-hole game, no errors, no fouls, no pain.

Jason Goddard was *not* her property. She did *not* have a thing for him. End of snit!

Melody patted Jason's cheek, ordered him to stir the sauce, and he saluted her and did her bidding.

He was playing to the cameras as he said he'd been taught, smiling for the cameras, kissing Mel for the cameras.

There had been *no* cameras to record his cocky grin in the shower that morning, however, which made Kira feel cheerful and . . . victorious.

Twenty

"THIS kitchen was once the height of domestic technology," Melody told her *Kitchen Witch* audience. "Let's see how it's stood the test of time." She went to the front of the counter and waved her wand.

> *"Glorious kitchen preserved in time,*
> *Make the success of the French chefs mine.*
> *Awaken ageless faith and fervor.*
> *Inspire this cook, sustain this stirrer.*
> *Bring us the best of the Gilded Age,*
> *Drawn from that century's cookbook page."*

To another round of canned applause, she returned to her position behind the counter.

"Most of the chefs during La Belle Epoch—the height of Newport Society—were French," Mel said, "so my menu is a salute to Gilded Age gastronomy. Among my selections are: Beauvilliers' Cheese Soufflé, Sauté de Volaille au Velouté Réduit, and for dessert, Meringues à la Crème."

Melody smiled. "Don't worry. I'll translate as I go. The Sautéed Chicken in Crème Sauce," she said, "calls for tender young fryers flattened slightly with the side of a cleaver, like so." She demonstrated and placed the chicken in a deep copper skillet with a long handle.

"After we sauté the chicken in butter, we'll cover it with the crème sauce and warm it in the oven to marry the flav—"

Melody stopped talking and looked up.

A soundman checked his equipment.

Jason and Logan exchanged glances.

The odd hum rose in volume, and Kira thought the stove was giving a death rattle, until two bugs hit her in the face, one after the other. *Buzz thwack, buzz thwack.*

A dark cloud of bees spilled from the copper vent above the stove. A swarm asleep in the vent, awakened by the heat, as if summer had arrived, were leaving their winter quarters, via the kitchen, and making a cameo appearance on *The Kitchen Witch* show.

The bees gravitated toward the exposed windows, sluggish and seeking sunlight, hundreds, it seemed, getting so thick on the panes they darkened the room like furry undulating shades, their buzz slowing to a dull hum.

"Keep rolling the cameras!" the director shouted. "This is good," he said. "It's so Melody to pull something like this."

"Hey," Mel said, battling the bees with a wooden spoon. "I didn't—"

Logan ran in and grabbed her by the hand to drag her out.

"I'm not allergic," she said.

"But I am," Logan said, "so the baby might be."

"Oh, gosh," Mel said, moving faster.

Jason called for an evacuation of the kitchen and told the director to shove his rolling cameras.

Kira wondered if they'd keep that in the show.

Jason lifted her off the floor, set her on her feet in the hall, and shut the kitchen door. "Call the exterminators!" he yelled to Weston, the caretaker. "Now!" Then he looked at Kira with a grin. "There were bees swimming in *my* sauce."

Mel did the second half of her show the next morning, starting with a spell to keep the bees away.

Jason talked about the mansion, the foundation, and St. Anthony's, while Mel slid a cheese soufflé into the oven. They'd started on the meringues, when the oven hiccupped with a bright flash, and everyone dived for cover.

The oven door flew halfway across the kitchen. Fortunately, no one was hurt.

The laughing cameramen did a close-up of the oven, the ancient heating element split but connected by a crackling blue and yellow arc, zapping the soufflé, literally, to death. When the dish exploded, only the cameramen had egg on their faces.

"I think we can safely call this a *Kitchen Witch* classic," Jason said. "Weston, cut the electricity."

Jason took Kira in his arms and leaned his chin on her head. "This is what we get," he said, "for cutting costs on mansion upkeep."

"The foundation is getting better every day," she said, to console him. "Three hundred people are coming to Mel's reception Saturday at five-hundred dollars a ticket."

"That makes me feel almost as good as your arms around me," Jason said.

They concluded the segment on the third day, station management chomping at the bit to get the show in the can.

On Saturday, for viewing during the reception, huge, flat-screen TVs were set up in each corner of a ballroom flanked by a swimming-pool patio with an ocean view where the orchestra was tuning up.

Melody did a live intro of the taped show in the kitchen—where electricians, carpenters, and conservators had been working for two days straight—and waved her wand for the fun to begin. Then she joined the reception upstairs.

With her show on in the background, Melody was the center of attention and a gracious guest.

The bees arrived on screen, and the room went silent. That Logan rescued Melody because the baby might be allergic started a round of applause and congratulations, turning the exploding oven into an anticlimax.

The *Kitchen Witch* crew, and several news crews, had set up on the patio. There Melody went live to end the show. She introduced Logan, Kira, Vickie, and Jason again. Then she handed her wand to Kira and faced the cameras for a close-up.

"In a minute," she said, "you'll see footage of the boys from St. Anthony's. You heard Jason speak about them on the show."

Melody became a voiceover to the footage of the boys. "I'm pleased to announce that the Seabright Foundation will be making a one-hundred-thousand-dollar contribution to St. Anthony's," Mel said. "Please jot down the address on the screen where you can send *your* tax-deductible donation."

She looked earnestly at the cameras. "I'm offering you a challenge. The Seabright Foundation will also match every hundred thousand dollars donated to St. Anthony's between now and December thirty-first."

Jason took Kira's hand and squeezed, and she thought he might as well have squeezed her heart, she was so hooked on him.

"Call the number on your screen if you'd like to make a donation, meet the boys, or if you're interested in adoption. The Pickering Foundation's development director and her staff of volunteers are manning the phones right now to take your pledge and answer your questions."

Kira and Melody raised their wands together, twirling them as practiced. "Until the next time we meet," Melody said, "we wish each and every one of you a generous heart, a giving spirit, and bright blessings for the Yuletide season."

The show ended to a deafening round of applause from the ballroom. Logan and Melody went inside, and Bessie was first in line to thank them.

Kira was pleased when Jason directed the orchestra to play and took her in his arms to waltz her around the pool.

"Sorry I'm not smooth. This is about as good as I get on the dance floor. I'm better on the ice."

"Feels good to me," Kira said, shivering in his arms.

Jason stroked the side of her breast with a thumb. "Feels good to me, too."

Since the guests and the cameras were focused on Mel, Kira felt free to indulge in Jason's seduction.

"Did you realize that we all asked Melody and Logan to visit St. Anthony's," Jason said, "and I didn't even know she had a foundation?"

"Guess it was destiny," Kira said.

Jason lowered his lashes. "Like us in the rabbit hole."

Kira gazed into the silver depths of his eyes. Her mother would call them bedroom eyes, and her father would warn her away from him. "I think the rabbit holes were more like—"

"What?" Jason slowed, held her tight, his breath tickling her ear. "What?" he whispered.

"Oh, I don't know. A natural charmer creating fantasies. A natural seducer setting up a seduction."

"Hey, who got into bed with whom?" Jason asked.

"I *said* I wanted to cuddle," Kira said.

Jason wiggled his brows. "And didn't we ever."

Kira smiled. "Just remembering gives me a mini . . . you know."

Jason groaned and slipped his hand between the folds of her full skirts to pull her against him. "Your hair brings out the tempting bits of scarlet in that gown. Have I told you how beautiful you look?"

"Yeah, a couple of times," she said. "Have I told you that I can feel Harvey knocking at my door, hard?"

"Let me help you take off that dress later and I'll show you hard."

Kira sifted her fingers through the hair at Jason's nape, raising her knee the slightest to tease his erection, the music closing the world out, and them in . . . until the floor disappeared from beneath them and a shock of icy water swallowed them whole.

Kira finally broke the surface and couldn't see Jason, but when he shot up, everyone applauded.

When had they become the center of attention?

Jason swam over and took her in his arms. "Are you all right?" he asked, holding her to his racing heart.

"S-s-sure," Kira said, warmed by embarrassment.

Jason looked up and saw the crowd, the cameras, so close, it was a wonder the videographers didn't fall in the pool with them, Kira thought. She shivered and pushed the hair from her eyes as Jason bent toward her, his lips offering the kiss she had anticipated, and yet—

"Let's give them something else to talk about," Jason said, and he kissed her for the first time.

She put herself into the kiss, but it didn't take long to realize that Jason wasn't . . . present to the experience.

He was kissing her as if he'd stepped away from himself, as if everything inside him had gone cold and vacant, the way he'd kissed Melody and every model and starlet on that reality show.

The son of a bitch was playing to the cameras. What had he said? Like kissing a rotten rutabaga? Well, now she knew what he meant.

Kira fought his embrace and levered herself, feet against his crotch, to push away from him and swim to the edge of the pool. Jason's groan of pain was something of a consolation as she fought to keep her cumbrous skirts from swamping her.

Logan pulled her from the water, then Bessie and Melody placed a warm leopard coat around her shoulders.

Jason pulled himself from the pool and stood outside her circle of comforters.

When he cut into the circle and gave her his best TV grin, Kira punched him in the nose.

That night Melody's gift to St. Anthony's was the lead story on one channel. But she and Jason had not been overlooked on the others. One news anchor began the story with "NHL's Best Kisser, Benched."

The instant media blitz included the bees swarming, the oven exploding, and, praise the goddess, Melody's gift and challenge grant, and where to send donations.

As far as Kira was concerned, they made too much of her and Jason kissing, of her world-class punch, and even of Jason's shock and nosebleed.

As far as the foundation was concerned, the publicity would likely be termed either wonderful or horrible, depending on who you talked to, and how they looked at it.

The next morning at brunch, Gram placed the Sunday paper beside Jason's plate. "Great publicity stunt," she said, "dancing into the pool."

"Yeah," Jason said facetiously. "Exactly as we planned, right, Stallone?" he asked, looking at Kira.

"Planned or not," Gram said, "it was worth the loss of that dress."

Kira groaned and buried her face in her hands.

Jason frowned.

The girls had stayed up half the night talking, after throwing *him* out.

He wished, then and now, that somebody would tell him why Kira had socked him. He'd waited in bed, and counted the hours until Kira came to his apartment, then when she did, she hadn't come to his room.

He remembered how scared he'd been in the pool when he realized she could drown in that dress. He'd gone back under when he couldn't find her the first time he surfaced, his heart beating so fast, he could barely swim.

When he came up for air the second time, Kira was there, thank God, looking like a drowned rat, but beautiful and dear, more dear than he could stand to admit, even to himself.

But the cameras had short-circuited his elation. Had they been caught practically making love as they danced? He went cold. He'd never wanted to go public with his emotions again. The reality show director used to say, "Don't think, kiss. Give the world something to talk about."

Jason tried to give the world something more sensational than their intimate, personal magic on the dance floor to focus on. He'd needed to overshadow it.

"The cameras only see what's on the outside," he'd learned well. "They're not in your head. Just do it. Shut down and kiss her, damn it!" The director's words had filled his mind.

Jason had done it. He'd taken the press's attention from the dance and centered it on the kiss, but Kira clocked him for it and hadn't spoken to him since. What was that about?

He looked at her now, sitting across the dining room table, gazing at him with open hostility. "Why the hell did you sucker-punch me?"

Melody huffed. "If you don't know, you're a lost cause," she said, placing an arm around Kira. "Too bad, too, because I was just beginning to like you."

"Yeah," Vickie said, and Logan just grinned.

Jason lowered his head and gave his attention to eating his eggs. There'd be no help from that quarter. Logan knew on what side of Melody's bed his bread was buttered, or . . . something like that.

Jason scowled at Kira for scrambling his brain and annoying the hell out of him.

"What?" she said in response to the scowl. "You got fresh; I hit you. End of story."

Jason cocked his head. "I'm guessing that means the pool *wasn't* a rabbit hole?"

Vickie and Melody's heads came up. If they were bugs, their antennae would be quivering.

Twenty-one

"NO," Kira said, looking at him as if he were nuts, "the pool wasn't a rabbit hole. And if you don't know why I socked you, then screw you! Sorry, Bessie."

His grandmother chuckled.

"I have *no* idea why you hit me," Jason said.

"Oh, please," Kira said. "Dancing was your idea, and the rest . . . well, let's just call the dip, and the kiss . . . calamities . . . compounded by bad choices."

"Yours or mine?" Jason asked.

"Right," Kira said.

"No wonder I never know who to thank . . . or fire," Jason said, sounding every bit as ticked off as he felt and not giving a damn.

"Feel free to give me full credit for the auction next Saturday," Kira said, employing her evil witch grin.

"Thanks for the reminder. Methinks our white witch is turning a bit gray around the aura . . . and don't you dare make a move on that wand."

"I want to come to the auction," Melody said, looking entertained and enthralled."

"Nothing doing," Logan said. "No more bachelor kissing for you, *Mrs.* Kilgarven."

"I'll come," Vickie said. "I might bid on Billy."

Gram laughed. "Get in one of his cars and he's yours for free."

Jason gave his grandmother a scowl. "Don't go giving her ideas. He'll eat her alive. The man's a wolf."

Kira snorted inelegantly. "But you run in different packs, right?"

"If you put Billy in that auction," Jason told Kira as he stood. "I'm out, and so are my buddies."

"Jason," Gram said, as if he were two and throwing sand, so he ignored her.

"Billy is a *great* date," Kira said.

"You should know."

"You don't mean that about the auction," Kira said, testing him.

Jason bent over the table and went eye to eye with the witch. "Try me."

She rose and threw down her napkin like a gauntlet. "I knew you were the kind of jock who'd take your toys and go home if I didn't play your way."

"Hah, so speaks the schoolyard bully." Jason touched his nose, which seemed to amuse the hell out of the women, including his traitorous grandmother.

Jason straightened. "I won't have Billy on the auction block, and that's my final word."

"Seven days, boss," Kira said, getting his point, "and I'm selling *you* to the highest bidder." She turned to his grandmother. "I don't need you to stake me, Bessie. I don't want him." She rose and left the dining room, her friends behind her.

Jason watched them go and fell back into his chair. "What the hell is eating her?" Jason said to no one in particular.

"I have no idea," his grandmother responded, patting his

hand. "When I asked her how she felt this morning, her answer made no sense."

Jason sat straighter. "What did she say?"

"That she felt like a rotten rutabaga."

Jason smacked his brow, cursed the vibrating pain in his nose, and left the table. As he rounded the corner to leave the dining room, he caught a grin on his grandmother's face and couldn't help feeling like he was losing a game in which she was making up the rules. And right now, he didn't freaking care.

The following week, Thanksgiving week, Jason gave Kira some breathing space, and himself time to think.

He went skating at the rink every afternoon after work to strengthen his legs and leave her in peace. He didn't cross their neutral zone of a kitchen at night, didn't get in her way at the office, and said yes to her every auction idea, including having him and Melody as emcees.

Kira never mentioned Billy, but she did begin to smile again.

Nevertheless, every time Jason thought about the auction, he wanted to run and hide in Kira's rabbit hole, except that he wanted *her* in there with him. But he wondered if she'd still want that. They hadn't even driven to work together since . . . the kiss.

How did a man apologize for making a woman feel like a decaying root vegetable? Jason wondered over the course of the week.

On Wednesday at hockey practice he let Kira dole out hot chocolate without asking her to put on skates, which left her free to sing Zane to sleep, which left Travis free to skate like a pro.

After practice they walked from the arena, through a light snowfall, toward Cloud Kiss.

"Will Regan be home for Thanksgiving?" he asked, a little worried about what a confrontation would do to Kira, never mind her holiday.

"Yes," she groaned. "Regan will be there."

"How about you?"

"I might go to Melody's."

"Don't you think it's time to decide? Tomorrow is Thanksgiving, in case you haven't noticed."

"I don't know what to tell my mother. If she finds out I bypassed Boston to drive to Salem, she'll be hurt."

Jason's heart skipped. "Stay and have Thanksgiving with us."

"Oh," Kira said, but her enthusiasm was short-lived. "No, I couldn't impose."

"Impose? You live here."

"But I'm not—"

"The fact is," Jason said, stopping her with a hand on her arm, "you'd be doing us a favor. See, even when small families have a lot to be thankful for, they don't make for a festive Thanksgiving."

"Your parents won't want—"

"They're not coming, and Gram wanted me to ask you weeks ago, but I assumed you'd be going home, until I remembered what you said about staying away if Regan was there. Tell your mother you're too tired to drive tonight."

"Well, I am."

"If you don't have to drive tomorrow," he coaxed, "you can sleep late." He was begging and he knew it. Hell, he wanted to spend Thanksgiving with her. Go figure. "No cooking," he added. "No cleanup. No argument with your sister. Just good food and great company."

"What time do you normally eat?"

"Gram likes to eat around two," he said.

"Yes! Tomorrow, I'm sleeping till *noon*!" She raised a fist in victory, then threaded her arm through his, and they continued on to the house.

"THIS is great," Kira said, forking another piece of turkey. Jason looked charming and gorgeous today. Even his face relaxed. He smiled, laughed, and grimaced as his grandmother told the kind of childhood tales that every man dreaded hearing.

Kira ate them up.

The phone ringing managed to plummet the temperature in the room on the instant. By the sudden set of Jason's and Bessie's shoulders, Kira could tell that an uncomfortable phone conversation was about to take place.

Bessie spoke to her daughter, Jason's mother, first, their conversation formal and stilted. When Jason took the phone, his expression turned stark, as if chiseled in granite. He listened, said, yes, he *was* planning to return to hockey, exchanged a polite pleasantry or two, said Happy Thanksgiving, and hung up.

Jason's father hadn't bothered to get on the phone, and Kira didn't need to ask why.

When Jason returned to the table, his unconcerned air, like a veneer of self-protection, reminded her of Travis the first time she'd seen him. As a matter of fact, the absence of Jason's parents from his life might explain his empathy for the boys at St. Anthony's.

Jason's smile didn't return until his grandmother covered his hand on the table.

Bessie turned to Kira. "Jason's mother takes after my husband, always looking for the next party, just like her father."

"And I take after both of them," Jason said throwing down his napkin.

"You do not," Kira and his grandmother said as one.

"Can't prove it by me," he said.

"How much did your husband do for the boys at St. Anthony's?" Kira asked Bessie.

"He never set foot in the place."

"But he made donations, like Jason does."

"*I* made our donations," Bessie said. "Jason makes his own."

"But if your husband had lived, he would have taken over the foundation, like Jason."

"That doesn't count," Jason said. "She blackmailed me, and I'm not staying. I'm going back to hockey, as I told my mother; therefore, I *am* looking for the next party."

His grandmother whacked him on the shoulder with the back of her hand. "You're nothing like your mother or your grandfather, and I can't believe you think you are."

He shook his head, denying her words. "How am I different?"

"You're here, having Thanksgiving dinner with me, like you did last year, and every year before, even if it meant flying halfway around the world."

Jason relaxed in his chair. "But that's—"

"When's my birthday?"

"June twenty-third; why?"

"Neither your grandfather, nor your mother, could name that date, and you've never let it pass without a gift, a call, a visit, or any combination of the above."

"You don't think I'm like them? Seriously?"

"I never did, and if I'd realized *you* thought so, I would have disabused you of the notion sooner."

Jason returned his napkin to his lap. "What's for dessert?"

FRIDAY morning, getting into the shower, Jason realized that the day before had been one of his best Thanksgivings. His grandmother had reigned supreme and held them in thrall with her stories, including a few he could have done without.

He'd let her show movies of him learning to skate as a toddler, and of the bright moments of his early career.

Kira was interested, beautiful, and amusing.

He enjoyed himself throughout, not so much during the phone call, but afterward, when that thirty-six-year-old weight had slipped from his shoulders.

He'd especially enjoyed their walk after dinner, the

three of them, Gram in the middle, strolling arm in arm down the snow-lined path to the garden.

While Gram sat in the snow-covered gazebo beside her rare copper weeping beach tree, Kira started a snowball fight, which he won, while Gram laughed, and he felt his heart open like the old days.

Though he and Kira had never discussed the reason she punched him, he guessed he was back in her good graces, for now, but he wouldn't stay long if he didn't come up with an excellent auction date that every woman would love.

Jason turned off the shower. No. Not every woman. He needed a fantastic date only *Kira* would love. He needed . . . an exclusive, made-to-order rabbit hole with the word *Kira* written all over it. "Yeah."

ON the night of the auction Jason tugged his tux out of the closet with all the enthusiasm of a puck in a face-off.

He was prepping for a journey to hell.

An hour later he walked into Summerton's silver- and gold-striped ballroom, no less magnificent for the rows of empty chairs between him and a bright stage in the throes of preproduction.

There stood Kira, the object of his search, beside a sleek high-res Plexiglas podium, her copper-fire hair and pearlescent skin kissed by the lights. She was as at home with a state-of-the-art techno production as she was with gay-nineties dresses and Gilded Age mansions.

A sorceress shimmering with power, she gave orders like a pro, making people laugh as they rushed to do her bidding, as if she were wielding her wand to control them.

She'd accented her simple black satin strapless gown with a mint-green scarf, bright with red and black lady-bugs. The scarf's foot of fringe all but swept the floor. Her mint green sandals were high and strappy, a bold ladybug nesting atop her sexy toes. Black, but not in mourning. Red, but still in hiding. Seductive, but unaware.

Kira the witch, invader of dreams, rejuvenator of the Pickering Foundation, creator of magic, of wishes, and of quilts that inspired forbidden dreams. She was the woman who sang a broken little boy to sleep, the one taking a broken man to places he never expected he'd *want* to go.

Truth be told, she had become the why of his every action and the subject of his every reflection, which just plain spooked him.

He should stay away, but she pulled him into her sphere, and he had no choice but to go.

She came gracefully down the stage steps when she saw him, and met him halfway across the magnificent room. Up close, he saw that, like her skin, her hair held a shimmer this evening, while her ears bore a pair of earrings he'd seen before. He touched a bejeweled ladybug. "Perfect," he said.

"They were Bessie's idea. I came down wearing plain rhinestones and she took me into her bedroom saying she had earrings that would match. The ladybugs are garnets and onyx, and the studs are diamonds." Kira shivered.

"Cold?" Jason asked as he lowered her wide scarf to her shoulders like a shawl and rubbed the fabric over her arms to warm her.

"No, I'm scared to death that I'll lose one of her earrings."

He tugged her lazy curl and tweaked her freckled nose. "What can I do to make you bid on me tonight?" he asked, taking her hand, cupping it, and bringing it to his lips to warm.

After kissing her fingers, he looked into her eyes. "I'm sorry for playing to the cameras. I didn't quite realize I was doing it—while I was doing it—but I hate that I took you to the rutabaga patch. Forgive me? Please?"

She stepped closer, as if seeking more of his warmth, said nothing for a surprised minute, and nodded.

"Bid on me?" he whispered, warming her ear.

"I'll think about it." She raised her chin to give him

room for a neck-nibble, and that gave him hope for a good auction outcome.

"I'll ask again," he said, stepping back and taking her arm. "Come on, I'd like you to meet my friends."

They went through a mosaic-tiled sunroom that led to a glassed-in patio, where a buffet was set with hot canapés, a champagne fountain, and priceless crystal.

Jason winced inwardly. The female "cattle-buyers" were beginning to arrive—some he'd dated, some he'd only slept with—all of them big-spenders and ready to throw their money at a night of fun, especially for a good cause. But not one of the women was his friend.

It was toward the men in tuxes at the bar that he led Kira, the first woman he'd wanted to show off since he was fourteen and high on testosterone.

"Kira," he said, "I'd like you to meet my best friend—"

"Santiago the Stealer," Kira said, needing no introduction and looking delighted. "Nice to meet you Tiago. Steal anything of interest lately?"

"What, you didn't watch the World Series?" He flashed a ring as bright as his charm-boy grin.

"Am I supposed to kiss it?"

"She doesn't like sports or jocks," Jason said, and his friends groaned as if they'd been shot.

Kira's eyes crinkled and her lips quirked as she focused on the baseball player known the world over as the Stealer. "Aw, come on, what are you packing tonight? Give me a peek."

"How come you know so much about him?" Jason muttered. "You didn't know who *I* was."

"I dated the Penis, remember?"

His friends looked at Jason questioningly and he shrugged. "Tillinghast," he said. "Pawtucket. She dumped him."

Their thumbs-up approval was genuine.

Kira turned back to Tiago. "Show me," she said, and the guys at the bar whistled.

Tiago winked. "I'd show *you* anything any day, Juguete." He pulled the corner of a red lace wet dream from his pocket.

Jason groaned, but Kira didn't seem to be the least offended.

"Do you really charm the pants off them," she asked with an eye-twinkle Jason would like turned *his* way, "or do women mail you their underwear by the truckload?"

Tiago tucked his badge of honor back into his pocket and scratched his head as if he'd been caught with his hand in a cookie jar.

"The truth is," Jason said, "women make it too damned easy for him. Find Tiago a girl he can't charm the pants off, and she won't be able to get rid of him."

Tiago slapped Jason on the back in a half hug. "Ah no, my friend. I couldn't let the ladies down and tie myself to only one." And then he slipped his other arm around Kira's waist and marched her possessively away. "Come, Juguete, there's somebody I want you to meet."

Jason watched Kira throw her shawl over her shoulder and look up at Tiago as if he were . . . charming the pants off her.

"Damn it, Tiago," Jason growled. "She's *my* date."

"Watch out," Billy heckled from the bar. "If he's got a hot car, you're toast."

"You wish," Jason said as he watched Kira and Tiago approach Tiago's grandfather.

Twenty-two

FROM the audience Kira watched Jason begin the evening with a formal welcome from the Pickering Foundation, then Melody started the first bachelor intro from her podium across the stage. "Our bidding starts this evening with the one and only Seth Arkwright, owner of the infamous Company of Rogues. Seth wants you to know that he and several of his rogues are *donating* their time to this event."

Vickie escorted Seth onstage, and Jason read Seth's bio. "When not renting high-profile bachelors for fun and profit, Seth likes to sail his ninety-foot schooner around the world. He has a house in Malibu, a castle in Wales, and a hideaway in Colorado."

Melody picked it up from there. "For his dream date, ladies, Seth will fly you to Los Angeles and take you for a leisurely sail on the Pacific, during which you'll share an intimate gourmet dinner aboard ship while you watch the sun set."

Jason gave his podium over to the professional auctioneer.

The bidding started at five hundred dollars and rose to ten thousand before it ended with Seth escorting a happy blonde off the stage.

"Santiago the Stealer, millionaire baseball legend, and owner of his own railroad train, hardly needs an introduction," Melody said as Tiago appeared, decked out in a tux, a baseball bat over his shoulder, and a pair of red lace bikini panties dangling from the bat like a victory flag.

Melody giggled. "Tiago's dream date consists of a private train ride from Boston to New York City for dinner, your choice of Broadway show, and a cast party into the wee hours of the morning."

After some hot bidding, Tiago went for twelve thousand five hundred.

No bachelor went for less than ten grand, and every hunk was enthusiastically bid upon. Kira bid on every one, to raise the foundation's profit, and the women bidding took to laughing, or booing, every time she raised her paddle.

"Hey, girl, you can't want them all!" one woman yelled.

"Oh, but I do," Kira said.

Jason was last up, or so *he* thought. She'd tricked him, because she'd been pissed about the rutabaga kiss when she made up the program, so she'd added a surprise at the end, for which Jason might want to fire her.

Kira was glad she did. An extra bachelor would mean more money for the foundation, but she was sorry now that she'd made Jason work so hard all evening, because she had *wanted* him to sweat, before he had to strut his stuff.

Melody whistled when Vickie escorted Jason onstage, so he took Melody into his arms and bent her back for a kiss, again for the cameras, in the way he'd kissed her on her show.

The crowd had been waiting for it, and they applauded it.

Melody grinned and winked afterward. "The Best Kisser in America," she said, "our own Jason Pickering Goddard, hardly needs an intro, but I can personally attest to the fact that he kisses as well as he plays hockey." She winked at Logan and looked at the auctioneer.

"His date?" the auctioneer said.

"Oh, I'm sorry," Melody said. "I got so flustered by Jason's kiss, I forgot tell you where he's taking his winning bidder."

Melody looked straight at Kira. "Tomorrow morning Jason will be taking his date on a sunrise balloon ride over the Newport coast, then for an attic picnic at his very own Cloud Kiss."

Kira sat straighter.

One of Jason's leggy airhead model friends bid three thousand on the spot. Kira had disliked her on the spot, and now she knew why. She was pushy. And before Kira could digest the fact that Jason had planned his date especially for *her,* the airhead, and several other women, got into a bidding war.

It probably wasn't good that Jason had known how to lure her into bidding, Kira thought. Then again, that meant he knew her, cared what she liked. He'd *listened* to her. So that was good, right?

As Kira questioned her judgment and her sanity in bidding, Jason caught her eye and gave her the connection she needed. He gave her a peek inside himself, where yearning, and the promise of adventure, pleasure, and intimacy, were hers for the taking.

Take me, his gaze said. *Come into* my *rabbit hole. I want you.*

Kira about melted. "Ten thousand," she said.

The auctioneer laughed. "Missy, you gotta keep up here. It's eleven to you."

"Eleven," she said, feeling a warmth climb her face.

Jason's shoulders relaxed. He grinned and crooked his finger her way. She'd won?

"Twelve thousand. He's mine!" the airhead shouted, outbidding her with no class.

Kira sat back down.

Jason scowled.

"Fifteen," came a bid from the back of the room . . . a male bid.

A female gasp rose from the audience, and Jason's expression could only be termed furious.

Kira stood and looked toward the back. Good grief, she thought, what did the rule book say about a man bidding on a man?

The bidder stood in the shadows. His voice had sounded familiar, but disguised. She wished she could identify him.

Jason went to the mike. "Give it up, Billy. I wouldn't go on a date with you for twenty grand. Hell, I'll outbid you myself."

Billy Castleton, Jason's rival since the sandbox, bid twenty thousand dollars.

"Twenty-one," airhead said.

"Twenty-five," Kira said, raising her paddle in panic.

Billy moved up the aisle into the light, winking first at her, then at Jason, and he bid thirty thousand dollars.

A shriek rent the air. The airhead in high pout was a sight to behold.

Kira turned toward Gram, who nodded for her to continue.

"Thirty-five thousand," Kira said. "Keep bidding, Billy," she added. "The foundation needs the money."

Billy stepped back as if he'd robbed a bank and faced the sheriff, hands up.

"Sold!" Melody crowed. "For thirty-five thousand dollars!"

The auctioneer turned to Melody gape-mouthed and she laughed. "Oops. Sorry. But the Best Kisser in America goes to the Best Event Coordinator in America for thirty-five grand."

Kira went toward the stage to claim her prize, forgetting to be sorry she'd caved. He'd seduced her with a look, the silver-eyed wolf. What a surprise. What a relief.

"Thank God it's you," Jason said as he took her hand to escort her up the stage steps. There he presented her with a single red rose, placed a possessive arm around her waist, and nuzzled her neck to catcalls and hisses from the audience. "And thank God this damned auction is over," he added.

"Not quite," Kira said.

Melody introduced Billy Castleton as the last bachelor up for bid.

"You rat," Jason said, abandoning Kira's neck to look her in the eye.

She tugged him offstage. "If I were a rat, I'd have let Billy win you. He's too ripe a plum to lose," she said. "For the sake of the boys at St. Anthony's, we need him. Watch him sucker those women into throwing their money at him. Besides, you should thank him for raising your price. I'm not sure you're worth it."

"You're great for my ego, you know that?" Jason held up a hand to stop the auctioneer and gave him a one-minute signal to wait. Then he walked away.

Kira wondered how angry she'd made him, wondered if he would make a spectacle of his dislike for Billy.

Jason approached his friends and spoke to them.

Tiago, Seth, and a couple other bachelors nodded, left, and returned with more men, and Jason raised his hand for the bidding to begin.

One bid after another, all of them made by men, the bidding dollars on Billy rose so high so fast, the women didn't have a chance. The men made it impossible.

In the true spirit of a power play, Billy went for fifty thousand dollars to Tiago's grandfather. Ninety years of age, if he was a day, Jose Santiago clutched his walker and laughed so hard, Kira was afraid he'd need oxygen.

Billy left the stage with good grace to meet his date halfway. He had promised to take his winner dancing in Paris.

Kira and Jason mingled separately, and later they sent Gram home while they stayed to clean up. They drove home in separate cars.

Kira got there first, but she sat on the floor beside the elevator and dozed while waiting for Jason. She still wanted to know if he was angry with her for putting Billy in the auction.

He gave her a hand up, when their eyes met, and pulled her straight into his arms. As he nuzzled her neck, she leaned over to push the Up button.

Too tired to discuss her decision about Billy, though she was pretty sure Jason wasn't angry, they necked in the elevator, lips never touching, by mutual consent, though his lips touched every place else on her that they could reach.

Actually, Jason was making a feast of her, and Kira was willing to let him slay her with passive pleasure.

He didn't let her fall out of the elevator this time; he was prepared.

"Hey," she said. "Good catch. Tiago would be proud."

"Would you please not talk about him at a time like this."

"A time like what?"

"You won me. I'm . . . your sex slave, right?"

"Wait a minute." She held him at arm's length. "I want the date."

"You *want* to get up at four in the morning for a balloon ride?"

"You did book one, right?"

"Well, yeah, but . . ."

"Then, hell yes, I want it."

Jason checked his Rolex. "That gives us an hour to play and two to sleep."

"No, that gives us three to sleep . . . in our own beds."

Kira raised Jason's jaw to shut his mouth. "Balloon ride. Attic picnic. Tomorrow. Meet you here in three hours."

"Nuts."

"For breakfast? Sure. Bring some."

"You're killing me here."

"Don't make me use my wand, Goddard."

AT four the next morning, bright-eyed and packing a wallop in black jeans and an off-the-shoulder sweater, one turquoise bra strap showing, Kira carried binoculars, a hamper, and a black wool cape.

Cranky and sleep-deprived, Jason forgot his car keys and had to go back for them.

"Yeesh," Kira said as he crabbed about it. "Nice date you're gonna make."

In the elevator she socked him. "Wake up. It's morning already."

He pulled her into his arms and rested his chin on her head. "I like you, Fitz; you're a real pain in the ass, like me. I like your body, too, right here. Sometimes I think we'd make a good coup—" Jason stopped talking.

Kira stepped from his arms. "Did you fall asleep in the middle of that sentence?"

"Yeah."

"Bad dream?" she asked.

"Scary," he said. "Nightmare scary."

"I suspected as much."

"Sorry," he said, "did I wake you?"

She took him by the hand to lead him from the elevator, and he was so tired, he surprised himself by getting into the passenger seat of his Hummer.

He tried to doze on their way to the balloon field, while Kira drove, annoyed him, and amused herself, by keeping him awake. If he didn't like her so much, Jason thought, he'd beat her.

"Bad weather for a balloon ride," the operator said. "Have to give you a rain check. I'll call next Saturday around three A.M., if it's a go."

Jason woke from another bad dream. "You're kidding. We got up this early for nothing?"

"Can't take a chance with these winds. Coming on hard winter, you know. You might want to wait until spring." The guy looked up and rubbed his hands together. "It's freezing up there."

Jason and Kira looked at each other, probably sharing the same thought; they wouldn't be together in the spring . . . not working together . . . or any other kind of together, despite his near-fatal statement in the elevator.

"Sure," Kira said. "We'll call you in the spring."

"I'm sorry," Jason said, walking her back to the car. "Our date's ruined and I've been a jerk."

"Yeah, well, that's been known to happen. But the date's not over," she said. "You're not getting out of it that easy. I've got an attic picnic coming, and I want it. I didn't pay thirty-five grand for nothing."

"Gram paid thirty-five grand."

"Oh, sure, shove that in my face. But it doesn't matter because I'm going to pay her back. We have a deal."

Jason couldn't contain his bark of laughter. "What does she get for her thirty-five grand, because I'm thinking it can't be cash."

"My firstborn."

Jason stopped walking.

"Honestly," Kira said, "she asked for my firstborn, then she corrected it to naming my firstborn after her."

"You could end up with one sissy boy on your hands."

"Okay, so my first *girl,* then, and Elizabeth is a pretty name."

"Bessie. My grandmother's name is Bessie."

"It's okay; she told me about the big family secret, that she was named after her father's mistress in a moment of wifely spite, so her father nicknamed her Bessie. But I like Elizabeth, so I said yes."

Jason tried to make sense of what Kira was saying. She knew a secret he didn't; his grandmother's secret. And she was going to have kids . . . without him.

"You didn't know your grandmother's real name?"

"I guess not, and I'm ticked that you do."

"I wanna watch the sun rise," Kira said. "Look, there's a rock where we can sit and wait."

"Nice rock. My ass hurts already. Come on. I have a better idea. Get in the Hummer."

Driving Kira back to Cloud Kiss, Jason kept thinking about giving "Elizabeth" a piece of his mind, and not just for the withheld name. It was that firstborn thing.

He knew damned well that Gram was angling for Kira's firstborn to be *her* grandchild.

"I wanted to watch the sun rise," Kira said into the silence.

"Did it rise yet?" Jason asked, indicating the darkness beyond the windshield, his hand, palm up.

"No."

"Then you haven't missed it."

"How come you're so logical all of a sudden?"

"You woke me up." He brought her to Gram's ocean-view greenhouse, an octagon garden room furnished in white whicker.

Lush with exotic plants, the scent of orchids permeating the air, six of the room's eight sides were windows. Kira had never been here before, Jason knew, because this was Gram's private wing.

"Goddard," Kira said. "*This* is awesome."

Jason pulled a velvet smocked fainting couch over to the window and invited her to lie on her side facing the ocean.

"Open the door so we can hear the tide," she said.

Jason cracked it open, letting in a fresh salty sea breeze, then he lay on the couch behind her, and pulled her against him like spoons in a drawer.

"Don't fall asleep," Kira warned, waking him.

Jason raised his head. "What? I was awake."

"Right. Mumble that again so I can be sure." She elbowed him in the gut. "*Stay* awake."

"Okay, okay. I'm awake. Annoyed, but awake." She fit perfectly against him, he thought, her head beneath his chin, her bottom exactly where it belonged.

"Look. It's beautiful."

"Yes," he said, "it is," but Jason wasn't looking at the sun, he was admiring the way the light spun Kira's hair to copper and shimmered against her skin. He sat forward to see the wonder in her eyes. He kissed her shoulder and she raised her hand to cup his cheek.

Jason closed his eyes and opened his senses to the moment.

There was indeed something magical about Kira Fitzgerald, and he decided to allow himself, for this one day, to accept whatever she was willing to give, and to give whatever she asked.

It was a date, after all, not a lifetime.

One day, all theirs. A day to make memories.

Twenty-three

GRAM stepped into her greenhouse room and stopped.

"Bessie!" Kira said, pulling her legs from under her. "Is it okay if we watch the sunrise from here? We didn't disturb you, did we?"

"Disturb me? No, I've been up for hours. I'll check my plants later."

"Stay, watch it with us," Kira said, patting the spot beside her, and Jason could see his grandmother was touched by her invitation.

When he nodded, Gram joined them.

They watched in silence, him with a hand on each woman's shoulder, the one who'd raised him and the woman she'd handpicked for him. Too bad she'd done it for nothing.

It wasn't Gram's fault that he wasn't ready, but he appreciated the attempt. If he weren't going back to hockey . . . well, Kira had been an inspired choice.

"What happened to the hot-air balloon?" Gram asked when there was nothing more to see but the ocean completing its endless cycle, mesmerizing in its own basic and primitive way.

"The balloon popped," Kira said. "I'm hungry," she told Jason. "What time's the picnic?"

"I didn't plan a breakfast menu."

"I'll get Rose in the kitchen to pack breakfast instead of lunch," his grandmother said. "Go on up. You'll like the attic, dear," she said to Kira. "It's been cleaned to Jason's specifications."

"Oh, no, I don't want to explore a clean attic, I want to rummage."

"There's plenty to rummage in," Gram said. "But now it has a year's less dust on it. Go and explore to your heart's content. Have fun, both of you."

His grandmother watched them get on the elevator. He was going to have to have a talk with that woman.

"She's gonna hate it when you go back to hockey, isn't she," Kira said as the elevator began to rise.

"She'll miss me, but she wants me to be happy. I've always known that."

"She's something."

"Something special," Jason said, thinking the description fit both the women with whom he'd shared the sunrise.

"I see we're skipping to the fifth floor," Kira said. "So what's on the fourth?"

"Staff quarters."

"A whole floor? Cool. And what's in the wing opposite Gram's?"

"The summer bedrooms."

Kira did a double take.

"The way the wind blows off the ocean," Jason said, explaining, "the rooms in that part of the house are cooler. No air-conditioning in 1889 when this was built, don't forget. Those rooms are decorated with lighter fabrics and softer colors, too, and the beds are made with coverlets, not heavy blank—"

"You're not freaking kidding. Your ancestors switched bedrooms with the seasons?"

"Yep."

"Where's the nursery?"

"This is not a nursery picnic," Jason said.

"Another day?"

"Maybe, but don't count on it."

"Why are you afraid of the nursery?"

"I'm not af— Because Gram's been trying to get me to fill it for a few years now. Her heart would give out if I took a woman there."

Kira pushed him against the wall and fell against him. "Rabbit hole," she declared, rescuing them both from the dangerous direction he'd been going, and giving his hands permission to wander.

The elevator opened on the fifth floor, too soon for him, not soon enough for her.

"I've never seen such a huge, bright attic," she said.

Jason examined it as if for the first time. The walls, whitewashed, the sunburst windows plentiful, the morning light streaming into a world of faded color and ageless chaos.

High-button shoes stood on steamer trunks. Dress forms wore corsets. Bric-a-brac, sandwich glass, and rare bronzes filled curio cabinets from several eras. Rare paintings sat stacked in corners. Gargoyles and angels guarded fringed Victorian lamps and fussy Victorian furniture.

Reverent and silent, Kira started a rocking horse to galloping. She picked up a glass-eyed china doll in a blue dress, rocked it in her arms, then placed it in a wicker doll carriage. She found a miniature quilt, rubbed it against her cheek, eyes closed—shooting Jason's heart with arrows—and placed it over the doll.

She pushed a pricey nineties perambulator his way and said, "Get in."

He didn't need to ask why she was enchanted. He'd

always felt the same when he was touching the past. He simply never expected to find anyone else who did.

"These are memories," she said, as if she'd been in his head. "Yours, your ancestors'. I don't know where to start."

"Tell me if you're looking for something special. I used to like to play up here."

She perked up at that. "Really. Where? Where was your fort?"

"Guess."

"So if I show you something, you'll share the memory that comes with it, whether it's yours or someone else's?"

"Rabbit-hole deal, and as usual, nothing leaves this room."

When breakfast arrived, they were caught sitting, Indian-style, beneath a mountain of furniture that had once, indeed, been his fort. Two hours had passed like a blink.

Cloud Kiss sat on the point at Lands End where Bellevue Avenue met Ocean Drive, so they were able to view the sea from a different angle than in the greenhouse downstairs.

Here the ocean met the rocks in a thunderous blast, like in one of those nature CDs that lulled the senses. They sat on a hemp patio rug and fed each other before a sunburst window, while watching nature's dance, feasting on crepes filled with fruit compote and marscapone cheese, medallions of ham with poached eggs, assorted fruit, and diet cola.

When they finished breakfast, Jason pulled Kira to sit between his knees with a view toward the room. "What do you see?"

"If this were my house," she said, "I'd put a huge four-poster bed in that corner and make it up with clean sheets and a bright quilt. Vickie has a room in her grandmother's attic like that."

"You mean you'd get rid of all this junk?"

"Of course not! We'd— I'd keep it, and I'd use the room as an escape, a place for romantic trysts."

"With whom would you tryst?" Jason asked.

"My husband, of course."

"You'd take that chance? After the Penis, I mean?"

Kira leaned way back and raised her chin, so they were looking at each other upside down. "This is a rabbit hole, don't go getting logical on me."

"Right, sorry." Jason started to speak and stopped.

Kira turned to face him. "What?"

He shrugged. "Okay, this is a rabbit hole, so let's say I'm your lover and we . . . tryst."

"Not my lover, my *husband*."

"Sorry, that word is not in my vocabulary. Besides, some people—not me—actually think one person can fill both roles."

"Not me, either," Kira said, "but let's play make-believe and say you *are* both, and we've come up here to escape the children. I want children."

"Fine. This is a rabbit hole. Gram will be happy to baby-sit. But if this were not a rabbit hole, I would need a nap before our tryst. I'm sorry," Jason said, "but I'm bushed."

"Oh, no, you don't," Kira said, taking her wand from her pocket and pointing it his way. "No nap on our date!"

"Okay, okay!" Jason raised a hand in surrender. "Then let's do some more exploring." Watching her bend over something should wake him right up.

They found Gram's wedding dress, and her wedding pictures, which made Jason realize that Kira could become soft and squishy romantic.

After Gram's wedding album, they continued rummaging, and Jason found what he'd been looking for, in the first place, a trunk full of his great-grandmother's quilts.

Kira went nuts.

She made him lay them out, one atop the other, but not before she crawled around on each—that sassy ass of hers keeping him and Harvey full awake—as she inspected the workmanship and design.

When she'd finish one, she'd ask him to spread out another.

The sun made its way around the house, slanting in from different windows. When she had examined all the quilts, Kira sighed with satisfaction and flopped onto her back in the center of a mattress made of quilts. "I'm in heaven."

"May I join you?"

She opened her arms.

Jason couldn't think of anything more beautiful than Kira atop those quilts, her red curls vibrant against their faded beauty, her body and arms open to his. Kira the witch, magic in every way, sandwiched between his past and his . . . future. . . .

"The auction date ends here," Jason said, falling to his knees beside her. "This is just you and me in a rabbit hole, got it?" *Goddammit, Goddard,* he thought. *Are you in trouble or are you in trouble?*

Kira nodded, her eyes as bright and multifaceted as emeralds.

As Jason sank into the quilts, he assured himself that this infatuation with Kira could be cured by going back to the NHL.

Relieved he knew the solution, and reminded that this was simply one day in the rabbit hole, a thirty-five-thousand-dollar day, he enveloped her in his embrace, rested his head on hers, and yawned hugely.

Kira yawned as well. "Cut that out!" she said, shoving his arm with little force. "It's contagious."

"Face it, we got up too early this morning," he said.

She threw a leg over his, one of her knees nestling softly against his groin.

Jason sighed in contentment. Good, she felt good in his arms, but he was almost too relaxed to respond sexually. Nevertheless, Harvey made a token attempt at rising to the occasion, but Kira's sudden soft snore against Jason's chest pretty much killed the big guy's enthusiasm.

Jason gave himself over to the drowsiness that had been dogging him since four that morning.

When he woke, he had himself a handful of breast and Kira had a handful of Harvey. He didn't know when she'd slipped her hand in his jeans, though he did remember dreaming about her gloving him, but Harvey was one happy camper.

Jason looked to see if Kira was awake, but she must have dozed off again.

To give her her fair share, he slipped a hand beneath her sweater, unhooked her bra, and fingered a nipple, tracing and tweaking it until she sighed and worked Harvey a bit before drifting off again.

Jason chuckled, managed to raise her sweater enough to take one of those pouting puppies into his mouth, and gave himself over to the pleasure of suckling her. With no other woman, not even with the hottest of starlets, had he been as elated, granite-hardened, and oddly enough, soothed, in the way he was now with Kira.

In her sleep Kira whimpered and shifted to his ministrations, especially when he took to fingering the neglected nubbin while he made a meal of the first with his lips and tongue.

When Harvey began to rise and throb in her hand, Kira roused enough to realize what was happening.

She soothed the big guy in the same slow and easy way Jason feasted on her, in a leisurely attempt to milk every nuance of pleasure from the extraordinary experience, as if by mutual agreement, their play should go on forever.

Jason had never felt so free and uninhibited. Time stopped, rules slipped away, and the bubble in which they pleasured each other floated above the earth, impervious to disturbance or fracture.

The situation required no rush . . . no need to act the stud, bed the hottest babe, carve a new notch in his bedpost, or keep score for a locker-room brag-fest. No whining demands or kinky requirements, no bimbo with a list of all-star studs with which to compete, just him and Kira, and foreplay at its finest.

They had all the time in the world. Well, not quite; his body's pulsing mandate was difficult to ignore.

The more remarkably keen the pleasure, the more Kira whimpered and arched, moaned and begged, the more Harvey wept and clamored for release.

When her hips rose in a rhythm too perfect to be denied, he undid her jeans and found a pair of pale turquoise bikinis. Geez, he could've come just looking at her, at Kira, visible through a shimmer of sheer turquoise perfection.

He slipped a hand beneath the gossamer fabric and found Kira slick, swollen, and budding with need.

"Yes!" she said on a breathless whisper, and he worked her with his thumb, plunged deeper into her, and her hips rose and she moaned, and Harvey wept again with need.

Jason found her perfect center, her sweet spot, and stroked it slow, switched breasts, adjusting his pull on her nipple to match the tempo of her hips and his strokes.

Kira gasped as he made her pleasure escalate, and she became more sensitive to the slightest of strokes. He brought her nearly to the brink twice, to the pinnacle of release, but not quite. She cursed when he slowed, made her rest, then he made her rise again.

Harvey was having the time of his life, getting lushly petted and lavishly woman-handled, coming often to the brink as well, but Jason remained strong.

He sank into a miasma of bliss, however, when Kira cupped his balls as she manipulated the big guy, a sensation he loved but rarely experienced. He wondered if she sensed his needs or if they enjoyed the same stimulating play, but this was not the time to ask.

When he slipped his hand from her slick center, Kira squeaked, or perhaps *shrieked* was the better word, and Jason chuckled as he rose to his knees, knelt between her legs, and slipped her jeans down her hips. He nuzzled her panties, lush with her musky scent, then he slipped those off as well and lifted her hips to his mouth for a feast of another kind, an unprecedented picnic of the sexual variety.

He stopped and waited. She opened her eyes.

"I'm just reminding you that this is not the auction date," he said. "This is you and me."

"Yes," Kira said, letting her head fall back, as he adored her with his mouth and brought her pleasure.

Her gasps and whimpers, each time she came, heightened Jason's pleasure as well. He'd never been driven to feast on a woman in the way he wanted to devour Kira. She was real, imperfect, sensuous as all hell, and as admittedly afraid of commitment as he was, which might perhaps be the biggest aphrodisiac of all.

After she came, and came again, and one more time, she begged for mercy, caught her breath, and took to returning the favor by giving Harvey her not-inconsiderable attention.

Her bra was still open beneath her black sweater, as proved by her budding nipples beneath the fine knit fabric.

As Jason about reached the end of his tether and Harvey was one *big* bundle of dynamite set to explode, she removed her talented hands and sat back on her heels, shaking her head.

Incredulous, Jason regarded her, unable to form a question.

She shrugged. "We *can't* ruin the quilt."

Harvey whimpered.

"The hemp rug?" Jason suggested.

"Too nice."

"Your quilt was in my bed the other day. That didn't stop—"

"New fabric; washable." She stroked the quilt the way he wanted her stroking him. "Old fabric," she said. "Fragile."

"I'll have it cleaned!" But Harvey was losing ground by the inch.

She stood on her knees. "How about my bra?"

"Huh?"

She raised her sweater over her head, pulled the iridescent turquoise bra off her shoulders, and got between his legs, her plump ripe breasts just there like shiny new toys waiting for his hands.

But when she bent to kiss his balls and nuzzle his cock, getting Harvey right back into the spirit, she took his toys with her. Then she capped the big guy with a silky C-cup, and rubbed him up and down, a study in sensual overload, while kissing Harvey's base and palming Jason's balls.

The pleasure of his release was so intense, Jason thought maybe he passed out, because he opened his eyes to find Kira grinning down at him, and he felt like he owned the freaking world . . . except for her. Kira, he did not own. He wanted her, however, the ache so deep, he was afraid to consider it.

"That was hot," she said. "I wanna come again."

Before the afternoon was over, in between finding his first pair of skates, and getting her naked, and putting his prep school hockey jersey over her amazing breasts, she got her wish . . . about five more times.

"*You* wanna come again?" she asked later, lolling on the quilts like a lazy hockey-playing cat.

"I'm a goner, Fitz. You ruined me with your greed. Twice in one afternoon is my limit."

"Oh, man, then we have to set a new record. Come on, Ice Boy, we're going for the gold."

Sometime later Jason regained slow consciousness.

"Tiago would be proud," Kira said.

Jason knew his grin was cocky, but he didn't care. "Damned if I didn't manage a hat trick."

"If you pull a hat trick in the rabbit hole, does that make you the mad hatter?" Kira asked.

"I'm mad, all right, with lust for you. Now I'm spoiled for any other woman—or at least for anybody else's underwear against Harvey's taut sensitive skin."

She flipped his limp self from side to side with a finger. "Taut my eye, he's a wrinkled marshmallow."

"Shh. He'll hear you."

She raised her chin. "Fact is . . . I'd prefer not to think

about Harvey nosing around in anybody else's underwear, if you don't mind."

"Not even his own?"

"That's different; he only sleeps there."

"Not when you're around. You've been a rude awakening, Glinda, and I mean that in a good way. In a big, embarrassing, but good way."

"Hah! Like he never did that before I came along. Please give me credit for some brains."

"Hey, I never said he was a monk."

Twenty-four

"NO," Kira said, "Harvey's not a monk, though you've been 'technically' celibate for a while. What happens when you go back to hockey?"

Jason sat up and rubbed the back of his neck. "I honestly don't know," he said. "I can only think of one woman at this moment that I'd like to . . ." He recognized the sudden heat and hesitation in Kira's eyes because it mirrored his own. "I don't know."

"Maybe that's because of the airheads you'll be going back to," she said. "What *did* you see in that leggy blonde who kept bidding on you?"

Jason was grateful to Kira for steering them from the emotional danger zone. "Leggy blonde? Oh, Tonya?" Jason grinned. "Whose panties do you think Tiago was flying like a flag?"

"I don't believe you."

"Tonya follows teams and picks out players every season. Once it was me, yesterday it was a New England tight end, today it's Santiago the Stealer. She was trying to make Tiago jealous by bidding on me."

"Well, I'm glad she didn't win you. I'd like to think she wouldn't have had quite the same date."

Jason felt the insult like a slap. "I told you, this wasn't part of it. The auction date ended when I climbed on the quilts."

"Right. Sorry." Kira's stomach growled, a physical reminder of the real world beyond the rabbit hole. "Too bad it's over," she said, but she raised a victorious fistful of silk turquoise with a grin. "Can't wear these home."

Jason pulled her down beside him, loathe to let the day go, to let her go. He grappled her for her underwear. "I want a souvenir," he said, "and turquoise is my favorite color."

"What do you want with them, you kinky man?"

He kissed her nose. "I figured I'd frame them."

"For our rabbit-hole retreat in the attic, you mean?"

"Ours? I thought that was *your* trysting place," he said, putting a bit of distance between them.

"Mine or yours, doesn't matter," she said, "we can both have one."

"Good. You scared me."

"Don't worry, Goddard, your commitment phobia is safe with me," Kira said. "I'll keep it on the altar of sanity where I keep my own. Help me fold these quilts and put them away."

Kira didn't seem to have any difficulty leaving their amazing day behind, unlike him, which bothered Jason.

She shoved her underwear in her pocket for the elevator ride downstairs, and he talked her into joining him in his shower, because it was bigger.

That she fell for his shoddy reasoning, or agreed despite that, meant she was up for a bit more playtime, which was good, and bad. Jason wished he could get his hands on a patch to slap on his arm, to help him kick his addiction to her. A "Kira" patch.

An hour later he was elated, sated, and drying her off, because she could barely stand. "I'm going to remember this," he said, "every time I step into a locker room shower from now on, no matter what state or country I'm in."

Jason's words knocked Kira from her sensual haze. She grabbed her clothes and stepped around him. "You can leave me the hell out of your locker-room fantasies, Ice Boy."

"Wait." Jason followed her, buff and sated, and half of her wanted to jump him again. "Where are you going?" he asked.

"I'm going to bed," she said. "I'm beat."

"What's in your bed that I don't have in mine?"

"My squishy pillow."

"You're kidding."

"There are some things commitment-phobics are allowed to become attached to," she said. "Pillows are one of them."

"And turquoise underwear," Jason said. "I'm pretty attached to that. I'll probably miss the puck every time I see a flash of turquoise in the stands."

Kira stopped. "You know, Goddard, I get it. Enough already. You're not staying. You're going back to hockey. Fine. Maybe you need to remind yourself, but you don't need to remind me."

"Okay," he said, backing away from her. "Geez, you got grouchy all of a sudden."

"Yeah, right." He'd probably screw every "ho" waiting outside the arena after he went back to hockey, but when he was in the shower, he was gonna be thinking of her? "Great. Just freaking great."

On Sunday Kira was still in a mood to stay away from the clueless jock, so she went shopping. At a local thrift store she found a turquoise scarf and a great pair of turquoise sandals. At the Brick Marketplace she found a sale and bought a clingy knit top, a low-cut silk top, and an awesome suit, all in shades of turquoise.

Not that she wanted Jason to stay at the foundation, she just wanted him to know what he'd be leaving behind when he went back to hockey.

On Monday she wore a black suit softened by a sheer turquoise top, her turquoise bra like an enticing shadow beneath, with a flowered scarf, largely turquoise. Gram saw her as she was leaving for work and offered her a pair of exquisite butterfly earrings, with turquoise, white, yellow, and pink stones that brought the outfit's colors together.

"Please tell me these are fake," Kira said clipping them on her ears and checking them in Bessie's mirror.

"Of course they are, dear," Gram said.

Kira kissed her cheek. "You're a terrible liar, Bessie Hazard," she said, and Bessie laughed. But Kira was guessing that aquamarines and topaz couldn't be too dangerous to borrow.

Jason froze when he saw her. "Glad to see you're coming out of your cocoon, Fitz," he said. "Great turquoise scarf."

Shut up, Ice Boy, she thought, *or I'll gag you with it.*

Working side by side, yet remaining emotionally and physically apart, they chose the Castleton Court ballroom for the Open Arms event, partly for its homey painted-leather wallcovering, and partly because its huge corner windows begged for a twenty-foot Christmas tree.

More than a hundred sets of potential parents had registered to attend, and calls were still coming in.

Sister Margaret dutifully explained to the boys not to expect miracles. None of them would go home with parents *this* Christmas. But Kira sensed anticipation, nevertheless.

They hung family-inspired Christmas decorations: a family watching a train beneath a Christmas tree, children in their beds with images of sugarplums, a family of carolers.

The boys set up the ballroom with chairs and a stage of risers with curtained space, behind and beside it, for props and dressing rooms. Sister Margaret held dress rehearsal there to get the boys acclimated. "I want them to see those empty chairs," she told Kira and Jason, "and realize that people who *want* children will be watching, to give them the courage to perform."

"Or scare them to death," Kira said. "The poor things."

"Speaking of poor things," Sister said to her, "they chose you, by popular vote, to play Mary in the Nativity scene. Will you?"

"Please," Travis said, tugging Kira's hand and employing the "look" he'd used when he'd asked her to adopt him.

"Please?" Zane said, his anxious gaze guileless and hopeful.

"Yeesh, talk about pressure," Kira said. "Will I have to memorize lines?"

"Nope," Travis said. "You just gotta act like a mother and hold a baby." He made a rocking motion with his arms to show her. "You know, the way you hold Zane at hockey practice."

"What is he, the director?" Jason whispered in Kira's ear.

She elbowed him. "I'll do it," Kira said, ignoring Jason's chuckled, "Pushover."

"And you'll be Joseph," Travis told Jason.

Jason's smile vanished. "Do I have a choice?" he asked. "*Kira* had a choice."

"Nope," Travis said. "Joseph watches over the baby like you watch over us at hockey. You're a natural," the kid said, stealing Jason's favorite affirmation.

Kira knocked Jason with her shoulder. "Pushover."

"Thank you, Sister," Jason said. "Do you give these kids lessons in salesmanship, or what?"

"Travis comes by it naturally," Sister said, watching him charm his friends. "He might make a success of sales someday, like cars . . . or swampland in Florida." The nun shrugged. "I'm guessing it could go either way."

Kira and Jason both chuckled, because they knew she was right.

"I guess we have to wear costumes," Kira said.

"Of course," Sister said. "Right this way."

Jason turned toward the exit with longing, but Kira tugged on his arm and dragged him backstage.

Her costume was turquoise, of all things, and when Sister left, Kira whispered to Jason that she knew exactly what to wear beneath it.

Jason was too busy scowling to take the bait. "Yeah, well, I'm wearing a burgundy freaking dress and I don't give a rat's tail what I wear under it."

"*Nothing,*" Kira whispered, "would be a turn-on."

Jason raised his head, and Kira was pretty sure that his radar was working again.

In the dining room that night, Jason ranted about his veil, "or whatever the hell they call that *thing* I have to wear on my head," going on about his dress, his itchy beard, entertaining Kira and his grandmother through dinner.

"Stop laughing," Jason said to Kira. "It's not funny. *You* have to act like a virgin!"

Kira raised her chin. "Do you have reason to believe it'll be an act?"

Gram's face was as red as her grandson's.

THE day of the event arrived in a flurry of stage fright, bad temper, and negative behavior . . . and the boys weren't much better. As far as they were concerned, the best part was that Sister had allowed the "angels" among them to choose the kind they wanted to be.

The Angel of Christmas Present was a maroon dinosaur named Larry.

Brad Davis, the bully Jason made captain of the hockey team, played Scrooge, an investment banker.

"You're cheap, Scrooge," Larry said. "You never give money to St. Anthony's at Christmas!" he shouted, and fell off the stage.

Scrooge helped the beached dinosaur get up.

Larry readjusted his head, and cleared his throat. "You have money, but nobody to love, Scrooge. Wouldn't you like to adopt a little boy and have Christmas every day?"

The curtain closed for a scene change.

The Angel of Christmas Future, a caped wizard in borrowed eyeglasses, blindly flattened Scrooge's gravestone and said his piece facing the donkey. "Scrooge, if you don't mend your ways, and find generosity and love, you'll die alone, and little boys like Tiny Tim will have a sad future."

Tiny Tim, played by Zane, pulled a red wagon piled with empty soda cans across the stage.

The curtains closed for a longer scene change.

Travis, the hockey-playing Angel of Christmas Past, brought Scrooge far back in time, to the Nativity. "This is a real family," Travis said. "See Mary trying to shush her crying baby, and Joseph making it shut up for her."

Okay, Kira thought, so Travis ad-libbed a little, but the screaming baby sort of made it necessary, until Jason took it away from her and patted it against his shoulder.

"See Joseph caring for a boy not his own," Travis said, "a boy who'll always try to be good, and make his new parents proud."

"I have to pee," said a four-year-old sheep, so Kira took him, while everyone waited for the play to continue.

Jason gave Kira a thumbs-up when she returned, and she gave him one right back. He'd put their borrowed baby to sleep.

To end the performance, a heavenly host of angels filed onto the stage to stand on both sides of the stable: Robots, cowboys, motorcycle and linebacker angels, and one yellow bear angel with a jar of honey in his backpack, sang two altered, off-key verses of "All I Want for Christmas Is a Fa-mi-ly."

When they finished singing, the children bowed to a standing ovation, cheers, and a couple of whistles.

Afterward, the boys made a beeline for the Christmas tree, where wrapped presents from Gram waited for each of them.

Potential parents watched the boys, read the program with pictures and bios, and gravitated toward the back to speak with Sister Margaret. Others went right for the boys. One couple left after learning that baby Jesus was not up for adoption.

Travis entertained several potentials, while Zane leaned on Melody's leg and watched his twin. "He won't go without me," Zane said. "He'll take me, soon as he finds the right ones."

"I'm glad we know the real Travis," Jason said. "Why does he think he has to act like Mister Cool when he's such a great kid?"

"He's scared," Kira said. "Can't you tell?"

"Scared but brave," Zane said. "Braver than me, but it's okay; we're *going* together."

When Travis and Zane *were* adopted, which seemed wonderfully possible, Kira realized she'd lose something vital in her life.

Jason questioned her tears with a look.

"Hope," she said on a shrug. "It's all around us."

And he nodded, looking like she felt . . . lost.

Donations followed the event, but it was the adoption applications that proved their success. Sister Margaret, however, would not give false hope, until all applicants had been screened.

Jason's Wednesday and Friday afternoon hockey practices had dwindled to fourteen regulars, boys who were willing to work hard at learning to play the game, Travis among them.

It snowed the Friday following the Open Arms event, and Zane came as usual, but he seemed sad and wistful. "Jason," Kira called, hoping Zane's idol could cheer him.

"Hey, Zane," Jason said, high-fiving him. "Your brother's skating great, isn't he?"

"Does it feel like flying?" Zane asked.

A simple question, but Melody's heart tripped, and Jason cleared his throat and sat beside them. "It does, Zane, until you fall and smack your face on the ice."

Zane giggled.

"Wait here for a minute," Jason said. "I'll be right back."

It took Jason ten minutes to return, but when he did, Kira and Zane both straightened, because he skated toward them. "Come here," he said, "both of you."

When Kira and Zane got to the edge of the ice, Jason turned his back on them. "Kira, put Zane on my shoulders."

"No! You're going to ruin your knee. Are you sure you can do this?"

"You know I've been practicing. The knee's much better. It really is. My doctor and my physical therapist agree. Wanna go for a skate around the rink, Zane?"

"Yes!"

"A short spin," Jason cautioned the boy, "'cause Kira's right; I don't know how much my knee can take."

"Okay, Jason."

Kira sat Zane on Jason's lowered shoulders, cringing when Jason rose, but his knee seemed fine.

He grasped Zane's ankles. "Now, Zane, lean forward so your chin's on my head, and grab my vest by the collar."

Zane did everything Jason told him.

Standing next to them, Kira could feel the excitement radiating off both of them, Jason as wired as the boy.

Kira laughed when Jason kicked off, and Zane screamed, as if he were flying, then she sobbed before she could stop herself. Travis skated over and took her hand. His grin must have tasted like salt, Kira thought, because his eyes were as full as hers.

Zane laughed with Jason's every move, especially his turns, but each time Jason spun, Kira bit her lip, afraid they'd go down. Yes, she was worried about Jason's knee, but she was more worried that Zane would find this one experience so exhilarating that he would become depressed over his handicap.

"I'm gonna go skate with them," Travis said, and he was off, while Kira wondered where her skates were.

Jason, his grin as wide as Zane's, was having an awesome time. The short spin he planned turned into a half hour, Zane the center of attention, so high in the air, he waved to her over everyone's heads every few minutes.

Kira loved Jason for that. Not that she was *in* love with him, precisely, though she might as well admit that she was in love with Travis and Zane.

But as for Jason and her, their rabbit-hole play meant nothing. They'd become quite close, physically and emotionally, though they hadn't had sex, not quite, but she wanted to. Who wouldn't want to, with a tender and generous lover like Jason.

He adored women. Women adored him. She was just another besotted fool . . . except that he only ever danced with her. She wondered if *he'd* noticed that. Though every event they attended seemed like a date, they were not dating, they were working.

Yes, they sometimes shared a bed, but they had only ever made one real promise to each other . . . and that was *not* to make any promises.

"Fitzgerald," she said to herself as she watched Jason and the twins. "Get a grip. That smooth-talkin' jock is the Big Bad Wolf of the fast-and-rich party set, and you're Little Miss Muffet with an empty tuffet. He's out of your league."

Jason Goddard was a world-class charmer, a jock, the kind of guy she detested, the kind she was, unfortunately, attracted to.

"He creates fantasies," she said. "This is one of them."

Kira wanted to go and skate with them. She just needed to keep things in perspective. She and Jason were not a couple, and the boys were not theirs.

"Right," she said as she went for her skates.

Twenty-five

"HEY, Fitz, you skate better every day," Jason said after a few minutes of watching her strut her stuff, as glad as the twins that she'd joined them. The dozen other boys, who'd abandoned their sticks to entertain Zane, became more animated as they vied with each other to make Kira laugh.

"I practice a couple of times a week on my own, plus you make me skate at practically every practice; what do you want?"

"What do I want?" Jason said, considering his options as he skated in a circle around her. "Hmm. Let me think about that."

"I'm getting dizzy!" Zane shrieked.

"Careful," Kira said, "I don't think you want him barfing on your head."

Jason winced and looked up. "You okay there, buddy?"

"Skate straight for a while," Zane said.

"Will do." Jason skated backward and winked at Kira. "Can I tell you what I want after hockey practice?"

"That would be now," she said. "I think I hear the bus."

"Okay, boys, that's it for today," Jason said, skating over and setting Zane down.

Zane threw his arms tight around Jason's neck, that chest-tug Jason had felt at Travis's adoption request turning to a full-blown ache.

"Thank you," Zane said, pulling away, almost before Jason was ready.

Travis hugged him, too, activating the ache's painful twin.

Jason ruffled the boys' hair and swallowed. "We'll set aside some time to do it again next week, okay?"

"Okay!" the identical carrottops said in sync.

"Boys!" Jason shouted, for more than the sake of being heard. "Get your gear together. Here's Mr. Peebles."

Jason watched the boys go, glad to get Kira alone. He took her hand, seeking the comfort of her touch, and skated her away. "I want," Jason said, slowing, and pulling Kira into the circle of his arms, "what I've wanted for a long time, what I hope you want."

They waltzed in place, her length bedeviling his. "I think we've danced around the subject often enough to know," he said, waiting for her gaze to meet his, and when it did, hope flared in him. "Screw celibacy," he said. "I want inside you, Fitz, and I hope to hell you want me there."

Kira raised her arms around his neck, her cheek against his ear, her sigh impossible to read.

"I hope I didn't catch you in my headlights," Jason said, "by putting it out there, but I want *you* to decide."

Kira nodded and Jason's heart about stopped.

He pulled from her arms to see her face. "Did that nod mean, 'Yes, I understand?' or 'Yes, I *want*'? Can you spell it out for me?" Jason said. "Use the words. I'm afraid to hope I got the right signal."

"Yes, I want," Kira said. "I want you inside of me."

Jason released the heart-tripping breath he'd been holding and brought her against him. "Half an hour? My whirlpool?"

Kira smiled. "Yeah."

They skated toward the bench, his arm and focus possessive. He helped her remove her skates, before he removed his own.

When they stepped outside, anticipation heating his blood, Jason was shocked to step in snow up to his calves. "I'm pretty sure," he said, "that these are white-out conditions."

"And I'm pretty sure," Kira said, "there's a bus full of boys over there."

"I was trying ignore the sound of wheels spinning," Jason said, sighing, as he went for his cell phone.

It rang before he could dial.

"They're warning drivers off the road," his grandmother said. "Sister Margaret called and asked if we could keep the boys overnight."

The rowdy boys hanging out the bus windows gave Jason an idea of what they would be in for. "Keep them?" he repeated, sounding stupid, he knew, but his libido had just short-circuited.

"Mr. Peebles can stay in one of my guest rooms," Gram said, "but you and Kira will have to take the boys."

Jason snapped his cell phone shut. "They're staying the night. I'd cry, but they'd make fun of me."

Kira's eyes dimmed. "Oh."

"Yeah," Jason said. "Oh."

"Do you have enough bedrooms?" Kira asked.

"I can't do that to Gram. Plus the rooms would need childproofing. And we'd never keep track of the boys, short of patrolling the halls all night. For everybody's peace, and for safety and supervision, I'm thinking the boys should camp out on my living-room floor."

"*Your* living room, with more bronze nudes than a French museum? Let's leave their innocence intact, shall we, and bed them down on the floor in my living room."

"Makes sense," he said. "Piece of cake, right?"

"I wish. They've worked up quite a sweat."

"Please," Jason said, "you're reminding me of the sweat I'd planned for *us* to work up. Your point?"

"Showers. While I look into feeding them, *you* have to supervise the boys' showers, which shouldn't be difficult in your bathroom. I'm thinking they could shower, three or four at a time."

"That is *so* not the shower I planned."

"Yeah, well, get over it, Ice Boy."

"Are you over it," Jason asked, "so soon?"

"No," Kira said with a grin, "but I'm trying to rise to the occasion."

"Funny," Jason said, "I stopped doing that the minute we stepped outside."

Kira patted his cheek. "Cute. You get them off the bus, and I'll see what Rose has in the way of food, because we have enough provisions in our kitchen to feed two chipmunks and a field mouse."

"Fitz," Jason said, catching her arm. "For the record, we would have had a hell of a night."

"Magic," she said, turning to trudge through the snow toward the house.

Jason went over, raised a hand for Peebles to stop spinning his wheels, and boarded the bus. When he told the boys they were staying, the unruly horde gave a resounding cheer.

Half an hour later Jason had stripped the five youngest, their sweaty clothes in a pile. "Travis, Larry, Chet, and Grady, into the shower. Zane, you get the tub." Jason removed his shoe brace and put him in. "Brad, you're bath captain. Watch them."

Jason got out towels, soap, and shampoo, heard the rush of his tub jets, and Zane's giggle. Smiling, Jason handed Brad the supplies and went to find Kira.

She was trying to fit another casserole dish into a full oven.

"They're naked and their clothes stink," he said.

"T-shirts," she said, "and socks, and turn up the heat. If

you don't have enough shirts and socks, some of mine will fit the little ones."

"How maternal of you."

"How big poor family of me," Kira said. "Put their clothes in a pillowcase and send them down to the kitchen. Gracie's gonna wash and dry them for morning. Do you have a blow-dryer?"

Jason perked up. "Sounds kinky. What do you have in mind?"

"Drying the boys hair, you horny beast. Do you have one?"

"A horn, yes, and it's lonely."

"There's a blow-dryer on the countertop in my bathroom. If you have one, set two of the older boys to drying hair."

"Check," Jason said. "What are we having for dinner?"

"Everything Rose had in the refrigerator."

"Fair enough."

Kira wiped her hands on her apron. "How many kids are clean?"

"Er, I'll check."

Another set of boys was in the shower, one of them trying to fill the sink across the room with the hand-held shower. "Cut that out," Jason said, disconnecting it.

Zane sat on the toilet seat wrapped in a towel watching a volcano of suds erupt.

Jason stepped into the suds and turned off his tub jets. "What'd you put in there to make the suds?"

"The shampoo fell in," Zane said.

"I hate when that happens," Jason said on a grin, wrapping Zane in a huge, thick bath towel and picking him up. "Brad?" he yelled. "You're supposed to be supervising, here."

Brad returned and went to work cleaning the suds.

Jason found Chet and Travis wrestling naked and wet on his bed. He tossed Zane into the fray with a promise of clothes and retribution.

The older boys, waiting for their showers, were examining Jason's bronze nudes with eager fingers.

Kira came in on Jason's heels. "I don't believe it," she said, hands on hips. "Go watch the food, Jason. Okay, boys, in the bathroom."

"Where's Travis," Jason called after them, but no one answered.

Jason went through Kira's apartment into the hall, and found a wet towel by the elevator. "Great," he said, hitting the Down button. "The kid's naked and lost in fifty rooms."

Twenty minutes later Jason returned to the kitchen with Travis wrapped in a blanket.

"I found Gram," Travis said. "And boy, was she surprised."

"I'll bet," Kira said with a grin.

The boys sat at the table, clean, dressed in T-shirts and floppy socks. It was a tight fit—some sat on stools, hassocks, and such—but like locusts, they ate anything not charred, except for the eggplant casserole. Kira picked up a black piece of . . . something, and shoved it in Jason's face. "You were supposed to watch the food."

"I had to find Travis, didn't I?"

Kira threw a T-shirt and socks at him.

"I raided your underwear drawer," she said, raising Jason's brows.

"Yeah, man," Brad said. "Thanks. Me and, er, the big guy were cold."

"What is that?" Kira asked. "Some kind of testosterone code you're all born with?"

Jason high-fived Brad, dressed Travis, and sat to eat. Kira gave the boy a chicken leg and macaroni and cheese. Him, she gave a congealed chunk of eggplant. "Yum," Jason said.

After she scooped coffee ice cream between chocolate-chip cookies to make ice cream sandwiches for dessert, and everyone had their fill, Kira sent the boys to play in the hall to work off their excess energy.

"Don't touch the buttons on the elevator," she told them, "or step inside, do you hear me? And don't open any of the doors off this hall. Disobey, and you can listen to Jason snore like a foghorn all night."

Zane tugged on her sleeve. "How do you know he snores?"

Jason watched Kira's freckles disappear. "I can hear him from my room."

"Wow."

"What *can* we do in the hall?" Travis asked.

"Look out at the snow; have a race . . . hey, you're in stocking feet, run and slide." And they were off.

While they played, Kira laid out fourteen amazing quilts—gorgeous, original works of art—thrilled they'd keep the boys warm. Some were squares, diamonds, circles, forming patterns; others depicted scenes: a lush green woodland; a winter cottage, smoke rising from the chimney; a spring garden, a city beneath a night sky with a quarter moon and stars.

The quilt Kira had given him was different. Each square revealed something about her, a classroom, cheerleading, her family, witchcraft. In the bottom corner a baseball bat in a red circle with a red line through it. No baseball players, it said, or no jocks. Some squares filled him with questions.

"They're beautiful," he said, "as vibrant as paintings."

"I'll take that as a compliment."

"I like the way you signed them."

Kira straightened. "Where do you see my signature?"

"It's the butterfly in the left corner of each, right?"

Kira's gaze softened. "You're the first to figure that out." She let the last quilt float to the rug with a smile, stuck her head out her front door, and called the boys inside for tooth-brushing and such. Once they were all snug in quilts, she turned off the light and lit the vanilla candle.

Jason sat on the sofa, opposite Kira for propriety's sake,

his stocking feet crossed on her coffee table, enjoying the peace, watching her enjoy the peace.

The boys giggled a bit, jockeyed for position, a few snored, or faked it, someone mentioned snorting pigs, then silence. Jason began sidling Kira's way, and Zane sat up.

"What's the matter, baby?" she said, going down and stroking his hair.

"I can't hear Jason snoring," Zane said.

"I'm here," Jason said, back on his side of the sofa. "I'm not asleep yet."

"Oh. Today was nice, and tonight, too, but . . ." Zane's voice cracked, and he swallowed convulsively. "Everything will be . . . the other way again . . . tomorrow."

Kira lifted Zane on her lap, quilt and all, and tucked his head beneath her chin like at hockey practice. She stroked his brow and let her gaze settle on each child in turn.

> *"Children in plight,*
> *Peace in the night.*
> *Let your sorrow*
> *Take fast flight.*
> *Forget your gloom,*
> *Your melancholy mood,*
> *And drift in dreams*
> *Of joyful interludes."*

Zane curled his small hand against Kira's breast. "That was nice," he said, his nose against her neck. "You smell good." He sighed and closed his eyes.

Travis sat up to watch Kira and his brother with a longing Jason couldn't ignore. He cleared his throat, caught Travis's eye, and gestured Travis over.

Travis perked up, grabbed his quilt, and climbed into Jason's lap. He scratched a small finger against Jason's chin stubble, into the dimple Jason hated, but it didn't take a minute before Travis closed his eyes and joined his twin in sleep.

While Jason appreciated the quiet, even enjoyed the small head against his chest, he found the experience of meeting Kira's gaze across the sofa, with kids in their laps, both breathtaking and frightening.

After a while they put the twins in Kira's bed.

When she tucked the blankets up to Zane's chin and kissed his brow, Zane gasped. "I . . . never been kissed good night before." He wound his arms around Kira's neck and hugged her so tight, Jason was afraid he'd strangle her.

"Me, neither," Travis said, clutching Jason's shirt, because Jason had just kissed him. "Nobody ever called me Trav, either."

"It's a good-night nickname," Jason said. "Don't tell, but Gram used to call me Jay when she kissed me good night."

The twins got tickled, tucked in, and kissed again, before Jason and Kira tore themselves away and went to the kitchen.

"Drink?" Kira offered, going for the fridge.

"Make it a double," Jason said, "straight up."

She poured him a ginger ale.

"This isn't gonna cut it." He was afraid that showering the twins with affection would only hurt them in the end.

Kira took out the chocolate sauce and a spoon.

"You still hungry?" Jason asked.

She dipped, and licked. "I'm drowning my sorrows."

"Tell me about it. I either need to get drunk or get laid."

"Not tonight, Ice Boy, I have fourteen headaches."

"Guess it's separate sofas for us."

Kira smiled. "Yeah, I saw your soaked sheets, but it was kinda fun, on the whole . . . until just now, in my room."

"Yeah," Jason said. "Domesticity always scares the crap out of me, but in there, that was the worst. Let's think about something else."

"Like?"

"Like what I had planned for tonight." He pulled her

onto his lap, took the chocolate sauce from her hand, and set it on the table.

"Hey," she said, but she quieted when he began to lick a spot of chocolate off her fingers.

"Do you have any idea what I wanted to do to you tonight?" Jason asked.

"Tell me," Kira whispered.

Twenty-six

JASON'S vivid description of how he'd planned to pleasure her made Kira shiver and cover his mouth. "Stop," she said. "I'm almost there." She abandoned him, left him wanting, and went to the other side of the table. "We should get some sleep."

"Right," Jason said, and the big guy wilted.

"Tomorrow, after the boys leave," Kira said, "let's do it, for the rest of the weekend."

"Do it?" Jason rose and went around the table. "You mean, the ultimate rabbit hole? The real thing? All weekend? I need verbal confirmation here, Fitz. This is too big a deal to get wrong. Harvey would never survive the disappointment."

"No strings," Kira said, "just two people, in the moment, giving and receiving the ultimate pleasure."

"Because you need to get over your jilt?" Jason asked, taking her into his arms.

She kissed his ear. "Because I need to get laid," she whispered, warming him.

"Yeah," Jason said. "I hear you. A-plus for your verbal skills. I need the same, desperately."

"That's true. You're in worse shape than I am," Kira said. "It'll be like . . . therapy."

Jason chuckled at her justification. "Right, mutual therapy, good for both of us. The ultimate therapy."

"Okay, then," she said. "After the bus leaves tomorrow, we're gonna spend the rest of the weekend having wild, hot, no-strings sex. Hot damn!"

"I couldn't agree more." Jason fisted his hands to keep from dragging her right down to the floor.

AT five the next morning Travis manually raised Jason's eyelids. By six most of the boys were awake. At half-past Jason sent them into the hall, where they couldn't break another lamp. He left the door open to hear them, and sipped cola on Kira's sofa to wake up.

Zane came from Kira's bedroom with a pearly pink pulsating tube. Jason might have taken it for a battery-operated toothbrush, in its case, if not for the vinyl rabbit vibrating at its base.

"Look," Zane said. "I found a bunny."

"Let me see," Brad said.

"There it is!" Jason said, turning it off and slipping it into his pocket, bunny first. "It belongs to the last people who stayed here. I'll go put it away for them. Why don't you two go and play with the others. Brad, you're in charge. Keep 'em out of trouble, will you?"

Jason followed Zane and Brad as far as the hall. After he counted heads, he went looking for Kira.

In the kitchen Jason shut both doors, closing them in.

"What?" Kira said, looking up from setting the breakfast table.

"I found Zane playing with a rabbit." Jason quirked his brow and held up the impressively long vinyl glow-bright tube. He hit the switch, and the rabbit began to . . . hop.

Kira squeaked and stared horrified.

Jason removed the cover, found another switch, hit it, and choked on a laugh. The sucker pulsed, it rotated, its embedded pearls swirled, and the rabbit freaking danced.

Kira snapped it from his hand, silenced it, and covered it, then she held it to her heart, looking around, as if to make sure they were alone. "That was *not* funny!"

Jason chuckled anyway; he couldn't help himself.

"Tell me the boys didn't—" Her face got redder.

"Zane thought it was a toy rabbit and Brad asked to see it, but I didn't give him a chance. The cover never came off."

"You rat!" She shoved him. "You scared the hell out of me for nothing! Tell you what," she said. "If they ask again, you can say it's what's gonna replace the ultimate rabbit hole this weekend, if a certain jock gives me any-more grief about it."

"Okay, calm down. I'm sorry. Just promise me they won't find any pink penis-shaped erasers hanging around."

Kira's jaw went rigid.

"This is not grief," Jason said. "It's damage control. Penis erasers?"

"Of course not." Kira slipped the vibrator into her pocket and turned back to the table. "I cut them up."

"Ouch?"

"They reminded me of Charlie."

Jason retrieved the bunny from her pocket.

"Hey, give it back," Kira said. "It's mine."

"You said it didn't work anymore."

"Well, that's not the one I was talking about that night, but at least those things don't have big mouths that give me grief."

"Do not discount the value of a big mouth; it can do amazing things," Jason said, "as you well know." He hit the switch and grinned at the rabbit. "How about we try this together later?"

"You're joking," Kira said, but her eyes smoldered, as if he'd touched her physically.

Harvey got a rush. "It's waterproof, right?" Jason asked.

Kira nodded, and Jason got to thinking about her using it, then he got hotter thinking about him using it on her. "I'll go put it by the spa tub, shall I, before we jump . . . the gun?"

"Who's watching the boys?"

"Brad. I checked on them before I came in. They're okay."

Kira followed Jason into his living room, where he shut his door and pinned her against it. He stared at her lips, parted as if waiting for his, at their rosy hue and perfect shape.

To distract himself, he took her breasts into his hands and teased the nubbins into hard pebbles, making her squirm and arch beneath his fingers.

After a gasp that said she wanted more, she scooted from his embrace and opened his door so fast, she caught his bare toe, and though Jason swore and hopped in pain, Harvey hardly cared. The big guy was too busy prepping for the ultimate rabbit hole.

Jason limped toward his replica of Bessie's octagon room, except that his held a huge center spa tub. The surrounding deck, however, revealed the same unrestricted view of the ocean.

He placed Kira's sex toy on the edge of the whirlpool and tried to adjust Harvey so as to make him more comfortable in the tight confines of his jeans. Then Travis called Jason's name, shouting that Grady got his head stuck between the spindles of a chair, and Harvey got small and comfortable again.

Cabin fever set in by seven, for the children and adults, but the snow continued coming down.

Jason thought he might cry.

Cartoons entertained the younger children, who sat on Kira's living room floor, while Brad and the older boys asked to watch the sports channel on Jason's television.

Some time later Jason found them watching the "adult" channel and sent them back to Kira's. A while after that, Brad said he had a theory about Zane's rabbit that Jason did *not* let him share.

Breakfast arrived with Gracie at eight, French toast with maple syrup and chocolate-chip pancakes. Eating quieted everyone for at least twenty minutes. Then Gracie brought up the boys' clean and folded clothes.

Jason went to collect every deck of cards he could find at Cloud Kiss, and entertained the boys by teaching them to play war, fish, and crazy eights, while Kira cleaned up after breakfast and sorted clothes by child.

The longest day of Jason's life lasted until two o'clock, when the roads were finally clear, and he watched the bus pull away from the arena carrying fourteen waving boys.

Jason took the elevator upstairs, half expecting to find that Kira had fled down the back drive and was halfway to Boston by now. She'd seemed that spooked when he said he'd be right back.

KIRA had showered quickly, and shaved her legs. She piled her curls on her head, and changed into the turquoise sleep set she'd once intended for her honeymoon, the one she'd been wearing the night she and Jason stepped into their first rabbit hole.

She generously blessed her wrists, neck, and the cleft between her breasts with her favorite perfume, Very Irresistible, rich with roses, star anise, verbena, and red berries.

She gathered scented massage oils and candles, and went looking for Jason's whirlpool. He told her the room mirrored Bessie's greenhouse, so Kira had an idea where to look. She had no idea, however, that she'd be stepping into a fantasy.

Centered by a huge cream translucent marble step-up whirlpool, its six windowed walls overlooked the sea, while its two inside walls were floor-to-ceiling mirrors.

Watery blue-and-green tiles, floor and ceiling, married the room to its view, the mirrored setting expanded to create an illusion of grandeur.

Beside a miniature Japanese garden, with a waterfall, sat a blue double-wide fainting couch, and a cabinet dressed as a side table, topped by a lamp with a clear ginger-jar base of seashells.

In the cabinet Kira found thick sea-green towels.

Kira placed the candles in clusters on the floor in front of the mirrors, instantly doubling each cluster, on the side table, by the windows, and on the edge of the spa.

She chose to ignore her bunny vibrator.

She lit the candles calling upon their power: indigo first to protect her defenses and emotions; ruby for passion; red for romance; gold for attraction; and pink to bind the magic.

When she felt their energy encircling her, she sat on the floor Indian style, to wait, gazing out at the sea, while letting the waterfall trickle over her fingertips and wash away her anxiety.

By the time Jason came in, still wearing his black jeans and T-shirt, peace and fate had seemed to form a bond to calm her. "I see you haven't changed your mind," she said, eyeing the awakening Harvey, as Jason stood on the threshold of the ultimate rabbit hole.

"I see *I'm* overdressed," he said, devouring her with his gaze. "God, you're beautiful, and wearing my favorite color, too." He lowered himself to sit facing her, reached out and traced the shadow of a nipple beneath her camisole.

"Take off your shirt," she said, rising to her knees to help. Afterward, she sifted her fingers through his luxurious mat of dark chest hair, kissed each nipple, saw that his jeans were becoming very tight, and went for his zipper. "Lay back so I can get these off," she suggested.

His boxers were black, too. They went the way of his jeans, Harvey springing proudly to life the second he was set free.

Naked, obviously aroused, Jason sat up. "No fair," he said, stroking her between her legs, through her panties, until she knew the fabric must be wet. "You're wearing too many clothes," he said.

Kira reclined on her arms. "Take them off me."

Jason removed her top, pulled her over his lap so she straddled him, and took to suckling her. She threw her head back and rocked against the big guy, slow and easy to make the sensations last.

"No one can see us, right," Kira said, "Even though we're surrounded by windows?"

"We own the land to the sea. Nobody's out there."

"I feel as if we're on display," she said.

"Yeah. Sexy, isn't it?"

She opened her eyes to catch Jason's grin. "Yeah," Kira said. "Almost kinky."

"I think your lady-boxers are ruined," he said, stopping suddenly and bringing her out of her pleasure-filled trance.

"Huh?"

"You got them nice and moist with need," he said. "Lay back and rest. That's it, and I'll just get them out of the way, shall I?"

"Hmm, sure." Kira closed her eyes and waited for Jason to slip into her, but he lifted her into his arms instead, making her gasp in surprise.

She hadn't even realized he'd stood.

He placed her gently into the pool of hot water, her every nerve ending coming alive with the massage of a thousand bubbles. She watched Jason step in as well, his wolf's eyes silver-hot with arousal. She admired his rugged beauty, nearly perfect, except for the scars on his knee, and the one crossing his brow, making him all the more dear.

No, not dear. No emotions allowed. Pleasure. Pleasure only, Kira reminded herself.

"This is like sitting in bicarbonate," she said, swept away by the bubbles, teasing her like tiny fingers . . . everywhere.

"The tub has whirlpool jets, too," Jason said, pushing a button and heightening her pleasure in the experience.

Neither of them had turned on the recessed lights, so as the gray day dimmed, and the view turned dark, becoming nothing but the sound of the sea fighting the moon's pull, candlelight bathed them in an aura of sensuality.

Jason played her so slowly, Kira wanted to beg for release and weep with joy. No one had ever taken such time, given such absolute attention to increasing her pleasure. Foreplay took on new meaning. Kira rose to the brink a dozen times, but Jason never let her fall into the abyss.

Beneath the water, amid the bubbles, she tried to play him the same way, reveling in the lowering of his lids, the set of his jaw, the way he controlled his own pleasure, as much as he controlled hers. She loved his guttural voice when he begged her to stop, as if the world depended on holding back.

"When I let go, sweetheart," he said, "I'm going to be deep inside you. Gimp jock's promise."

Sweetheart, he'd said, but Kira wouldn't let it matter.

Jason pulled away before he came, sat higher in the spa, looked about as if for rescue, and grabbed her vibrator, his grin suddenly evil.

He removed the cover, hit the switches, and toyed with each embedded pearl. He let the rabbit ears play against his hand, his expression confounded, until he grinned. "Aha! Now I know where these belong," he said. "Let's see how they work. Here," he said, patting his shoulders, "put your feet up here."

"You're joking!"

Jason took matters into his own hands and lifted Kira's feet to his shoulders, then he played her with the rabbit beneath the pulsating waters, working himself into one hell of a case of lethal infatuation.

He caught his breath and tried to concentrate on how great Kira looked coming. "Hey," he said, pulling the plug on the vibrator to save himself. "I thought you said this didn't work. Looks like it works great."

He'd surprised her into opening her eyes.

"Are we done?" she asked.

Guilt pricked him. "No," he said. "Of course not. Let's put it on high," but Kira lowered her legs and threw herself into his arms.

"Nobody," she said, looking into his eyes. "No other man, has ever—"

Jason watched her eyes fill with tears; clearly, she was the most beautiful woman in—

Before he realized what he was doing, he cupped her face, pulled her close, and opened his hungry lips over hers.

For half a beat she seemed as startled as him, but he kissed her again, and again, and she welcomed the assault.

A kiss, but magic, like his first. Shiny, new, and gleaming gold. A moment to treasure, a newfound simmer.

She had lips like ripe plums, and he was a man starving.

She tasted of honey and joy, sunshine. Freedom. Destiny. He hadn't kissed a woman for more than a year, hadn't slipped inside one for nearly as long, but he wanted this woman, this one woman, so much, he feared he could expire of want.

But first, he wanted her lips, couldn't get enough of kissing, licking, suckling them.

He found her warm wet center with a finger and matched the rhythm, their tongues mating in the truest sense.

She arched her hips, while he all but consumed her with his mouth.

For more than a year he hadn't been able to bear the

thought of touching his lips to another's. Now he couldn't bear the thought of taking them from Kira's, of kissing anyone but her.

How dangerous the sentiment; how enticing the notion.

He should stop. He couldn't.

Jason continued to devour Kira's mouth, celebrating his lack of willpower.

Twenty-seven

IN the midst of that kiss, which had gone on so long, it might be their first, or their fortieth, Jason slipped inside Kira for the very first time ever, there with the hot water bubbling about them, sensitizing them to every level of rising pleasure.

Bliss.

The feel of her slick womanhood bore no comparison to anything of earth, only heaven. Jason had never known a sensation so incredible.

Kira broke the kiss by throwing her head back and offering her breasts.

Jason feasted on her ripe rosy nipples while entering her, and leaving her, in a painstakingly slow and methodical dance, like a form of torture, until he could feel his climax coming.

But he gathered his strength to stop, and rose, water streaming from their bodies, her ass in his hands, him, a steel rod inside her, and stepped from the tub.

She roused from a sensual haze to squeal and hold on. "Where are we going?"

"To the quilt in front of the fire."

"Wait. I brought massage oil."

He backed up; she grabbed it, and he carried her into his living room, her legs around his waist, his pace erotic, as he moved inside her in a new and thrilling way.

When he set her down on her quilt, he slipped from her tight silk glove, both of them gasping in disappointment.

"I want to make it last," he said, "though it might kill me."

She giggled and stroked Harvey's bold length. "Didn't think I'd find anything bigger than the pink rabbit."

"All for you," Jason said with pride.

"Just like a jock," Kira said.

"I *am* a jock. Face it, Fitz. You're about to get . . . dazzled . . . by a jock."

"Promises, promises."

"The only promise I can make is that I'm nothing like Charlie."

"I'll say."

He growled possessively.

"What were you planning on doing to me when you got me here?" she asked leaning on her elbows.

"I was going to give you a massage."

"Hah, I had the same plan. You first."

"Why me?"

"I have *magic* oil."

Jason stilled. "Please don't make Harvey disappear, not now. Where's your wand?"

"Beside the whirlpool. I can get it?"

"I think not."

They laughed. "You first," she said. "Lie on your stomach. You'll like my magic touch. You'll see."

Jason jumped when the oil hit the small of his back, but it warmed and disarmed him at once, and when she rubbed it into his butt, the oil got hotter, and Harvey got harder. "Mmmm, magic."

She massaged down his spine, and up, his shoulders, arms, his hips and legs. He might have been able to sleep, she massaged him so completely, if he wasn't so achingly hard.

When she told him to roll over, Harvey did a happy dance, but Jason was skeptical. "Be careful not to get any hot stuff on the big guy. He's plenty hot already, and watch the family jewels, too, will you?"

Kira grinned. "Don't worry, I'll massage you everywhere . . . but."

Jason sat up and rolled Kira onto her back. "Never mind the *buts*. My turn, and don't touch anything important with those lethal hands, because we don't want you spoiling this with hot oil in the wrong spot. I have plans. Big plans."

Massaging her didn't last, because Kira was on her back looking up at him, with trust and longing, while Harvey teased her entrance, and she arched . . . and swallowed him whole.

Jason shouted with shock, and victory, and buried himself to the hilt. Then he stilled and took deep, deep breaths to last more than half a minute. "How did that happen?"

"The law of inevitability," Kira said with smug satisfaction, her inner muscles working a sensual magic of their own.

"No kidding," Jason said. "I'm set to explode." The feel of her gloving him was . . . incredible. "Er, maybe we waited too long."

"Gee, Sherlock, you think so?"

He stopped. "You're sassing me like in the stairway. Is something ugly going to come out of your mouth and eat my head?"

"Only if you don't start moving, Ice boy. Now. Fast."

"The lady wants it fast," Jason said, so he thrust, fast, and hard, inside her, where he'd ached to be. In Kira . . . this was Kira, taking him, begging him . . . fulfilling him.

She climaxed on the instant, making him harder, if that were possible. Jason held on, so she could climax a second time, before he spilled his seed deep inside her.

They slept, and woke, and made love again, through the night, moving from the quilt to his bed, as if they'd been starved for each other.

Sunday at noon they stopped long enough to find sustenance and were reduced to calling downstairs and asking Rose to send something, anything, up to them.

"Bessie is going to figure this out," Kira said. "We haven't come out all weekend. I hope she isn't upset."

"Please," he said. "She's down there on her knees—"

"Why?" Kira asked. "Praying for us to reform?"

Jason was sorry he'd spoken, because Gram was likely praying for the opposite. "Yeah, something like that," he said, "but don't worry, she's too polite to say anything."

"Great," Kira said.

Jason kissed Kira's brow. "Gram is hardly upset. I'm certain she's thrilled. And since we can't tell her this is no-strings sex, we'll let her be happy for a while."

The blunt reminder caught Kira off guard, which she supposed meant she needed it.

A few hours later, while they soaked, sated, in the whirlpool, and swapped life stories, Jason sat up. "I have an idea," he said. "Any chance you can do a spell for me to go back to hockey?"

After everything they'd shared over the past twenty-four hours, Kira couldn't believe Jason could talk so easily about leaving, but she appreciated the reality check.

"I can't change your future," she said, putting on a good face, "but I can cast a spell that will give you the courage to accept your destiny, whatever that is."

"Great," Jason said, "since hockey *is* my destiny."

Kira got out of the whirlpool and remained naked, sky-clad, wearing nothing but a cloak of stars. This way her magic would not be hindered by clothing, and Jason would remember what he'd left behind after he returned to hockey.

"Since you perceive that hockey is your destiny," Kira said, "I want you to visualize yourself playing your best, your knee stronger than ever. Imagine the crowd watching, cheering. You might want to close your eyes to concentrate."

"No," he said. "I can't take my eyes off you, not now, but I can always imagine myself playing hockey, whatever else I'm doing," he said.

"Okay, fine," Kira said. "You concentrate and I will, too."

Jason watched Kira take up her amethyst-tipped wand, and swirl it, her magnificent body burnished and glistening in the light of a dozen candles, the black night and bright moon behind her, turning her into a goddess before his eyes.

His goddess.

She twirled her wand above and around him.

> *"May you follow the stars,*
> *Grasp your dreams,*
> *Listen with your heart,*
> *Open to adventure,*
> *Strive for balance*
> *And live in peace."*

Kira the goddess, suspended between the sea and the stars, replaced Jason's vision of hockey in his mind.

> *"May your life be full,*
> *Your fate accepted,*
> *Your future blessed*
> *With joy and passion.*
> *This is my will.*
> *So mote it be."*

She ended her spell with a flourish and a sigh, as if the spell had exhausted her.

"With a spell like that, I can't lose," Jason said. "I'll be back on the ice in no time. I—"

Jason caught his breath. He had nearly said, "I love you," though he would have meant, "I thank you" or "You're a doll," but Kira would not have understood. Neither did he.

Those words never came to his mind, much less his lips.

Kira gave him a tired smile. "I did my best," she said. "I really did."

"I know. The spell was beautiful; you're beautiful. Come," Jason said, and the moon goddess stepped into the sea, dissolved disquiet, and took him to heaven.

Late Sunday afternoon they went ice dancing at the rink, and at midnight they made love standing on the deck, outside the whirlpool, wrapped in her quilts, the snow falling about them.

She was a witch, all right, Jason thought, still hard inside her, magic from her copper curls to her peach-tipped toes.

KIRA woke in Jason's bed Monday morning, hating the thought of facing work after the intimacy of the weekend. Not sure what to say, she left his bed, and his side of the suite, in silence.

She hoped they hadn't ruined their working relationship.

In the Hummer, talk was strained, but as the day progressed, they finalized plans for the Christmas Ball. She needed a costume for that, so she went looking for one in the vault, hoping to get away, and think straight, but Jason followed her.

"What are you doing here?" she asked.

"As your date for the ball, I reserve the right to approve your choice," he said, and she made a face at him, but he chuckled and sat to wait.

She came out modeling an emerald velvet twenties gown, and Jason locked the door. She knew what was coming and should stop him, but she let him peel it off her. And when he found the Victorian corset she'd worn beneath, almost hoping he'd find it, he pulled her down and made love to her on the floor. Love. Yes. No. Maybe. For her. Not for him.

"Bessie would kill us, if she knew we were fooling around up here," Kira said when Jason fell beside her and gathered her close.

He chuckled. "I told you, she'd raise a flag."

Kira had to face facts. Their working relationship had taken a new turn, not a wholly bad turn, but probably not good in the long run.

They worked in comparative ease for the rest of the day, and settled details for the Christmas sleigh-ride tours of the mansions.

Determined to ease her need for Jason, Kira went to her own suite when they got home, leaving him silent and surprised in the hall. She shut the kitchen door, and didn't go down to Bessie's for supper.

Still awake at midnight, Jason wondered how Kira could have left him like that, after everything they'd shared. She'd hurt him, which was rare, and startling, and awakened him to a harsh reality.

Over the years he had left a good number of women expecting more. *He* was guilty of hurting dozens of women, in the same way Kira had hurt him tonight.

A hard lesson, Jason thought, vowing that in the future he would try to think of his dates' feelings. Except that there was only one woman he cared to date, only one he cared to . . .

Kira came into his room, and stood beside his bed looking down at him, as if she'd sensed the change in him, or couldn't stay away . . . or he'd conjured her by wanting her so badly.

"I missed you," Jason said, pulling the quilt aside.

As she climbed into his bed, Jason realized that he needed Kira the way he needed air to breathe, which scared the hell out of him, but when he slipped inside her, pleasure blocked alarm.

In the morning he woke her, made love to her again, but the alarming thought amplified his pleasure as he spilled his seed inside of her. Air to breathe equals Kira.

Jason saw his doctor at eight, and called his agent at ten from the office. "Hey, Sam. This is the day. I'm ready to go back to hockey. Yep. How long do you think? Okay, see you then."

Hockey would pull him from her spell. Hockey was all he needed.

She'd worn a turquoise suit today, sexy, inviting, and Harvey-hardening. Knowing what she wore beneath it, intimately knowing, nearly pushed Jason over the edge of sanity.

Sam arrived at three o'clock. Jason had never been so glad to see anyone. "Sam, this is Kira, my assistant. Kira, my agent, Sam Van Zandt. Whatcha got for me, Sam?" Jason rubbed his hands together, in anticipation, he supposed . . . or anxiety, because he couldn't seem to stop.

"How about a contract offer?" Sam said.

"Yes!" Jason turned to Kira. "The Wizards want me back!" He lifted her off her feet, twirled her in a circle, and kept his kiss short and friendly. "That's for your excellent magic."

Kira watched Jason take Sam into his office, and shut her out—of his life.

If Jason's dream came true, this place was headed for disaster. Jason Pickering Goddard made the Pickering Foundation a success, not her, with her planning, lists, and knowledge of special events, but him, with his wild ideas, star-quality charm, and smiles that enslaved their donors.

Jason made the difference. If he left, the Pickering Foundation would be finished.

She remembered him in his tux, slow-waltzing her, her heart pounding, her palms sweating just for being in his arms.

She remembered him coming inside her that first time,

making her feel complete and whole . . . and loved. Kira mocked herself for her foolishness.

Jason threw open the door between their offices, while Sam, his agent, exited Jason's office at a run.

"We're catching a plane to Minnesota," Jason said. "I have to sign a new contract, then I'll be back to settle things here. No worries. I just have to run upstairs and tell Gram."

"Right." No worries. "Congratulations." Kira watched Jason go and couldn't believe he was leaving for good.

She called St. Anthony's to cancel hockey lessons for the rest of the week. Maybe she'd start taking the boys for free-style skating in a couple of weeks. Maybe. She'd see.

Bessie came into Kira's office looking like she'd lost her best friend.

Kira's empathy rose when their eyes met, and they both broke down. How weird was that? But they consoled each other with a hug, cried a bit more, dried their eyes, and chuckled at their foolishness.

"Hockey makes him happy," Gram said, accepting a tissue.

"And that's what we want for him, right?"

"Right," Gram said, looking at her in a new way.

"What?" Kira asked.

Gram shrugged. "I'm willing to let him go, for his sake, but you're surprising me."

"I knew from day one that he was going back to hockey, and he must have reminded me a dozen times this weekend," Kira said, seeing Gram's surprise through a blur of tears, not bothering to be embarrassed at what she'd basically revealed.

"I thought *you* might change his mind," Gram said.

"I hate to admit this, but I might have helped him achieve his goal. Who knows? He asked for a spell to go back to hockey, and I gave him a spell that I put everything into."

"Because you care about him."

"Guess so." Kira shrugged. "If he's happy, I'm happy." So why was she miserable? "I . . . can I have the rest of the week off, Bessie? Christmas events are set. I'll check my E-mail from home, and you can call me if you need me?"

Kira went to Cloud Kiss to pack. She would go home for a couple of days to get her bearings and catch her breath. She didn't even care if Regan was there. It was time to stop running, from ghosts, and jocks. Life was full of both. Better she should face them and move on.

That was the deal she and Jason had made, wasn't it? A weekend out of time, the ultimate rabbit hole, sex before they moved on.

She just hadn't expected him to move on so fast.

She had a good case of whiplash from his speedy exit. So much for no strings, no pain.

She left the quilt she'd made him for Christmas, wrapped and tied with a big red bow, in his living room beside her Argyle boots. He might not find them till spring, but what difference did that make? It was a matter of principal.

The boots pretty much represented their relationship, and she didn't have the heart to keep them.

Driving home, Kira decided she was definitely *not* in love with Jason, but she *would* miss him, a great deal. After all, the sex had been great.

Crap, she forgot her bunny. Ah hell, she didn't have the heart for that, either.

At home she and Regan avoided conversation, and each other, for three days. Kira took a lot of solitary walks, and came to terms with her future at the foundation, accepting the gift her time with Jason had been.

She cared for him. She wanted him to be happy. End of story.

He would come to visit Gram. She'd see him on occasion. So why was she crying?

Friday night her father woke her from a sound sleep. "Daddy?" Kira said, sitting up. "Is anything wrong?"

"No, Kitten, nothing's wrong, but you have company downstairs." Kira looked at her clock. Midnight. "Who?"

Her father grinned. "He insisted I wake you, but I'm going back to bed. He can have Aiden's old room. Tell him we're looking forward to seeing him in the morning. Night."

"Daddy, who is it?" But her father didn't answer, and why was he so pleased?

"Crap," Kira mattered, slipping her ancient red plaid robe over her faded red plaid pajamas. "Must be Charlie." Her parents had really wanted her to marry the Penis, so of course her dad would be pleased if he showed. Shit.

"I do not need this right now!" Kira snapped as she entered her parents' living room, the sight of her visitor tripping her heart and stopping her cold.

Twenty-eight

JASON dwarfed her parents' living room, standing there dripping snow, carrying her Argyle boots, looking as if he'd lost his best friend.

Kira squealed and ran.

Her boots hit the floor as Jason caught and lifted her in his arms and opened his mouth over hers.

The kiss was like their first, glorious and unending, voracious and demanding, made of emotions, not skill, though that was a given.

This kiss, however, conveyed a great deal more . . . affection and yearning . . . on both sides.

For her part, Kira stopped trying to hide her feelings and let herself go. She didn't care to be logical right now. She wanted Jason inside her.

"I want you," Jason said, his voice gruff with need. "I want inside of you."

"Upstairs," Kira said between nibbles and slow sweet kisses.

"Your bed," he said. "I want you in your private rabbit hole."

"My brother's bed," she said.

Jason chuckled and teased her lips, tugged the curl on her brow. "Kinky."

Kira giggled. "My father said you should sleep in my brother's bed, so let's go mess it up to make it look like you did, before I crawl back into the womb and take you with me?"

Two hours later, sex hazed but ready for more, Kira let Jason carry her to her own bedroom.

"Wow," he said when he saw it. "I really need to fuck you here, you know, break you out and make you fly and splinter into a riot of color."

"Yes," Kira said as Jason dropped her on her old twin bed. "Make me fly, Ice Boy." And she opened her arms and took him to her heart. This time was different, she thought afterward. This time they had made love.

The following morning around ten, hand in hand, Kira led Jason toward her parents' crowded kitchen, for the usual Saturday morning gathering of the Fitzgerald clan.

She knew the Ice Wolf's presence would raise her brothers' eyebrows, as his best-kisser status was bound to raise some envy from her sisters, but she didn't expect to come face to face with the promise of sweet revenge.

Regan stared, shocked, at the celebrity her loser sister dragged into their kitchen, but that was nothing compared to Charlie Freaking Penis's slack jaw. He looked like a beached fish sucking air. Kira bit off a giggle.

Charlie extended a hand to his idol, but Jason placed his arm around Kira's waist, instead, and nuzzled her neck and ear until another giggle escaped her. Then he pretended to see Charlie's extended hand, and shook it. "Tough year in the minors," Jason said, tormenting Charlie, and abetting Kira's revenge.

Kira loved Jason for that. Well, not that she actually

loved . . . Shit, she did. She loved him. Honestly, terminally loved him.

Hell of a time to figure *that* out.

Regan sipped her juice and cleared her throat. "You might as well know, sis, Charlie has asked me to marry him, and I said yes."

"Hey!" Jason said. "Congratulations. You totally deserve each other."

Kira's younger brother barked a laugh and her mother cuffed his ear. Her father smirked down at his plate of eggs. When Regan brought Charlie home, her father must have figured out what really happened.

Charlie snorted in disgust. "She got herself knocked up."

"Not without your help," Regan snapped, starting an argument and drawing her family in.

Jason turned his back to the table and leaned into Kira. "Looks like your spell didn't work," he whispered.

"The spell was for him to get what he deserved and take responsibility for his actions. He's marrying her. It worked."

"What?" Jason said. "You mean I read the spell wrong?"

"You did."

"So I've been afraid for nothing."

Kira winked. "Oh, I wouldn't say that."

Jason kissed her, and she kissed him back, which pretty much silenced her family and stopped the fight.

She and Jason squeezed in at the table, and everyone started talking at once. Her brothers asked questions about hockey, and her sisters asked about the kissing show, as if they expected Kira to answer. She felt like a star.

Jason asked about Kira as a child, charming her parents into sharing the kind of tales Gram shared about him, which warmed Kira, and ticked the hell out of Regan.

Kira had never enjoyed a family breakfast more.

When the talk turned to hockey, Jason said he was returning to the Wizards in a few days. "But I'll be back for every foundation event," he told Kira, "until my six months are up. I promise."

"Great," she said, not sure why his announcement surprised her. She guessed she'd assumed, when he showed up here, that he'd changed his plans.

What a time to realize she'd fallen for him, despite the indigo candles to raise her defenses, and her recent solitary pep talks, and the many promises she'd made herself, and him.

She was such a loser.

Jason stayed the weekend, laughing and playing with her brothers and sisters, with board games indoors, and football and baseball in the park, excluding Regan and Charlie whenever he could.

"You're lucky to have such a big family," Jason said after a cataclysmic bout of lovemaking on Sunday night.

Yeah, right, she thought. Lucky. She'd just slept with the man she loved for the last time. How lucky could she get?

After dropping Jason at the airport on Monday morning, she went back to work without him.

The minute it hit the news that he was back on the ice, people began to cancel their reservations for the Christmas sleigh-ride tour of the mansions.

Jason showed for that event, surprising her, but he didn't notice that attendance was down, and she didn't mention it. He didn't stay around long enough to talk anyway, never mind make love.

"I'll be back next weekend for the Christmas Ball," he said, leaving at ten to catch his plane. No good-bye. No kiss.

It was official. Jason Goddard had ice water running through his veins.

Bessie came into Kira's office on Friday morning, the day before the Christmas Ball. "Jason called," she said. "He's sorry, but he can't make the ball. He asked us to forgive him. He has a game the next day. He said he'd be home for Christmas, though."

"Yeah, right," Kira said turning to look out her window. She'd just been stood-up by the man she loved, through his grandmother.

Gram squeezed her shoulder and left.

Billy came sailing into her office ten minutes later. "Bessie said *somebody* needs a date for the Christmas Ball."

God bless Bessie.

"I'm available," he said. "Want to hit the ball with *me*?"

Kira dredged up a smile. "I'd love to. Thank you."

DURING the ball, Kira turned off her cell phone, because it kept ringing and showing Jason's name on the display. She got home at two in the morning, watched her clock instead of sleeping, and didn't turn on her cell until four.

It rang immediately.

"Are you out of your mind?" Jason said before she had a chance to say hello.

"How did you find out?" she asked, knowing full well they were talking about Billy taking her to the ball.

"Gram called and told me. She said you had a blast."

"This bothers you? I should go into mourning maybe, start wearing black again, just because you went back to hockey? I don't think so."

"You're insane; you know that. Billy's nothing but a lazy, candy-ass out for one thing."

Kira scoffed. "And again I ask, how does that make Billy different from you?"

Jason went silent.

"Life is *not* a rabbit hole," Kira said. "You have no claim on me. I can date, or fuck, anyone I please!" Kira hung up, hating herself, and she wept.

A minute later Jason called again, and while she tried not to answer, the phone stopped ringing. A second later the display indicated that she had a message.

She punched in the code and listened to what the jerk had to say. "Watch my goddamn game tomorrow!"

"Like hell I will."

HALF an hour after Jason's game was supposed to have started, Kira got tired of pacing in front of her television and turned it on. "Might as well watch the stupid thing," she said, a spoon and a jar of chocolate sauce handy.

Two seconds into watching, Kira was conflicted. Did she want Jason to win or lose?

She flinched every time a puck flew his way. She lost count, but she thought maybe hundreds did. Nevertheless, Jason blocked every one, and shortly before the Wizards won the game, the announcer started calling Jason the Ice Wolf again.

Evidently a shutout was a big deal.

The score was one to nothing. The crowd went ballistic.

The press swamped Jason outside the arena after the game.

"The Ice Wolf is back!" the interviewer said, shoving the mike into Jason's face, and Kira felt his excitement as he grinned into the cameras.

"How does it feel?" the interviewer asked.

"Like magic," Jason said, looking straight at her, Kira thought, as if he were speaking only to her. Then the bimbo from the auction threw herself into his arms, and Kira turned off the set.

That was it. She'd not only lost him to hockey, she'd lost him to the bimbo as well.

Funny how you never realized how much you loved someone until it was too late.

It was time for a change of job. No way could she bear having Jason run in and out of her life every time he visited Bessie.

The following day, however, Kira got a panicked call from Travis that forced her to call Jason, but the bimbo who answered his cell phone didn't know where he was.

To hell with him, Kira thought, hanging up to go to St. Anthony's, herself, conflicted now about the twins getting adopted. They needed to be adopted, together, as much as they needed *two* loving parents. It was simply that losing them was not what *she* needed.

Then again, losing Jason had not been what she needed, either, but she'd tried to help him get what he wanted. As she would try to help the twins find parents, whatever the cost to her.

Maybe she wouldn't quit the foundation just yet.

Her cell phone rang, identifying a number she didn't recognize, but after Travis's call, she answered anyway.

"Kira," Jason said, "I'm on my—"

"You got my message already?"

"What message? I forgot my cell. I'm on a pay phone."

"Call Travis at St. Anthony's," Kira said. "He needs you. And Jason, don't let him down. You're his idol. He thinks you can fix anything."

"Sounds like he believes that more than you do."

"Whatever."

"You didn't watch the game," Jason said.

"Screw the game," Kira said. "Travis needs you."

Jason sighed. "What does he want me to fix?"

"He says somebody named Cruella wants to adopt him, but she doesn't want Zane."

"That can't be right. I'm on it, and halfway home," Jason said. "Meet me at the Providence airport in two hours."

Jason hung up before Kira could ask him what the hell he was talking about. He had a game on the West Coast tomorrow. How could he be on his way to Rhode Island?

Two hours? Kira's heart raced.

She knew exactly what to wear.

Twenty-nine

WHEN Jason cleared the airport gate, it was like seeing him in her parents' living room all over again.

Kira ran.

Jason dropped his bags and lifted her into his arms to kiss her, melt her, and make her want him so much, she could barely breathe. The kiss was so hot, Jason lifted her high against him, and Kira had no choice but to kiss him back, ignore the news crews, and hold on.

"You're not kissing me for the cameras," Kira said, breathless, and needy. "I can tell."

"I don't see any cameras," Jason said. "I see only you."

Outside, in the parking lot, the snow coming down around them, Kira apologized for what she'd said on the phone, and Jason said it was his fault, and apologized for hurting her.

Before she could question that, a porter brought his bags, then they saw the news crews coming.

Kira gave Jason the keys to his Hummer, and he got them out of there.

"I called St. Anthony's," he said, turning south on the highway, "and everything is fine with the boys for the moment, so you can stop worrying. I spoke to them both. That Cruella dame, or whatever her name was, talked to Travis in the schoolyard, and scared him, but Sister Margaret said they sent her packing."

"I can't tell you how relieved I am," Kira said. "Thank you, Jason."

He regarded her for too long. "I brought you a tape of the game," he said.

"Oh, goody."

He smiled and grabbed her hand to squeeze it, squeezing her heart at the same time. Something was off. Kira was confused.

At Cloud Kiss, Jason steered her toward Gram's greenhouse where a candlelight dinner was set.

Jason removed her coat and whistled.

"Vickie sent it," Kira said, looking down at the sequined dress, its bright butterfly wings wrapped around her, its wingtips covering, almost caressing, her breasts.

Kira modeled it, front and back, so Jason could see the entire butterfly. "I planned to wear it to the Christmas Ball . . ." She looked into his eyes. "But I couldn't."

Jason took her into his arms, waltzed her around the room, and sang an off-key rendition of "That Old 'White' Magic," as if he really were in her spell. She knew she was in his.

But he stopped, and pulled out her chair, and sat opposite. "Eat," he said, "before Rosy's feast is ruined."

He tasted the lobster and sighed. "You can't get seafood like this in Minnesota."

Kira tasted it, too, agreed it was good, and raised a brow. "What are you doing here? Don't you have a game halfway across the country tomorrow?"

"I like the quilt you gave me for Christmas."

"It's not Christmas for another few days. You opened it too soon."

Jason shook his head. "Why did you make the hockey side black-and-white?"

"Because it suited you and the game."

"The opposite side is alive with color—Travis's and Zane's handprints, mansions, ghosts, magic, a staircase, a birdcage, bees, a rabbit in a rabbit hole . . ." Jason wiggled his brows. "A hot-air balloon, things we've experienced, or almost experienced, together."

Kira nodded. "It's a memory quilt, for when you're far from home playing hockey."

"I don't get the toad-on-the-lily-pad reference, though."

Kira smiled. "Remind me to tell you about that sometime."

"Do you realize how well you defined my life?" he asked. "I thought you were hiding in black, because I had been hiding in a black void, where no hurt could touch me, no emotional rejection, but no love or joy, either."

Kira put down her fork as her heart sped. "Really?"

"Being away from you gave me time to think, mostly about you, but the most important thing I discovered was that if I'm not in a rabbit hole with you, I'm in a black hole missing you."

He took her hand. "I'm letting go of the past, Kira. I found something that I want more than hockey."

Kira had to blink against hope, and fear, and all the possibilities in between.

Jason kissed her. "I played a game in a rink far from home, the crowds cheering, but it was an empty victory, because the one I wanted most was not in the stands. I knew then that my dreams, my magic, existed elsewhere. That was when I understood, and accepted, my destiny."

Kira took a ragged breath. He'd said so much, but not enough, and she was afraid to want more.

"Can you let go of the past?" Jason asked. "Can you forgive me for running, and make room for new dreams? Will you help get Zane's leg fixed, help save the foundation and St. Anthony's?"

Kira didn't understand what he was asking. "But you're back on the team," she said. "You have games to play, a contract to fulfill."

"Too bad you missed my postgame interview," he said.

Kira understood that she'd missed something important.

"I quit," Jason said. "I broke my contract. I knew going into the game today that it was my last, so I played my best . . . for you."

"But . . . you need hockey to be happy. You need the screaming fans, the beautiful women."

"I need you, Kira."

"Me? I can't make you give up hockey. I'm boring. I can't make you happy. I certainly can't hold an Ice Wolf's interest."

"Oh, yes, you can!" Jason chuckled. "You're the most fascinating, exciting woman I've ever met. A witch. My favorite witch. A goddess. You enchanted Gram, the birds, the boys, and most of all, you enchant me." He combed his fingers through her hair and brought her close. "I love you, Kira."

Jason swallowed her gasp with his kiss. She could have kissed him forever, but he stopped, took her hand again, kissed her palm, and traced her lifeline.

"Life without you is empty," he said. "I think we haven't been stepping into a rabbit hole so much as climbing into a cocoon, hiding, the both of us, from what we really want, from what we need to make us whole. Look at you, you're ready to spread your wings and fly. Take me with you? Take *us* with you."

He got on one knee before her, a gentle wolf, almost tame, but not entirely.

Hope rose in Kira's heart, her deepest most secret dream there before her.

"Will you marry me, Kira Fitzgerald? Will you adopt the twins with me, and give Gram someone to spoil?"

Kira released her breath on a sob and looked into

Jason's eyes, but she was afraid to believe the impossible, incredible, love she thought she saw there.

"We can't raise children in a suite," she said foolishly.

Jason chuckled. "You've been arguing with me since the day we met. It shouldn't surprise me that— Wait! Was that a yes?"

"I . . . yes," Kira said, breathless, her heart opening. "I love you."

Jason whooped, kissed her, and kissed her again. Some time later he took a ring from his breast pocket and slipped it on her finger, a gem-struck butterfly.

"I almost wrapped it," he said, "but I was afraid I'd have heart palpitations waiting for you to open it."

Kira laughed. "It matches the earrings I'm wearing."

"They're yours, too. Gram wants you to have them, and so do I. Nothing but a butterfly would do, as a symbol of our commitment."

Jason rose to his feet and took her with him, up and into his arms. "By the way, Gram lied. They're not fake. They're diamonds, every one. Rare."

Kira caught her breath.

Jason kissed her, tender, yet greedy, but with something new added to the kiss, love, commitment, and the promise of a bright new future. That kiss fired their passion, until a bump against the door caught Jason's attention.

Kira nearly wept with disappointment when Jason left her.

"Remember where we were," he said, stepping away, then back, for one more kiss. He backed away, as if he were fighting her pull. "Cloud Kiss is mine," he said. "We'll convert the east wing. Who needs summer bedrooms?"

Kira smiled. He was a wolf, hungry yet tame, his aquiline features as sharp as the gleam in his silver-gray eyes, the dimple cut deep in the center of his chin . . . adorable. A wolf, sexy, gorgeous . . . and all hers.

"Okay, Gram," Jason said, opening the door. "You can bring in Kira's Christmas presents now."

Bessie came in with Zane and Travis by the hands, and Kira let her weak knees take her down. She covered her heart. "Oh," she said, catching the boys in her arms and kissing them all over their faces.

Gram swallowed hard, her eyes full, as she turned to Jason. "Judge Attleboro got the papers you signed and faxed. He granted you temporary custody about forty minutes ago. When you two sign the final papers, he'll rush them through."

"They're really ours?" Kira asked.

"We are," Travis said. "Aren't we, Zane? Gram and Sister Margaret said so."

"They're ours," Jason said, hugging a nodding boy on each side. "We need your signature on a few papers," Jason told Kira, "to make Travis and Zane Pickering Goddard legal." He ruffled each head. "But first, you and I have to sign a marriage certificate and make *you* legal." He bent over the boys to kiss her. "Judge Attleboro does weddings, too. How does Christmas Eve sound?"

"Awesome," Travis said. "Can we call you Mom and Dad now?"

"Oh, God," Kira said on a sob. "Yes!"

"Is that *our* hockey rink now?" Zane asked, looking up.

Kira laughed and hugged them all. "You're the best Christmas gifts ever."

"We brought you another one," Zane said.

"It was the coach's, I mean, Dad's idea," Travis said on a grin, looking up. Dad. It hit Kira then; all of it. She was in love with this man, with these boys, and they were hers.

Yes, Jason Pickering Goddard created fantasies, and this was one of them . . . come true.

Bessie left, and a kitten—the Rainbow's Edge kitten— came running through the door and leaped into Kira's arms. It swished its black tail, pawed its black ear, and licked Kira's thumb.

"I figured she had to be yours. She found you," Jason said. "Plus, she reminds me of you. White, solitary, with only a touch of black, to keep life interesting." He winked.

"She likes to be vacuumed." Zane giggled. "Old Sister Clean discovered that by accident this morning."

"You're kidding?" Kira said.

"Deering was right; she is deaf," Jason said. "Gram took her to the vet yesterday."

"Yesterday?"

"What?" Jason said. "You think this was all spur of the moment?"

"Misty." Kira stroked her soft white fur. "Does her name remind you of anything?"

Jason shrugged. "You can rename her."

"I don't think so. I think she's from the edge of the rainbow in the void of the mist."

"Son of a . . . hockey stick." Jason cupped his nape, and Kira smiled and kissed him.

Misty mewled, jumped to the floor, and ran to touch her tiny paw to the glass, where three crows stood on the snowy deck outside, looking in at them, heads tilted.

"Uh-oh," Jason said. "Kira . . ." He stepped back, taking them all with him. What do three crows augur?"

Kira smiled, and gazed into his silver gray eyes. "Three for a daughter," she said.

"Elizabeth," Gram said.

Travis shook his head. "A girl?"

"She can't play hockey, if she's a girl," Zane said.

"Oh, yes she can," Gram said.

Turn the page for a special preview of
Annette Blair's next novel

The Scat, the Witch & the Wardrobe

Coming soon from Berkley Sensation!

"MUST be Friday, if the mad MacKenzie's deigned to leave his fancy cave to watch the antiques on the telly." Old Angus slammed his shot glass on the table, startling more than one man into spilling his ale.

"Right, well then," Rory MacKenzie said, letting the door shut behind him, ignoring the inebriated Knight of The Sacred Star . . . The "Star" being the organization, dressed in ceremony, that had helped the locals turn drinking into "lodge business" more than a century before.

"Turn on the telly, will you Liam?" Rory asked.

"Give it up, damn your eyes!" Angus shouted. "Drummond's unicorn sits at the bottom of the sea. It might be your family's curse, but it's our families who suffer."

The MacKenzie curse, Rory thought. He cut his teeth on talk of that. Uncanny how his "mad" age-old search to end it had been shot through with vigor-reincarnated of late. He scratched his tatty beard and claimed his favorite bar stool.

"You're in rare form tonight, Angus. Took to the bottle a wee bit earlier than usual, did you?"

Angus refilled his shot glass. "Damned hermit. You're as mad as old Drummond," he muttered.

"Ach, go vent your spleen in the loch, and sober up, you old blatherskite," Rory growled. "I'm here to watch the telly, not listen to your twaddle."

In the days before the curse, according to local history, as told by Angus and his ilk, visitors from all over the world swarmed to Caperglen to ride Drummond MacKenzie's Immortal Classic Carousel. Because of it, the village thrived . . . until Drummond broke his engagement to rumored-witch Lili Lockhart.

After Lili fled to America, Drummond destroyed the carousel—and village prosperity—by breaking up the twelve zodiac figures and sending the Aquarius unicorn to Lili in America. The villagers said Drummond had been bewitched, and *they* suffered his curse.

Whether fact or fiction: the unicorn, Caperglen's prosperity, and Drummond's happiness, never resurfaced.

Without the unicorn, the Immortal Classic stopped running and became a broken whirligig in a pavilion on the family property. And the MacKenzies became local pariahs—from that day to this.

Rory's grandfather, another in a long line of carousel artisans like Rory, had, in fact, carved a unicorn from Drummond's original plan and tried to repair the carousel, but he failed to resurrect it. According to legend, only Drummond's unicorn could bring the Immortal Classic Carousel, and the village of Caperglen, back to life.

Rory dreamed of reversing the curse. Talk about mad: Lately, he'd been dreaming about the Immortal Classic—music merry, lights bright, turning beneath a pale blue sky, him kissing a woman beside it.

Aye, sure, and he might have time for a woman, if he ever found the unicorn.

Maybe the dreams were responsible for his new zeal, or maybe his zeal was responsible for the dreams.

"Mad and cursed," Angus mumbled.

"Seems so," Rory said. "But it's a matter of public record that the ship carrying the unicorn docked safely in Salem Harbor the year Drummond sent it. I found the ship's records on the Internet."

Angus stilled, shot glass half way to his lips.

Like clockwork, Liam set a bowl of tattie drootle before Rory.

By his fourth ale, Rory was paying more attention to a bit of a dispute over a golf game than to the antiques.

"Rory!" Liam shouted. "Look, a unicorn!"

The lodge went silent, and Rory about choked on his potato soup, because he saw someone who looked amazingly like his dream woman, there, on the antiques show, bold as brass, laying claim to a carousel unicorn with the sign of Aquarius carved on its forelock.

"That *our* unicorn?" Angus asked, shocked sober.

Her name was Victoria Cartwright. Her unicorn belonged to her ancestor who brought it from the old country more than a century before—all the proof Rory's mates needed for a lynching. His own thoughts darkened as he became one with their dissonant ire, and while no proof could be found, and no sense made of their garbled shouts, the general consensus fit his mood. She stole our unicorn! Off with her head!

"Wisht!" Rory snapped to silence them, so he could hear the telly.

The woman issued an invitation for viewers to "come and see" her unicorn at her vintage dress and curio shop, The Immortal Classic, on Pickering Wharf in Salem, Massachusetts.

"Why don't she just take out an ad," Liam said.

Rory raised a quieting hand. "Her shop is named for the carousel, did you hear?"

"Odd that you call your shop The Immortal Classic," the carousel expert said, "since the workmanship on this figure indicates it could have been carved by the Scot whose Immortal Classic Zodiac Carousel won him world recognition at the 1867 World's Fair in Paris."

In counterpoint to the woman's pleasure, Rory's heart firmed to tempered steel. Did curses get passed, like blue eyes and red hair, from generation to generation? If so, he'd fight Victoria Cartwright for Caperglen's treasure with a claymore honed by decades of village bitterness.

"Did you know?" the appraiser asked, "that your shop was named after a famous carousel?"

"No," she said. No. I'd never heard of it. I made the name up, I thought, in reference to the kind of classic clothing that never goes out of style."

"But you come from Salem, right? Land of witchcraft? That's enough to raise the hair on my arms," the art dealer said. "I wonder if fate or magic gave you the words?"

"Coincidence," Victoria Cartwright said with conviction. "I thought it was good advertising." She sighed. "So the Scot who built The Immortal Classic Carousel; he was my unicorn's carver, then? How weird is that?"

"The Scot *might* have carved it, except that Drummond's figures were last seen on his own carousel around 1880, I believe, and no collector since has come across one. It's been generally believed that they were destroyed by fire, as so many wooden carousel figures were over the years."

The reverent appraiser touched the unicorn's glass marble eyes, the sign of Aquarius below its forelock. "It almost has to be a Drummond," he said.

"Why?" Victoria asked.

Rory fisted his hands. Too much knowledge and he wouldn't have time to claim it before the dealers and collectors started circling.

"Until later in the nineteenth century, astrological

magic was linked to the occult," the appraiser explained. "Because of that, I only know of the one carousel artisan who took a chance with astrological signs midcentury. But, as I say, nothing of Drummond's has ever come up for auction. Anywhere."

The pleased carousel aficionado tilted his head toward the unicorn. "Nevertheless, this certainly looks like the real thing. Without knowing whether it's a Drummond or not, because of it's age, its condition and patina, its rare astrological reference, and because the semiprecious stones set into its bridle are real, I'd put a price of one hundred and fifty, to two hundred, thousand dollars on it. If we can prove it's a Drummond, we can safely double that. At auction, the sky's the limit."

"I'd never sell," the woman said. "It's a family heirloom."

Rory groaned. Her adamance was a classic case of good news/bad news. Reclaiming the unicorn might prove as great a challenge as finding it, he thought, but with her determination, she might just keep it long enough for him to get to America. The hermit in him cringed at the thought.

"With more research," the appraiser said, "your unicorn could prove to be a national treasure. Congratulations."

Liam turned off the telly.

"That's our unicorn," Angus said, without question, his gaze expectant, like every other gaze turned Rory's way.

This was as close as any MacKenzie had got to respect in more than a century, and by God, Rory wasn't going to let Caperglen or the MacKenzie name down again. He tossed back the dregs of his ale and slammed his tankard on the sleek mahogany bar. "I'll go fetch it, shall I?"

A resounding cheer followed him out the door, warming him as he walked the length of Caper Burn toward Mackenzie Manor.

If Drummond Rory MacKenzie had carved Victoria Cartwright's unicorn, a hidden compartment sat beneath its saddle. Ach, and if he found the compartment, that unicorn was his National Treasure, *not* Victoria Cartwright's.

Development director, journalism adviser, and award-winning author **Annette Blair** became an overnight success with her first sale eleven years after beginning her first novel. That process has made each of her thirteen contracts and nearly fifty writing awards that much sweeter. Yes, her tenacity is legendary, though some just call her stubborn. After ten historical romances, Annette turned to writing single title contemporary romantic comedies, and she loves her new home at Berkley Sensation. Visit her website at www.annetteblair.com, or write to her at Annette@AnnetteBlair.com.

The Kitchen Witch

by Annette Blair

Do you believe in magic?

When a single-dad TV executive hires Melody Seabright—a flaky rich girl and rumored witch—as his babysitter, she magically lands her own cooking show... and makes sparks fly.

Annette Blair's novels are:

**Available wherever books are sold or at
penguin.com**